Star Light,
Star Bright

Also by Katherine Stone
in Large Print:

Home at Last
Illusions
Imagine Love
Thief of Hearts
Damascus Gate

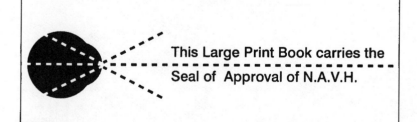

This Large Print Book carries the
Seal of Approval of N.A.V.H.

Star Light, Star Bright

Katherine Stone

Thorndike Press • Waterville, Maine

Published in 2002 by arrangement with Harlequin Books S.A.

Thorndike Press Large Print Americana Series.

The tree indicium is a trademark of Thorndike Press.

The text of this Large Print edition is unabridged.
Other aspects of the book may vary from the original edition.

Set in 16 pt. Plantin.

Printed in the United States on permanent paper.

Library of Congress Cataloging-in-Publication Data

Stone, Katherine, 1949–
        Star light, star bright / Katherine Stone.
            p.   cm.
        ISBN 0-7862-4207-8 (lg. print : hc : alk. paper)
        1. Triangles (Interpersonal relations) — Fiction.
    2. Female friendship — Fiction. 3. Virginia — Fiction.
    4. Large type books. I. Title.
    PS3569.T64134 S73 2002
        813'.54—dc21
                                                        2002022589

For Paula Eykelhof —
with appreciation, admiration
and many thanks.

Prologue

In the Snow Shadow of Popocatepetl

Thirty-Four Years Ago

His name was Rafael and he was a born warrior. It was an authentic inheritance, though far from pure. Rafael was a hybrid of ancient enemies, of conquered and conqueror, slave and master, vanquished emperor — yes, emperor — and triumphant conquistador.

And within him the battle raged still.

Genetics as a formal science was unheard of in the village where Rafael was born. But the ancestry of every villager was known to the elders, a pedigree preserved in Nahuatl, the language of their forebears.

It was within Rafael's mother that the blood of emperor and conquistador had wed, the consequence of a futile gift: a daughter, a princess, given by the proud ruler to the man who would destroy him. The lineage on Rafael's father's side had remained pure Nahua for three hundred years. Then it, too, had mingled with New World descendants of the conquerors from Spain.

The villagers didn't know Rafael's pedigree. But the elders, the keepers of royal lineage and sacred lore, forecast a perfection of flesh and bone five hundred years in the making.

And when the firstborn child of the many-times-great granddaughter of a princess was born? His skin was so pale that only when he was old enough to spend from dawn till dusk beneath the springtime sun did it become bronze and remain bronze through the summer rains. That was the conquistador legacy, the elders knew, the alabaster of European aristocracy. Rafael's mother was almost as fair. And her hair, like her son's, fell in soft curls of midnight. But her eyes were ebony. As were his father's. As were the other eyes that would stare — and glare — throughout his boyhood.

For Rafael's eyes were blue.

Five villages clung to the steep hillside where Rafael was born. His village was the oldest, five centuries, the uppermost and most remote. Like Rafael, many villagers had both Spanish and Nahuatl names. But

Spanish wasn't spoken — or even known, except to the elders.

Spanish was the language of the villages at the base of the mountain. And in the world beyond. Only the elders made the near-vertical descent, the precipitous journey from ancient to new, and it had been several lifetimes since a stranger had climbed even to the fourth village — which was as far as any outlander had ever been allowed.

There'd been such visitors once, nineteenth-century explorers in search of sixteenth-century artifacts. There'd even been a dalliance between Rafael's paternal great-grandmother and a blue-eyed, black-haired Scot.

He'd had warrior blood, too, that descendant of the Celts. But far from fierce, and with a gift for language, he'd faithfully translated into English the Nahuatl poems of love.

The elders were unaware of the clandestine liaison with the Edinburgh poet. Nor had they imagined a blue-eyed gene within Rafael's mother, the vestige of a long-ago marriage between a Scandinavian princess and a Castillian prince. But there was such a wisp of DNA, and it placed a fourth warrior, a Viking, in the mosaic that was Rafael.

The stunned and troubled elders had no doubt the blue-eyed infant had been sent to earth by one of the pantheon of Nahua deities that had been devastated, too, by the soldiers from Spain.

The gods had stormed away following the final battle, into a black sky that thundered their rage. And now, one of them had sent this boy. But was he a sign that a dethroned god was planning to return? Or was he an enemy disguised as a gift, a reminder from an angry deity of Rafael's imperial ancestor's catastrophic mistake?

The emperor had misidentified the conqueror as a long-awaited Nahua god. The elders must not repeat that fatal error.

Rafael was welcomed with wariness. And he was taught and tested constantly.

The elders had no choice but to reveal to Rafael the secrets of the ancient empire. Selected secrets, judiciously disclosed. It was the only way to determine who he was. What he was. Gift or trick.

The elders believed they'd have their answer in his reactions to the revelations they did — or did not — make. But Rafael was as circumspect as they were.

They got nothing from the solemn boy . . . except excellence in the lessons they taught him. He recited Nahua poetry as if he'd composed it, and drew with perfection the sacred glyphs. And he could retell the elaborate stories of the gods as if they were his own.

But, as if his own, he mastered, too — and quickly — the language of the conqueror.

He preferred Nahuatl, some elders thought. Just as some thought they saw pain — he couldn't hide it — when they told him of the devastation the Spanish-speaking soldiers had wrought.

The elders had to be certain. They would take their pupil down the mountain to the world beyond — a journey forward in time, but back in history. They'd retrace his Spanish ancestor's march from the sea . . . to the city he'd destroyed.

They'd leave in three days' time. On the boy's fourteenth birthday.

When Rafael was told of the impending journey, he concealed, as always, the bewilderment he felt.

What did they want from him? Who did they expect him to be?

He had no answers despite a lifetime of listening to every word his teachers uttered. He'd listened to their silences, too, tried to hear in their hush the words they chose not to speak.

Rafael didn't want to see the conqueror's world. Loathed it without needing to see it. He wanted to remain, forever, on the mountain he loved . . . with the family he loved.

His father, for whom Rafael was named, who spent his life farming a small patch of earth to keep his wife and children fed.

And his mother, who prepared the maize that always appeared, and who, like his father, looked with wonder at the son they'd relinquished to the elders. They'd had no choice — even though they had no idea, either, who the elders hoped the blue-eyed boy would be.

And the younger sisters, two of them, whom Rafael adored — and who adored their brother back.

Rafael had very little time with his family, precious moments between the lessons that were so different from what the other village boys were taught. If only his lessons could be the same as theirs. To be husbands. To be fathers.

To be farmers.

Rafael knew the conqueror's blood flowed in his veins. Seethed there. He hated that part of him, just as he hated the world he had no wish to see. He would kill the conquistador within him, if he could. In his heart he already had.

And if, by some magic, he could summon the spirit of his beloved ancestor — the emperor — he would restore to his mountaintop home the splendor of the world before the conqueror had destroyed everything he could . . . and forbidden what he could not: the poems, the music, the enchanting stories of warring suns and flying serpents and gods who slept in clouds and cavorted with stars.

Rafael's ancestors had loved those legends. His sisters would love them, too. And his parents.

What harm could there be in permitting the forbidden tales to be told anew?

And . . . why, moments after informing him of the hated journey that lay ahead, were the always-stoic elders smiling at him? And why did their eyes shimmer with hope?

Because he'd been speaking aloud. Revealing *his* secrets. The wishes, held in silence, all his life.

Was this what his teachers had wanted from him all these years? These simple truths?

Yes. Yes! Rafael was welcomed, without wariness, at last.

His joy was so overwhelming he needed a little time alone.

He wandered into the forest in search of a place so private that when he shouted his happiness to the heavens only the resplendent quetzals would hear. Perhaps the birds in the cloud forest would even sing with him. . . .

Rafael found a private place. But he didn't shout. And his song grew silent when he caught sight of something wondrous, something unexpected. The statue was tangled in a web of vines; it took all of Rafael's strength to free it. But he needed to. He'd just been freed from the heavy mantle of aloneness that had cloaked him since birth. The statue's imprisonment had been even longer — five centuries — as had the god whose mythic adventures the Nahua people had been forbidden to tell.

Only after removing many ropes of vine could Rafael tell which deity he was setting free. Tlaloc. The Rain God. Rafael could draw his glyph perfectly: his goggled eyes, his fanged mouth, the rattles he carried to make thunder.

Rafael believed the elders would be thrilled with his discovery.

He could not have been more wrong.

The elders assembled around the weather-beaten carving as if carrying the mammoth stone on their backs. When eventually they spoke, it was to Rafael.

"What do you want from us?" one of them implored.

"The tears of children?" whispered another.

Rafael had found what he wanted . . . only to lose it, to destroy it. "The tears of children?"

Rafael's question went unanswered in words. But too late, too late, the listener heard the truth that had eluded him in the elders' silence.

The stories weren't legends. And the gods were real.

The emperor had believed in the all-powerful deities. The Nahua people had believed in them.

The elders still believed in them.

They hadn't told him. They'd expected him to know . . . unless his true allegiance lay with the conqueror.

It didn't. Couldn't. He was Nahua farmer. Like his father. That was all he ever wanted to be. And Rafael believed in many things: his parents, his sisters, the quetzals that sang, the crops that grew, the stars that shone, the volcano that puffed smoke into the azure sky.

Rafael had been enchanted by the ancient stories — but had he believed them? No.

The elders prepared to meet their fate, which would be harsh, even though they hadn't been entirely wrong about Rafael. He *was* a sign from a god planning to return. But they'd guessed the wrong god. It had been a logical enough guess, given the fourteen years of bounty the village had enjoyed.

Even the relatively good-natured gods had their foibles — and extravagant tantrums and fits of pique. Tlaloc, not good-natured to begin with, could be particularly difficult. On the sheerest of whims, he'd darken the sky with the promise of rainfall, only to withhold the moisture from a thirsty earth. Or, if the mood struck, he'd hurl lightning from the heavens or beckon a hurricane to howl.

If sufficiently provoked, the Rain God might send fiery torrents of volcanic rain.

And when truly annoyed, as surely he must be now, enraged that his gift, Rafael, had been welcomed with such joy as a token from a rival god — what happened then?

The elders expected a parching that would wither plants and humans alike.

16

But Tlaloc tricked them again.

It was a rain like no other, a sobbing of the heavens, a drowning of the land.

Just moments before the hillside gave way, a great roar filled the air, the battle cry of an offended deity exacting his revenge.

Then the avalanche began, lava without fire, an ocean of huts and forest, crops and mud.

And people. Families. Rafael's parents didn't know, even as they died, who their son had been. But they understood all hope had been dashed and were remorseful for the creature they had borne.

Rafael's sisters didn't forsake him. They clung to him, trusting him. Rafael ran with his precious cargo, fueled by a warrior's courage and a brother's love. But it wasn't enough. The crumbling mountain, propelled by the rage of a slighted god, drew ever more near.

They didn't drown when the ocean of mud overtook them, were swept up instead, riding the earthen wave as Quetzalcoatl had ridden to sea on a raft of feathered serpents.

Rafael held his sisters tight, even when their wave crashed.

Of the many levels of heaven, the Rain

God's hovered just above the mountain-tops, in that shimmering space between snow and sky. Tlaloc's heaven was reserved for those slain by lightning or drowned in the sea.

And if a brother and his sisters perished in an ocean of mud?

It was too late for Rafael to believe in the God of Rain. But, for his sisters, he prayed. *Let my sisters, oh please, my sisters, live forever in the shining clouds.*

Rafael felt peace then, even as mud clogged his lungs and shrouded his too-blue eyes. He *felt* their ascent, all three of them, their feathery flight, and in those moments before blackness, he was home.

He awakened hours later atop the ocean of mud. It was a hot ocean, seared by the sun, and its baked earthen waves no longer surged.

The god that tormented earthlings with rain clouds, only to withhold the rain, had tempted him with paradise, only to withhold such grace. Punishment, Rafael had no doubt, for failing to hear in the elders' silences the truth they'd withheld.

But he was hearing truth in this sunscorched silence. His sisters were alive and calling to him. He needed merely to dig, just a few handfuls, and there they'd be.

What do you want from us? the terrified elders had implored. *The tears of children?*

If the Rain God had thirsted for such an anguished offering, the craving had now been amply slaked. Rafael's buried little sisters were crying. Sobbing. *Help us, Rafael! Rafael, please help us!*

Rafael wept, too, as he dug. And dug and dug. And his fingers bled tears that painted the earth.

He knew it was a trick long before he stopped digging. His sisters were dead, all but their screams. Everyone was dead. He was alone.

Alone.

With Tlaloc.

Night had fallen by the time Rafael looked up from the screaming earth. The statue, too, had survived. It hovered nearby, shining silver in the moonlight, its goggled eyes satisfied, its fanged mouth smug.

Rafael shouted at the gloating stone — as, not so long ago, he'd planned to shout his happiness to the heavens. Shouted and shouted until he had his reply.

The mountain roared anew, then moved. Anew.

When the statue lurched toward him,

Rafael stood his ground in its lethal path, waiting, not fleeing, waiting, not screaming, waiting, waiting, waiting to be crushed. . . .

1

Forsythe, Virginia

Friday, April 8

Twelve Years Ago

He was twenty-two, the man who'd been
since birth a warrior. But to those who
knew him, he was twenty-six. And he was
Rafe, not Rafael.

He hadn't meant to vanquish Tlaloc on
that moonlit night eight years before. Nor
had he. The screaming earth had devoured
the Rain God, parting at the final moment
and swallowing the statue whole.

Rafe was the sole survivor from the village in the clouds. The village itself was
gone.

The other four villages had perished as
well. The villagers who'd survived huddled
at the base of the mountain . . . and welcomed the blue-eyed orphan not at all.

Even the most shivering of refugees

insisted that Rafe be evacuated first. Dressed in a twentieth-century ensemble of faded denim, he was taken to the city he'd never wanted to see.

The freefall through five centuries was stunning enough, and his soul cried for the loved ones he had lost. But now he was here. Mexico City. The modern metropolis built on top of the island city where his Nahua ancestors had died.

Rafe wandered the crowded streets, oblivious to all but the screams that came from the tons of pavement beneath his feet. His sisters weren't alone in that crushing coffin. The choir of screaming voices was young and old, male and female, all imploring him, depending on him . . . failed by him.

He would hear, forever, the screams of the lost empire — its children and its poets, its farmers and its mothers. He deserved, forever, to hear the screams.

But he would leave Mexico City far behind. Rafe wasn't thinking. It was a *feeling*, desperate yet confident. He was to journey north, a reverse of the odyssey his ancestors had made from the desolation of Aztlan to their Tenochtitlan home.

Rafe expected desolation to the north. But the valley was lush. And home to majestic creatures he'd never seen before.

The horses came to Rafe willingly and so generously, nestling their velvet muzzles in his hands, warming him with breaths that whiffed and blew.

The horses gave him fleeting comfort. Phantom peace. Rafe had to journey on. But their grace sustained him, a nourishment as fundamental as air and more essential than sleep.

Rafe was many days and miles north of Mexico City when a car slowed beside him. A girl, pelted by raindrops but smiling, called out, "Would you like a ride?"

The language was foreign to Rafe. One he'd need, perhaps, in his journey north. He interpreted the girl's offer correctly and, in Spanish, answered yes.

Spanish was just fine, although a surprise, to the three college girls from Texas. They'd assumed he was an American — a fellow student who'd argued with his girlfriend, they'd theorized as they debated the safety of offering him a ride. She'd be waiting in the feuding couple's car a few soggy miles ahead.

The girls didn't rescind their invitation. He looked awful, starving and pale, and yet . . . he was remarkably attractive even in his ravaged state.

His rain-washed hair fell in black curls around a face at once fierce and gorgeous. Harsh bones. Sensual eyes. A mouth that — He was young. Seventeen or eighteen. Too young for them.

And safe enough, especially in his weakened condition, a worthy project for the final leg of their Mexican adventure. His village had been destroyed, he told them — without clarifying further. He asked them to teach him English. It felt, in fact, like a command, as if he had family, friends, *someone,* he must speak to in the States.

He learned quickly, startlingly so, and his accent — well, he had none, save for the soft Texas drawl that was theirs.

By the time they reached the border, he'd be a perfectly convincing American teen. The girls decided he should be Rafe, though, not Rafael, and he'd need an Anglo surname. Preferably one of theirs. Of the three possibilities, the most unambiguously north-of-the-border was McClure.

Rafe listened to his rescuers plot the story that would accompany his new name. He was a younger brother whose wallet — with his driver's license ID — had been lost during the forced evacuation of a hotel beside the rapidly rising El Rio Santa Maria.

The girls' middle-of-the-night evacuation was a bona fide anecdote. It added the perfect note of authenticity to the fiction of Rafe. The entire story sounded great in rehearsal. But when the time came to present it to the border guards, the girls balked.

Rafe knew nothing of the consequences of lying to federal authorities. He knew only that he had to journey north.

So it was he, in soft and fluent Texan, who recounted the story — a plausible tale, as luck would have it. Many unhappy vacationers had been separated from their belongings in the deluge.

Eighteen-year-old Rafe McClure and his rescuers parted company at a horse ranch south of Dallas.

The ranch wasn't Aztlan, nor was it home. But it was where the desperate, confident feeling permitted him to stop. Rafe was grateful for the respite here, for there were horses, that grandeur, that nourishment . . . as long as they couldn't hear the screams that traveled with him, wouldn't shy away in terror.

No horse ever shied away from Rafe, and the screams were his alone.

What he'd thought would be a respite lasted eight years. His bosses wished it would never end. He had a connection with horses, even — especially — the high-spirited champions the ranch prided itself on being able to train.

And he was a hard worker. They'd never seen anyone who'd worked harder . . . or better.

They'd been surprised that he had no identification of any kind, and more surprised that he was from Mexico. They were impressed when, having learned the gravity of misrepresenting himself at the border, he'd confessed the deception to the proper authorities — and was allowed to stay. He was, after all, an orphan of the storm that had caused such terrible devastation.

His bosses and fellow ranch hands were impressed, too, by the seriousness with which he pursued the citizenship that was eventually his. And they respected the way he studied his dictionary late at night in the bunkhouse, learning new words — which, as far as they could tell, were spoken during the only real conversations he ever had, the ones with the horses in his care.

Then there was the matter of his women, the daughters of Texas whose champions he trained. . . .

Rafe would have found lovers if they hadn't found him. They wouldn't necessarily have been heiresses, however, had he been doing the searching.

But Rafe didn't have to search. And all that mattered was the sex — which the heiresses were happy to provide. They wanted his wildness, his daring.

His need. That was what sex was for Rafe. An essential if fleeting escape. The escape became more fleeting over time. Even in the midst of passion the loneliness remained. In fact, over time, the loneliness during intimacy surpassed what he felt when he was truly alone.

As months became years, Rafe doubted he'd ever leave the Texas ranch. There was no reason to. He was meant to be with horses. He wanted nothing more. And there was no proof, quite the opposite, that a true home for him existed anyplace on earth.

Then the feeling returned, even more powerfully than in Mexico City. But its mandate was the same. He was, once again, to journey north.

Rafe could have resisted. He was no longer a devastated teen. But he chose to surrender. To follow wherever it led.

North, the feeling guided him, and east, a route that took him from Texas to Tennessee. Then Kentucky. Then Virginia's verdant south. And in each state, he drove the country roads . . . the places where, on either side, horses beckoned.

Rafe's parched soul needed the solitude of rural living and the companionship of horses. But it was as if the god who tempted thirsty earth with clouds, only to withhold the rainfall, was tormenting him. . . . As if Tlaloc had found him anew.

On he drove, even when, in northern Virginia, the warnings began to appear.

Washington, D.C. 60 miles.

Then 50.

40.

Rafe was still in horse country. But he felt the metropolis that loomed ahead. Felt it and hated it.

Then he saw another sign.

WELCOME TO FORSYTHE, VIRGINIA
FOUNDED 1764
POPULATION 4,228
(INCLUDING HORSES)

2

Forsythe was charming, historic and blanketed on that April afternoon with a cherry-blossom snow.

Here was where Rafe's journey would end. Should end. But would there be work for him here?

Only if the unimaginable had happened and another horseman had chosen to leave.

He almost stopped at the Saddlery, the logical place to inquire about jobs. But he would allow no one, except the receptionist at the Silver Fox Inn, to see him at his most ruggedly road-weary.

Rafe apologized at once when she did.

"Nonsense!" the receptionist, who was also the innkeeper, replied. Harriet was an excellent judge of character, if she did say so herself. The entire town agreed. Here was a young man *with* character.

As she checked him in, Harriet provided answers to questions Rafe didn't even ask. It might seem surprising, she acknowledged, that she'd have a vacancy on a

Friday. Especially since today was also the beginning of spring break.

But Forsythe really wasn't a spring-break kind of place. Thank goodness! The town wasn't even a tourist destination. It could be with any encouragement — which no one was about to give. The residents of Forsythe, many of whom spent the work week in D.C., were quite militant when it came to preserving the tranquility of their country homes.

The Silver Fox Inn, Forsythe's only overnight lodging, had eighteen rooms. There were no plans, never would be, to expand.

With the exception of this hiatus in April — wasn't it lucky he'd arrived now? — the Inn was booked solid for months in advance. For those in the know, Washingtonians mostly, Forsythe was *the* place for romantic getaways.

Forsythe was also renowned for its lilacs, which explained today's vacancies. This was the calm before the "blizzard of blossoms and visitors" that would begin in about two weeks and last until July.

The town council had voted down the notion of an official Festival of Lilacs. But since people came anyway, to see the blooms, the Garden Club had started hosting formal tours. It was the only gracious thing to do. The lilacs were simply too splendid not to share. Besides, the organized tours controlled congestion on the narrow country roads.

"You should make a point of coming back in a couple of weeks," Harriet said. "Not, I'm afraid, that I'd have a room for you."

"I'm hoping to still be here. To find work here."

"What kind of work?"

"With horses."

"Well! You've come to the right place. I have no idea what openings exist at the moment, but there must be *something*. I do know the sure way of finding out."

The Lilac Cottage, a property management company, handled all work for all of the estates. The estate owners loved the convenience. Most of them were far too busy to deal with routine maintenance, much less the unexpected, and thanks to Lilac Cottage proprietor Marla Blair, not only was all the work done, it was done *perfectly*.

An application bearing Rafe's neatly typed name awaited him at The Lilac Cottage. Harriet had made a call. She'd also advised Rafe to provide the names and

31

phone numbers of his references as soon as he walked in the door. Lorraine, in charge while Marla was in Switzerland, could then be making calls while Rafe completed what Harriet knew, everyone knew, was a comprehensive questionnaire.

Harriet had offered helpful information, too, about the twenty-eight-year-old woman who held Rafe's destiny in her hands. Lorraine was very good at her job. A "consummate" professional. But she *could* be a little reticent when it came to making negative disclosures.

It was an admirable reluctance. If you couldn't say something nice, you shouldn't say anything at all. But it wasn't always practical, or even desirable, in business.

Lorraine was getting *much* better about being direct. She was, after all, learning from the best. No one could be nicer and more forthright — at the same time — than Marla Blair. Still, if Rafe sensed that she was withholding something, he should ask her what it was.

Lorraine was very pretty, Harriet had also said — as if, businesswoman though she was, she felt a little guilty about the negative comments she'd made. The inn-keeper had swiftly added something else. Lorraine would be a beautiful bride at her wedding, to a Delta Airlines pilot, in June.

Twenty minutes after Rafe's completed application had been taken to Lorraine's office, Rafe himself was escorted there.

"There are a couple of points I'd like to clarify," the consummate professional began when he was seated. "You arrived in Forsythe today, yet you indicated that you're interested in a job commitment of at least a year."

"I am."

"Even though you have no family in the area?"

"Even though."

"Friends?"

"No."

"Why Forsythe?"

"It looks like a nice place to live."

"It is." Lorraine's smile was transforming. She *was* very pretty. "You wrote that you're interested in 'anything' having to do with horses."

"I am. As long as the horses aren't harmed."

"There's nothing, we wouldn't — that's *not* a problem. You don't have a strong preference for working with polo ponies, though?"

"No."

"Or being involved in the Hunt?"

"No. In fact, I'd prefer not to be."

"What about taking care of elderly horses? Ones too old to be ridden and requiring special care?"

"I'd like that."

"Do you have a horse?"

"No."

"But you could get one if you felt it was important to ride."

"I could. If it was. Which it's not."

"Well. Your references are excellent. I'm sure you know that. The ranch manager in Texas, Ed, asked me to tell you he wishes you'd return to your job there."

"I'd like to be here."

"Okay. Good. Because we do have an opening. It's at FoxHaven Farm. Forsythe's premier estate. You could live there, if you wanted to, in the carriage house beside the stable."

Rafe would have detected Lorraine's reticence even if Harriet hadn't foreshadowed it. He also sensed the internal nudge Lorraine was giving herself — and waited.

"There *is* a slight . . . problem I should tell you about. It's awkward because it involves Marla Blair, who both owns The Lilac Cottage and lives on the Farm. But, as she herself would say, 'No surprises.' Of course," Lorraine reflected, "what *hap-*

pened is a surprise. Last week, before leaving for an extended trip to Geneva, Marla hired a man, Jared, to care for the horses. Yesterday, he quit. I don't know the details. Jared wouldn't say — except that it had something to do with Brooke."

"Who is?"

"Marla's seventeen-year-old daughter. I haven't spoken to her yet. She's at school. And Faye, who also lives on the Farm, didn't know Jared was gone until I told her. So I'm afraid whatever happened remains a bit of a mystery."

Not a mystery at all. Rafe had eight years' experience with heiresses.

"Better tell me about Brooke."

"She's terribly bright. Like Marla. She's graduating at the top of her class in June. Until today, I would've said she was . . . different, I suppose. But not difficult. I don't know her well. I'm not sure anyone does. She spends most of her free time with the horses."

"How many horses?"

"Six. The three seniors I've mentioned. And two FoxHaven-bred horses that only Brooke rides. And Rhapsody. He's a recent Farm rescue, the only one in the past seven years. He's young — five, I think — and has a pedigree that should've made him

35

the best show jumper Loudoun County's ever seen. He *does* jump, sky-high. He just doesn't permit humans to jump with him. He threw his previous owner one too many times. Despite the investment, she wanted him . . . gone. Everyone's rescuing doomed horses these days, but no one except Brooke wanted to save Rhapsody. Marla agreed to it, so long as Brooke promised never to ride him. Which made Rhapsody Jared's to ride. Marla told him as much. And this autumn, when Brooke's at Vassar, he'd have been riding the Fox-Haven purebreds, too." She gave him a puzzled shrug. "Jared's a known quantity. Well-respected in Forsythe and a champion in his own right."

"Not the kind of man who'd quit because Brooke decided she didn't want him riding her rescued stallion, after all."

"No. Definitely not. So there you have it. A fabulous estate. Three exceptional horses — I'm including Rhapsody — that you may or may not be able to ride. Plus a little mystery, which might or might not turn out to be a problem."

And, Rafe added in silence for the too-nice Lorraine, a spoiled teenage heiress named Brooke.

3

The restlessness that had kept Rafe wakeful throughout the night urged him to see the Farm at dawn, when the day was new.

He parked near the estate entrance on Canterfield Road and considered for a moment the Farm's distinctive fence. He'd seen white fences during his drive through Virginia's horse-and-hunt country. And black ones. And fences painted red or green.

The FoxHaven fence was lilac.

The newborn sun gilded the estate's private road, a cobblestone drive that followed the contours of the land. Rafe walked the dips and crests of nature, a journey of pasture and forest, with flowers, *flowers* everywhere.

Rafe had never gardened for the sake of gardening. But he was a farmer's son. The memory of working beside his father on the hillside had been eclipsed by the last time his hands had dug into the mountain, when its blood-soaked mud had pleaded and screamed. But now, as he beheld this first act in the drama that was spring, Rafe remembered the joy of working the soil, of tending the crops, of reaping the harvest.

Such attention to the earth had been essential. They'd survived on what they grew. And if the purpose of his labor was beauty, not sustenance?

Rafe's hands opened as if in greeting to the flowers. The farmer's son could tend these gardens, would do so willingly — and might there even be joy?

The job with the horses was his if he wanted it. Lorraine had said as much. As for the mystery that wasn't a mystery at all, Rafe hadn't given her — Brooke — much thought, much less worry, since leaving The Lilac Cottage yesterday afternoon.

But as he considered the petulant heiress who lived within these lilac fences, he recalled the last heiress with whom he'd been intimate — and lonely — and clenched his hands again.

She'd been like all the others, a few years older than his fictional twenty-six, and like the others, her interest in him had been limited to sex — as in fairness, and as with all the others, had been his interest in her.

But unlike all the others, she'd told him she might be pregnant with his child. A pregnancy *scare,* she'd called it, although she'd been quite unalarmed. She'd have an abortion and that would be that. The procedure might curtail their fun for a while, but just think of the reunion they'd have.

There'd been alarm however, *horror*, when Rafe suggested she have the child. It wasn't a fear of scandal. Given her wealth, no one need ever know. She could spend the final months at her favorite haunt in the south of France, after which he'd raise his baby far from Texas and on his own.

It was an imposition. Nine months of her life. But —

Her expression had spoken volumes. She didn't want his child inside her. Because she feared even its temporary residence might taint her with whatever alchemy of enemies and their gods had conspired to create him? No. She knew nothing of his mestizo ancestry and would never have guessed.

She was an heiress, and he was a cowboy, and it wasn't *personal.* Surely he understood!

She hadn't been pregnant.

The scare for her was over. And for him? There'd never been alarm, only hope. And when there was no child, the lessons of the mountain were affirmed anew: there might never be, for him, a place to call home.

The heiress could have had him fired.

She'd been furious when he'd refused to touch her again. But she'd been only a spoiled goddess, not a vengeful one.

Rafe left Texas a few weeks later.

And now he was here, in this heaven of flowers, and he was going to stay. There was nothing a teenage heiress could do, not one thing, that would make him leave.

The cobblestone drive opened to a circle at its final crest, a sweeping loop from stable to mansion with a cottage between. All three structures were white, trimmed in lilac, and colonial in grandeur and style.

It was the stable that beckoned him, a tantalizing invitation to which he surrendered without a fight.

He saw the white-brick home for horses as he neared, and the carriage house that could be, *would* be, his.

His fists uncurled.

His aching soul felt release.

A horse show was underway in the paddock. A horse show for horses. The gymkhana's sole participant was a roan filly, three or four in human years, an equine teen. She performed for an audience of four mares, three of whom, obviously the rescued seniors, were very old.

They seemed most attentive, those elders, watching — and testing?

The ancient faces were appreciative, not judgmental.

They were horses, after all.

The roan filly was being ridden by a roan-haired girl. Their long red ponytails swayed as they cantered and flew as they jumped.

Rafe didn't sense the balk coming. Nor did the girl. It was a last-second decision made just before flight and solely by the horse. The girl catapulted onto the neck, rested there a moment, hands entwined in mane, then slid gracefully to the ground.

And then . . . there was a thoughtful fluffing of the sunlit forelock accompanied by worried words. "Did I set the jump too high for you? I'm sorry. I didn't want you to be scared. You know that, don't you?"

Rafe expected a whinnied reply. The girl would understand it, as would he. Of the languages he'd mastered — Nahuatl, Spanish, English — this one, equine, had been the easiest, the most familiar, from the start.

It was the oldest mare, the palomino, who whinnied . . . at him.

The girl spun, and saw an imposing male silhouette backlit by the sun.

Rafe approached her as he would a skittish horse, with care, with calm.

41

No horse had ever shied away from him. Never.

But when he moved from shadow to light, she recoiled a single startled step. Her retreat halted just as abruptly, for what had compelled her to withdraw was now compelling her to stay.

Him. And the dark blue eyes that seemed to be searching, wanting — what?

"Who are you?"

"Rafe McClure."

"Oh. You're here about the job?"

"Yes. Are you Brooke?"

Her answer was a nod and a shrug. An apologetic yes.

No surprises. A favorite caveat, according to Lorraine, of Marla Blair's. Well. Everything about Marla's daughter was a surprise. Her solemn brown eyes. The utter disarray of auburn hair. The profusion of freckles on her nose and cheeks.

Rafe's vocabulary was vast, far more than the loner — and lover — needed it to be. There was, in his lexicon, a perfect word for her. A word unused by him. One he had never imagined he'd use.

Lovely.

And blushing, at this moment, embarrassed by his silent appraisal, approving though it was — as if it was the approval itself that embarrassed her.

Lovely.

The other roan filly was quite bold. She nudged his hands and got what she wanted, a cradle of warmth.

"She likes you," Brooke murmured.

"That's a start," Rafe replied. "What's her name?"

"Fleur."

"Hello, Fleur."

"Are you going to take the job?"

"That depends on you."

"Me?"

"I'll take it if you want me to."

"You might not want it."

"I already do, and I know the rules. Only you ride the FoxHaven horses. Fleur and —" his gaze traveled to the four mares and settled on the youngest "— her mother."

"Meg."

"Meg. I also know the rescue horses require special care."

"They really do. But I can do that. I always have."

"You've taken good care of them. The palomino must be thirty."

"She is. Thirty and a half. And she's happy, I think."

"She looks very happy, whoever she is."

"Minerva. Minnie to her friends."

"And the other two?" *Introduce me, Brooke, to all your friends.*

"The chestnut's called Snow — I have no idea why — and Grace is the gray."

Rafe repeated the names, hellos to Meg, Minnie, Snow and Grace, then to Brooke, "I don't see Rhapsody."

"He doesn't spend much time with us girls. There's a greenhouse behind the stable — you can't quite see it from here — and beyond that a pasture beside a pond. That's the only place he really likes to be. He must've been traumatized at some point, but no one knows how or when." Brooke's frown became a smile. "I'm just glad he likes his place by the pond."

The horse she'd saved had found a little peace from his demons. And it was enough for this lovely girl. But there could be so much more healing for the tormented stallion. He needed only to permit Brooke to fluff his forelock as she comforted him with quiet words.

"I can't believe Rhapsody doesn't like you."

"Oh! Thank you. We do all right, I guess. He's not hostile, of course. What horse is? He's withdrawn, but very polite."

"Unlike Jared?"

"Did Lorraine tell you that?"

"No. She doesn't know what happened. Jared wouldn't say. Did he get rough?" Rafe meant rough with the stallion. But it occurred to him suddenly, fiercely, that Jared's mistreatment might have been of her. Her expression didn't reassure him. "Brooke?"

"Jared's reputation is excellent, and, as far as I know, he's trained very difficult horses without resorting to violence. But Rhapsody wasn't responding to his usual technique. I think his plan was to break Rhapsody's spirit so completely that he'd be able to reassemble the pieces any way he liked." She shook her head. "I'm not sure Rhapsody would ever have broken."

Jared *had* hurt Brooke. By hurting Rhapsody. "You weren't about to let Jared try."

"He *was* trying when I got home from school on Thursday afternoon."

"But you convinced him to stop. And to leave. How?"

"I told him I was going to have Curtis Franklin — he's an attorney — initiate an animal cruelty action against him. In the meantime, I'd be notifying the sheriff, the *Forsythe Banner* and the SPCA."

"Jared didn't call your — it wasn't a bluff."

"No."

Rafe had come to this place for the horses. But the farmer's son would have stayed for the flowers.

And now he was looking at the reason he would never want to leave.

"Good for you," he said to her softly. "Good for you."

4

Rafe was a loner and a listener. And so was she. But encouraged by him, Brooke became a storyteller. She had stories to tell, true ones, heard as a girl and learned by heart.

The estate was Forsythe — not Fox-Haven — Farm in the beginning, and, like the town, was a generation older than the nation itself. Indeed, both Farm and town provided winter haven for General Washington and his troops. Daniel Forsythe and three of his sons joined the battle for freedom. Daniel perished in the conflict, as did his youngest son.

For the first century following the Revolution, the estate passed from Forsythe father to firstborn male. In 1879, with Charlotte, the era of Forsythe women began — and might have ended. She conceived only to miscarry, year after year and baby after baby, devastating losses that endangered her health.

Delicate but intrepid, Charlotte braved all risks and, at forty, she and her James became loving parents to the only baby they'd ever have. And what a baby she was, the long-awaited Emma Anne, the Forsythe woman destined to send shock waves through her northern Virginia home.

The fact that Emma married for love was not a shock. Romance was a family tradition. It was her ladylike but resolute prohibition of foxhunting on her property that shook the community to its very core. Forsythe Farm was the Hunt Country's most sprawling estate, and there'd always been a gentleman's — and, one had presumed, gentlewoman's — agreement to permit pass-throughs for purposes of the chase from one estate to the next.

But Emma forbade pass-throughs. Nary a foot, hoof or paw in pursuit of a fox would be permitted on her land. At other times, of course, all were welcome. Especially horses. Although not a huntress, Emma was a rather spectacular equestrienne.

When it became clear that Emma wasn't going to budge, the Farm became known, with affection, as FoxHaven. It was impossible not to love the iconoclast in their tradition-steeped midst, even when she added fifth boards to the estate fences and planted a wall of lilacs, just in case.

Emma did more than plant her favorite flower. Throughout the difficult years when she, like her mother, conceived only to miscarry, she gave birth to new lilacs — which in turn gave birth to new fortune for the town.

Emma hadn't intended her lilacs to become a commercial enterprise. "Charlotte" and "James," named in loving memory of her parents, would have bloomed only in the gardens of her friends had not those bedazzled friends intervened.

Canterfield Nursery had flourished ever since, as had every Forsythe artist who'd chosen to specialize in a lilac motif.

Emma flourished, too. Like her mother, and at last, she had her baby, her only child, her daughter — Carolyn.

The storyteller's voice shimmered when she spoke the name.

She shimmered.

"Carolyn," Rafe echoed. "I thought your mother's name was Marla."

"It is. *Oh.*" Comprehension dawned, shadowed with worry. "I'm not Carolyn's daughter, Rafe. Or Emma's granddaughter. Not a Forsythe at all. I'm sorry. I didn't mean to mislead you."

"You didn't mislead me, Brooke." It was

true, and not true. Who else could this lovely girl be but the granddaughter of Emma Anne? Just ask Rhapsody. Or Jared. Brooke was as ferocious as the Forsythe matriarch when it came to the lucky creatures for whom she provided safe haven on the Farm. "Your mother's Marla."

"Yes. She and Carolyn met during their senior year at Georgetown. . . ."

And became instant best friends. Carolyn married the following May, beneath a trellis of FoxHaven lilacs, with maid-of-honor Marla on one side and husband-to-be John on the other.

John Rutledge, a D.C. attorney, commuted to work — for a while. The nation's capitol was a possible commute from Forsythe. Many Forsythe residents made the drive every day.

But it was too far for John. Too much time away from his bride. Carolyn needed to live on the Farm, with Emma, who was lonely without Charles, her husband of fifty years, and whose own health was beginning to fail.

John opened a law practice in Forsythe, risky though such an endeavor was. The wealthy landowners needed attorneys of course. But for generations their legal work had been handled by prestigious Washington firms like the one John had left. Competence mattered, however, and that was John. It also described Curtis Franklin, John's partner when the practice became more than a single attorney could handle — especially when that attorney wanted to spend extra hours with his grieving wife following Emma's death.

John had long since abandoned the commute between Forsythe and D.C. But Carolyn's best friend made the drive often during her MBA year at Georgetown, and after, when she worked at a property management company near Embassy Row.

And when Marla's pregnancy made her decide to leave D.C., Carolyn and John insisted she live on the Farm for as long as she liked. Forever, Carolyn hoped.

"Why did she decide to leave Washington?" Rafe asked.

He'd been listening without comment. But now, as he sensed that Brooke's learned-by-heart story wasn't going to linger as long as he'd like on the baby Marla had been carrying, he interrupted her.

"Because of my father . . . I think. I don't know anything about him. My mother's never wanted me to know. He wasn't *worth* knowing, she told me once, and that was that. I didn't care. It didn't matter. Because of John. I thought he was my father. I was six before I realized he wasn't."

"And?" Rafe prompted the storyteller who needed prompting when the story was hers.

"I also believed, for a very long time, that Carolyn was my mother and that Lily was my little sister."

"Lily."

"Carolyn's daughter. Carolyn's and John's. I took charge of Lily right away, apparently. In a bossy big-sister way. I didn't need to, of course. Carolyn was always there, with Lily and me. Always . . ."

Carolyn was twenty-eight when Lily was born. Unlike the Forsythe mothers before her, pregnancy was easy for Carolyn. Pure joy. But like those mothers, Carolyn welcomed her daughter as the miracle she was — just as, twenty months earlier, she'd welcomed Marla's baby girl.

Carolyn became the *Mom* mom, spending every waking moment with the girls and missing them desperately when they napped. And the other mother, the Georgetown MBA, loved both daughters dearly, too. But Marla couldn't *play* with them the way Carolyn could. She simply wasn't any good at it.

Which was fine. Carolyn was a born mother, just as Emma and Charlotte had been. Had Marla Blair followed in *her* mother's footsteps, she'd have married often and well, and divorced with such finesse that she remained adored by every ex.

"Grandmother Elise couldn't even organize a grocery list. Or," Brooke amended, "so she said. There was quite a bit of speculation that she was more steel magnolia than swooning petunia."

"What do you think?"

"I don't know her very well. She moved to Beverly Hills when I was seven. She and my mother talk all the time, though, at least once a day and often more." Brooke said it wistfully, as if such mother-daughter communication was a treasure she missed. "I talk to her, too. Sometimes. And she always seems perfectly capable to me. And smart, like my mother. She's very beautiful, of course. Like my mother."

Marla Blair could have made a career out of marrying well. But she'd chosen a more modern path. The *Entrepreneur* mom's Lilac Cottage began casually enough. With John and Carolyn's blessing, she assumed all management responsibilities for the Farm — which included giving the property itself a makeover. Riotous pastures were subdued to manicured lawns, and weeds were banished from the gardens, and the FoxHaven lilacs bloomed even more bountifully with artful pruning and expert care.

Other Forsythe landowners saw the Farm and wanted estate makeovers, too. Those who tried it on their own discovered far more was required than a skilled workforce. Vigilant — and persuasive — supervision was essential.

Ever gracious, but a steel magnolia in her own right, Marla induced the best from everyone she employed. Like Elise, whose every ex-husband remained loyal, Marla knew how to make her professional relationships flourish, even when she insisted that a given job didn't meet her standards and needed remedial work.

As Marla's client list grew, she moved her office first to the guest cottage on the estate and then into town.

Branch offices were planned. In Middleburg. In Warrenton. Even in D.C.

But.

Then.

But then, Brooke's story faltered.

Rafe and Brooke were sitting on sun-warmed grass in Rhapsody's pasture by the pond. The equine girls grazed nearby, and from across the mirror-smooth water the night-black stallion observed the scene.

Rhapsody had reacted immediately to the arrival of visitors in his private place, a reaction unseeable by those who didn't know horses. But Brooke and Rafe saw the way he moved even as he remained statue-still — the retreat ever deeper within.

The powerful creature stood his ground, aloof yet watchful — and listening, Rafe thought. To whatever chorus of screams tormented the animal.

Rafe's own screams were muffled on this day. Soft. Softened.

They fell mute as Brooke's story faltered.

As she faltered.

But there *were* screams in the sudden silence. Rafe heard them clearly.

"But then, Brooke?"

"But then," she whispered the quiet scream, "Carolyn died."

5

"Tell me what happened."

"Carolyn died."

Brooke had been reciting the stories she'd been told, the sagas of patriots and horses, and foxes and flowers, and best friends and loving mothers.

But it was a daughter's story now. Brooke's story. It lived in her heart and could be told — only — by her.

Her vocabulary, like Rafe's, was vast. But she'd found the two words that mattered.

Carolyn died.

There had to be more words the lovely girl could speak. Should speak.

Rafe saw her sadness. Felt it.

"Tell me, Brooke." *Trust me.*

"It was seven years ago. In late July. We gathered raspberries that morning for our raspberry toast. It was Carolyn's favorite summertime breakfast."

Which made it the favorite of her girls, her daughters, her Lily and her Brooke. . . .

Faye Holloway was in the kitchen when

Carolyn and the girls returned with their bounty of raspberries. Faye was Carolyn's most recent rescue, having arrived in June, and although Faye was new to the girls, she wasn't new to the Farm.

She'd been a frequent FoxHaven guest when Carolyn's father, Charles, was alive, and after Charles's death there were times Emma had needed Faye, too.

Faye and Carolyn met in their early twenties, when Charles's diagnosis of congestive heart failure was made. His diet for the rest of his life would be salt-restricted and potassium-enhanced, a bland and bitter regime until a novice dietician was assigned to his case.

Faye's dietetics degree was recent, but she'd been a lifelong cook, a baker's daughter who — had family finances been different or had Faye been bolder — would have pursued her love of the culinary arts.

The love and the art were there, however. Faye prepared special dishes in the hospital kitchen, custom recipes just for Charles, and on his discharge home, she spent weekends cooking, and visiting, on the Farm.

Faye cooked for Emma, too, when her health declined, creating imaginative concoctions that buoyed Emma's spirits and prolonged — with quality — her life.

It was Emma's idea, and Carolyn readily agreed, to ask Faye to make Carolyn's wedding cake. The result was a five-tiered masterpiece of buttercream lilacs, satin sugar ribbons and crystal sugar bows.

Faye was married the following year and moved with her neurosurgeon husband to New York. She became a full-time wife and a half-time mother, except in her heart, to his five-year-old daughter, Jen.

Carolyn and Faye kept in touch, a correspondence that invariably included a reminder that Faye and her family were always welcome at the Farm. Carolyn imagined that if Faye ever did visit, she'd come alone. There were so many weekends Faye was alone, when her husband was on call and Jen was with his ex-wife.

Just months before the raspberry-toast morning in July, Faye's aloneness became more permanent. She was no longer needed or loved, her husband told her. Not that he'd ever loved her, anyway. The neurosurgeon had subsequently discovered true love with someone else.

Thanks to the Manhattan divorce attorney John found for her, Faye was financially secure, and thanks to Carolyn — and John — she had a wonderful place to live. Permanently, if she liked.

Faye was not to cook for them. She was a guest. The mansion's shamefully underused kitchen was all hers, however. To make wedding cakes, perhaps? There was a precedent, Carolyn and Marla reminded her, for successful businesses being launched from the Farm.

Faye *was* baking cakes — wedding and birthday — and she was also cooking the family meals. She wanted to.

Cooking provided a welcome riddance of unwelcome thoughts. Such as . . . what a fool she'd been, and so bewitched that she'd acceded to her husband's every edict, including the one that she mustn't ever become pregnant.

His new bride, of course, the one he truly loved, would be giving birth to their first child in a matter of weeks.

It wasn't too late for Faye to have children. Her biological clock would be ticking for another ten to fifteen years. But a trusting relationship with a man felt unimaginable in her present state.

Besides, Faye had a child. Jen, with whom there'd been such closeness . . . until, and with a vengeance, the girl's teen years had arrived.

The newly fragile Faye-Jen bond

snapped entirely when Faye's marriage to Jen's father fell apart.

Jen blamed Faye in a way that made perfect sense to a troubled fifteen-year-old. It was Faye's fault Jen wasn't important enough, relevant enough, to keep not one but two marriages from failing.

Maybe, Faye would think when she wasn't cooking, she was to blame.

So she cooked, permitted her mind to downshift into neutral and coast awhile.

Faye was coasting when the raspberry gatherers appeared. The timing was perfect. Faye had perfected it. The toast was warm and buttery, ready for the raspberries to be lavishly layered, lightly sugared, gently squashed.

The confection was savored as the day's plans were discussed. Carolyn and the girls were going to the stable. Naturally. Faye was welcome to join them.

Faye smiled but declined. Three birthday cakes awaited her today, and a wedding cake tomorrow.

So it was the usual threesome who walked to the stable after the breakfast dishes were done.

Well, Brooke and Carolyn walked.

Lily skipped, twirled, flew. And between pirouettes and chasées, Lily Forsythe Rutledge spun perfect cartwheels.

Brooke beamed at her remarkable little sister. She and Lily were spring and autumn, daffodil and redwood, ballerina and its clumsy opposite — whatever that was. Something sturdy and clumping.

It couldn't matter less that Brooke was ungainly. And big. In Lily's sunny estimation, Brooke *was* the sun.

Carolyn rode FoxHaven's Nutmeg Lady — Meg — that morning, soaring over jump after jump with ease. Or so it appeared. The jumps might have been a breeze to Carolyn's five-year-old champion. But, Carolyn confessed during lunch, they'd been a stretch, literally, for someone as old as her.

"You're not old!"

"Thirty-six doesn't seem ancient to you, Lily?"

"No!"

"Well, you know what? It doesn't seem ancient to me, either." Carolyn touched her abdomen just below her right jeans pocket. "But I seem to have a muscle that doesn't quite agree. If you ladies don't mind, maybe we could play upstairs this afternoon?"

Carolyn's girls didn't mind. Upstairs meant the playroom adjacent to the bedroom Brooke and Lily shared. There were many vacant bedrooms in the mansion. But neither eight-year-old Lily nor Brooke, who in six weeks would be ten, could imagine a time when they'd want separate rooms.

Nor could they imagine a time when their playroom wouldn't be the best place to do their homework . . . and create their art.

There was only one real artist. Lily. At the moment, her fascination was mosaics. Her parents suspected the fascination would endure. Even before she'd discovered mosaicking as art, Lily had rescued crumpled flowers the way Carolyn rescued discarded horses and shattered friends.

Lily's talent was surprising, and true. Brooke, by contrast, was as artistically inept as she was at spinning cartwheels.

But the discovery of a paint-by-number kit during a craft-store visit with Lily enabled Brooke to *feel* artistic . . . just as, when she rode, her innate gracelessness disappeared. The horses gave her grace.

On that July day, and unbeknownst to Carolyn, an artistic collaboration between the daughters was underway. It was a present for Carolyn, a Christmas gift, which she would love. In fact, the girls had decided, she'd love it so much they really needed to pace themselves. If they finished it too soon, they'd want to give it to her right away.

Carolyn's gift-to-be was hidden in Brooke's rolltop desk. Other works in progress were in plain view.

Brooke and Lily were quite happy to spend an artistic July afternoon while Carolyn's pulled muscle convalesced, a recovery abetted, they hoped, by the pill Carolyn had taken. Carolyn rarely took medication of any kind. Nor did Marla. All their lives, both friends had enjoyed bountiful health.

But when Faye, whose thirty-six-year-old muscles occasionally proclaimed their age, offered her an over-the-counter muscle relaxant, Carolyn said yes.

Carolyn, too, had an artistic work-in-progress in the playroom. Like Emma, she hoped to create new lilacs. Carolyn's art supplies included a stack of books and one very special journal.

Emma's "Adventures in Horticulture" detailed how "Charlotte" and "James" had come to be, as well as results of each pollination, promising and otherwise, from every floral union she'd tried. The diary provided valuable science to Carolyn, and an invaluable remembrance of the mother she had loved.

Carolyn had started her own, as yet untitled, journal. And with the assistance of her two eager young helpers had recently done three couplings of six carefully selected lilacs, including Emma's "Charlotte" with "James." The seeds would be planted in September, on Brooke's birthday, and who knew if anything would ever come of it?

Who? Carolyn's artist daughter. Lily had long since predicted spectacular lilac-making success, beginning with the first two lilacs her mother would create — named for the grandparents Lily had never met but knew so well.

Lily had also forsaken her own mosaic projects in favor of working on the colors of Carolyn's lilacs-to-be.

The "Emma" lilac could be almost any pink, from delicate to shocking; Emma herself had been both. Mixing leftover paints from Brooke's paint-by-number kits, Lily had arrived at various possibilities and painted the most appealing ones on the *Emma* page of Carolyn's journal.

Then she'd turned her attention to "Charles." Her grandfather's favorite color was blue, her mother told her. Cobalt meets sapphire. Carolyn would know it when she saw it . . . and on this afternoon, she did.

"You've got it, Lil! Would you mind dabbing that color in my journal?"

Lily dabbed. Smiled. Looked up. "How's your muscle feeling, Mommy?"

"Much better, sweet pea. Faye's muscle relaxant really did the trick."

So much so that Carolyn took another, as the dosing recommendations on the bottle prescribed, before she, John and Marla left for a charity dinner-dance at the Silver Fox Inn. Lily and Brooke spent the evening helping, primarily by marveling, as Faye created horsey adornments for tomorrow's wedding cake. The nuptials were to take place at the Polo Club, the bride and groom both avid players.

The girls fell asleep to the fragrance of baking bread and the promise of raspberry toast. They should have awakened only to the scent of warm vanilla, the Polo Club cake itself.

Vanilla did fill the air when Brooke awakened. But it was sound, not scent, that woke her.

She thought, at first, the sound couldn't be real. A creature so wounded couldn't possibly be alive. The injury was too deep.

65

The pain too great.

But the sound *was* real. She needed to get Carolyn to help her find the wailing creature. Rescue it.

Carolyn . . . who slept just down the hall with John . . . in the bedroom from which the anguished sound was coming.

John's sound. John's anguish.

While Carolyn slept. Forever.

She looked so peaceful in death and she was smiling, as if her final dream had been a happy one.

But Carolyn was unable, in death, to rescue her John. He kissed her face, so cold, and held her body, so dead. And to the ears — now deaf — John whispered, wept, *Caro, Caro, Caro.*

And moments later, Lily — so wounded — cried, *Mommy, Mommy, Mommy!*

6

"What happened to her?"

Brooke answered Rafe's question with a startled frown. She'd been speaking aloud — hadn't she?

"I know she died, Brooke. But do you know —" *Why?* Rafe didn't say the impossible word. *Why* was too vague, too open-ended, and too likely, he knew — oh, he knew — to evoke a cascade of torments. Why had the rains come? Why had the mountain crumbled? Why had his family drowned? "Do you know, medically, what caused her death?"

"No. I don't. But there *was* a diagnosis. I overheard my mother telling my grandmother that if only she'd known — whatever it was — or John had, or Faye, or even Carolyn herself, she'd never have taken the muscle relaxant."

And Carolyn might have been saved. The *if only* made the survivors' anguish all the worse. Rafe knew. If only he'd listened *even more* carefully to the elders.

Brooke stared at a blade of grass and

gnawed her lower lip. There was more story.

More confession.

"Brooke?"

"I was so afraid after that."

"Of sleeping?" *Never to awaken?*

"Of Lily's sleeping."

Carolyn's daughter, however, had no such fear. The grieving eight-year-old welcomed the reunion with Carolyn in her dreams.

Lily slept and Brooke kept vigil — as, in the darkness, did John. He stood over his dreaming daughter, listening to her breathe.

Lily was watched. Constantly. But she became sick, near death, right before their eyes. Blinded by happiness when Carolyn was alive, her loved ones had become unsighted by sadness since her death.

When Lily's sepsis finally declared itself, it did so with fury.

Everything plummeted, her temperature included, ominous evidence of how overwhelming the bacterial infection was. Her blood pressure collapsed; her blood counts did, too. She bled, a mass exodus caused by DIC, the series of coagulation miscues that caused a patient to both hemorrhage and clot. Lily's consciousness cratered, her kidneys failed, and she became so perilously acidic that her heart forgot even the most rudimentary steps of its once rhythmic and joyful dance.

Lily had been having abdominal pain for a while, they'd later learn, in the right lower quadrant just as Carolyn's had been. But Carolyn's appendix had been removed without incident — or the slightest hint of rupture — when she was Lily's age.

When Lily's appendix finally burst, the pain vanished temporarily. The pressure was relieved, and the countless bacteria that spilled into her peritoneum needed a little time — not much — to settle into the nooks and crannies of their fertile new home.

Once settled, the tiny invaders multiplied at an astonishing rate, and when a microbial neighborhood became too crowded, entire families relocated, quite happily, to Lily's lungs, bloodstream, kidneys, bones.

When Lily's abdominal pain returned, it was accompanied by septic shock and its myriad sequellae.

Despite the best weapons of modern medicine, and the best practitioners, Lily's very survival was in peril. And even when, with cautious optimism, her doctors acknowledged that she seemed to be turning the corner, a major setback loomed ahead. A loop of small intestine was in danger of strangulation by the "violin string" adhesions that would permanently memorialize the ferocious battle waged within.

The pediatric surgeons operated emergently again, the fourth such assault. Lily survived. Again. And eventually Lily Forsythe Rutledge came home.

A small pharmacy of medications arrived with her, a medley of tablets, powders, liquids and caps, the equivalents of which she'd received intravenously throughout her hospital stay.

Lily needed round-the-clock dosing, a responsibility that John, Faye and Marla were eager to assume. They were determined to keep their precious Lily home where she belonged, and to make her well. The frail little girl was no less determined. She hated the worry she'd caused, especially for her father. He'd already lost so much.

She'd take her medications, every one, and in no time she'd be back to normal. But Lily couldn't swallow the pills, no matter how hard she tried. Her throat closed, she couldn't help it, and she choked and gagged.

Lily had been unafraid of sleep following Carolyn's death and had been stoically silent when her stomach ached. She'd wanted to sleep like Carolyn, to hurt like Carolyn.

But when it came to taking pills, as her mother had on that fateful afternoon, something within Lily balked. Her subconscious, perhaps — or maybe her heart — voiced the protest she wished she'd known to voice on that summer day. *Don't take Faye's pills, Mommy! Please don't!*

The same *if only* haunted Faye, even though she'd been told categorically it should not. Still, it was the trained dietician and clever cook who ensured that Lily's meds would work their magic.

Faye made life-saving shakes for Lily, delicious concoctions into which the small pharmacy could be ground, sprinkled, poured.

Did Lily know her medications were hidden in the shakes? Maybe. Or maybe she simply chose not to know.

Eventually she did acknowledge it. And, eventually, Lily could swallow without gagging every medicine that was prescribed. But there were still times, when Lily was especially weak, that Faye would blend Lily's pills into the shakes which — meds or no meds — Faye made for Lily every day. Lily needed the supplemental calories. Every day. And a shake just before eating often encouraged her finicky digestive tract to accept solid food without rebellion.

Lily's wish to spare her father further worry didn't come true. No one knew what it was, this illness that taunted with unexpected periods of wellness only to return with no warning at all.

It affected every organ system, just as the sepsis had — as if lingering wounds reopened on whim, wept again, bled anew.

Lily's illness "felt" autoimmune to her team of doctors at D.C.'s Swedish Medical Center. And, the physicians at the renowned hospital concurred, an autoimmune process made scientific sense.

Lily's sepsis had been accompanied by a massive antigenic assault. The bacteria were foreign; so, too, the numerous pharmaceuticals she'd received. Her besieged immune system had done its best to custom-make antibodies directed at each and every invader. But such precision was impossible even under a far less aggressive attack.

The antibodies were more bomb than bullet, a scattershot in which her own tissues couldn't help but be harmed.

Damage caused by such friendly fire had ample precedent in medicine, and although Lily didn't have a *known* autoimmune syndrome, her illness was in many respects "lupus-like." Her central nervous system symptoms especially — including the hallucinations she occasionally had — were reminiscent of lupus cerebritis. And, albeit in low titer, an anti-nuclear antibody was detected in her blood.

Lily's immune system had turned against her, creating antibodies whose only purpose was to attack her normal cells.

"She'd always been so healthy," Brooke said. "And so happy. Every cell inside her should have *loved* being part of her life. But now . . . she must wonder why her body decided to betray her. She must wonder about that all the time."

Rafe had been listening, again without interruption, and making mental notes of all the medical words Brooke used. It was as if they belonged to her. She seemed to believe, almost, that if she put them inside her, they might leave Lily alone.

He'd look the words up later, including one he thought he'd correctly deduced.

73

Hematemesis, Rafe felt quite certain, meant to vomit blood. Lily's hematemesis had been a consequence of vomiting itself, a retching so violent that her battered esophagus had bled.

Understanding each term would clarify the scientific details of Lily's ordeal. But the most important truth was crystal clear: Brooke ached for her little sister.

Missed her.

And blamed herself for the estrangement that had so obviously occurred. Brooke had watched Lily become ill. Her loving vigil hadn't been enough.

If only she'd watched her little sister *even more* carefully.

It was time to interrupt the storyteller's solemn tale. Rafe did so with a question to which he already knew the answer. "Have you talked to Lily about the fact that she must feel betrayed by her own body?"

"We don't talk much anymore."

"Where is she now?"

"In Switzerland with my mother and John. Her nephrologist thinks she may have a potassium-wasting nephropathy. There's a research institute in Geneva that specializes in electrolyte disorders."

"*You're* not in Geneva."

"No. I never go to the hospital, even

when Lily's admitted to SMC. I was too young, and she was too ill, the first time, and since then . . . my mother thinks it's best if I don't. I'm sure she's right. I might not be able to hide my worry. It's hard enough for John, although he does, at least from Lily. But sometimes, when her doctors send him home to rest, he looks as if he's just found Carolyn again, lying dead beside him in their bed. He must feel that way every time Lily has a relapse."

"What about your mother?"

"She's *amazing,* an absolute rock. She's devastated, too, by Lily's setbacks. But all anyone ever sees is her complete confidence that everything's going to be all right. She's protective of Lily, but not overly so, and, both medically and emotionally, she's a huge help to John."

"Medically?"

"I'm sure it's helped John to have her with him when he talks to Lily's doctors. She's really good at being direct without offending. And she's so smart, she knows what questions to ask — and she's read everything there is to read about every sign and symptom Lily's ever had. So have John and Faye, of course."

"What about you?"

"Me?"

"You." *You, you, you.*

"Oh. Well, I've read everything there is to read, too."

Rafe and Brooke had nine perfect days together. All day, every day, from dawn till dusk. They spent those days — all day, every day — with the horses.

But neither rode.

They would ride. Later. When Rhapsody was ready to be ridden by Rafe. But riding was such a small part of being with horses, and Rhapsody was their priority now.

The stallion made progress during those days of spring. He tarried in the morning until it was clear that all of them would be following him from paddock to pasture, and when the rescued seniors returned to the stable for their teatime meals, he wandered to a crest from which both pond and stable could be seen.

The meals were like the shakes Faye made for Lily, digestible and nutritious. One of Faye's wedding-cake blenders, in fact, an older model, puréed the fruits and vegetables, to which were added just-warmed oats.

Minnie, Snow and Grace liked their oatmeal warm. Minnie had become a little hesitant about eating, though, as if after thirty-and-a-half years she couldn't quite remember how.

Brooke had begun adding maple syrup to Minnie's oatmeal. The fragrance seemed to entice her to take the all-important first taste. Still, sometimes a handful of the sweet purée needed to be held directly under her reluctant nose.

"If that doesn't work," Brooke explained to Rafe, "you have to hand-feed her a bite or two, to get her going, to remind her how nice it is to eat. She eats slowly, once she starts. She likes to think about every swallow. Don't you, my Minnie-Min?" Brooke cradled the velvety muzzle and smiled at the attentive brown eyes. "I always stay with her the entire time she's eating. I don't want her to feel abandoned."

Brooke's Minnie-Min was cradled, not abandoned. But what about the abandoned girl? Who cradled her?

"Brooke?"

"Yes?"

"Tell me something true."

"Everything I've told you is true!"

"I know. What I meant was tell me something about you. Just you."

When I'm with you I feel like a ballerina. She couldn't tell him that, even though it was the most important truth of her entire life. The only truth, it seemed at this moment. She looked away. Down. The sight of her jeans, her cowboy boots, tripped an embarrassing truth looming just a few days away.

"I wear a uniform to school. Sweater and skirt. I have to. For the past century or so, the color everyone's required to wear is a *very* bright green."

"Some people believe that a *very* bright green is magical."

"Really?"

"Really."

"Rafe?"

"Brooke."

"Tell me something true."

My heart doesn't scream when I'm with you. "I'm one of those people."

7

"Who needs diamonds when you have the stars?"

Brooke's question was posed to the sparkling sky. It was the final night of Brooke's spring break, and the first time she and Rafe had been together after dark.

"My mother loves jewels," she explained. "Especially diamonds. I don't really . . . get it."

The voice Brooke heard in the darkness a moment later was Rafe's. But the language was music.

"What did you say?" *What are you singing to me?*

"What you said. 'Who needs diamonds when you have the stars?' "

"But in what language?"

"Nahuatl. The language of Mexico at the time of the Spanish conquest."

"The Spanish conquest. We learned about that in fourth, no, third grade. I don't remember being taught the name of the language."

"But were you taught about the emperor

Moctezuma and his empire of farmers and poets and — Brooke?"

"There was a Mo*n*tezuma. But he was the emperor of the Aztecs."

"The Nahua are the Aztecs. That's who I am, Brooke. What I am." *All I ever wanted to be.* "A Nahua — Aztec — farmer."

"No, you're not!"

His different — wrong — looks had mattered so much on the mountain. Could such differentness matter, so much, to her? "I know I don't look like an Aztec. But I am."

"You can't be! The Aztecs weren't farmers, Rafe. Or poets. They were brutal sadists who —" Where was her vehemence coming from? And how could she possibly say something so hurtful to Rafe? "I'm *sorry.*"

"Brutal sadists who did what?"

"Nothing! Third grade was a million years ago. Obviously, I'm misremembering."

"You don't misremember, Brooke. Ever."

"Well, it doesn't matter, anyway. It's ancient history. And even if it weren't, it has nothing to do with *you.*"

But it did have to do with him, and the history was quite modern: a family drowned in a mountain of mud.

"Rafe? Please forgive me."

"There's nothing to forgive."

"Yes, there *is*." Rafe was beside her in the blackness. But so far away.

"It's late. I'll walk you to the mansion."

"Rafe . . ." But he'd withdrawn from her, retreated without moving, the way Rhapsody withdrew.

"It's a school night, Brooke. Let's go."

The elders who'd told him of the bright-green magic of quetzal feathers — but neglected to mention brutal sadists or that they believed gods were real — had nonetheless described the sun's nightly battle against the forces of darkness. It was a ferocious fight, its outcome always in doubt. Only with dawn did Rafe's ancestors know the sun had triumphed and the world would survive another day.

The forces of darkness owned the night sky now. Brooke's gemstone stars had vanished with her. A ceiling of clouds promised a rainy day ahead — assuming a triumphant sun.

The rain would arrive.

The day would.

The sun would triumph, always, for Brooke . . . and for him. At least until he'd learned the truth.

A friendly librarian escorted Rafe to the area of the Forsythe Library where the Aztec books were shelved. Additional books could be requested from other branches throughout the county.

Rafe wouldn't need to make such requests. On the very first page of the very first book was all he would ever need to know.

It was a modern depiction of an ancient ritual. The artist had recreated the horror, with its agonizing detail, in living — dying — color.

The temple steps were particularly bright. Crimson. And the priests, their faces painted black, wore bloodstained cloaks embroidered with skulls as they offered to the heavens the victim's still-beating heart.

The painting was eloquent. And ample.

But Rafe studied every image — there were so many — in every book. He ignored the less brutal images, and those that weren't brutal at all, until he came to a photograph of a statue identical to the one he'd found. It wasn't the same Tlaloc he'd untangled from the vines. The statue pictured here had been discovered in 1908.

The Rain God demanded tears, the photograph's inset noted. Preferably of children. Sacrificial raindrops from innocent eyes.

Fearful parents induced such offerings by piercing delicate flesh with thorns, or holding young faces over steaming peppers. The tears were collected for Tlaloc and placed at his shrines, in the hope that his vengeance would be averted.

The Rain God's demands could have been worse, Rafe found himself thinking. And sometimes were. At certain times, the inset concluded, only tears from children's hearts would do.

The elders had never asked Rafe to take sides in the battle that raged within him. He'd made the decision on his own, had chosen, on his own, which ancestor to love and which to loathe.

He'd chosen to love the Aztec Moctezuma, the emperor of priests who carved hearts from chests with obsidian knives.

Rafe staggered, his soul did, out of the library. His heart was long gone, beating wildly amid the raindrops that wept from the sky.

It was surprising that a man without a heart — and with a dying soul — could think. Or drive.

But Rafe drove, safely, the rain-slick streets, and his thoughts were clear.

It shouldn't matter that his ancestors had been monsters. Brooke had said as much, despite her perfectly remembered horror. And Rafe agreed.

Rationally, it shouldn't matter at all.

But there was nothing rational about the images Rafe had seen. And, once viewed, they were impossible to forget.

Rafe had vowed, that first morning at dawn, that nothing and no one could make him leave the paradise of horses and flowers he had found. Especially not a spoiled teenage girl.

But it was because of her, that lovely innocent, that he had to leave. He'd take the rain with him, would lure Tlaloc and his furies far, far away.

Rafe needed to leave soon. But not without talking to Brooke.

He'd become a storyteller for her, a talker, though he'd been a listener since birth. He'd explain that the images would always be there for both of them — no matter how much neither wanted them to be.

Rafe would talk and talk and talk, the truth, the truth, the truth. To no avail.

Brooke would want him to stay. She'd rescued Rhapsody, after all, asking nothing more from the tormented creature than the chance to offer him a peaceful home.

Brooke might even decide she'd failed Rafe as she'd failed Lily. If only she'd been more vigilant, she'd have sensed Lily's engorged appendix before it ruptured. And if only she'd been more sensitive, insightful, *nice* — the sensitive, insightful, nice girl might believe — she'd have kept silent about the Aztecs.

Truth had been paramount during their nine perfect days of hello. But it would be useless, even harmful, when they said their goodbye.

He'd have to lie. A woman in Texas, he'd explain, was pregnant with his child. He'd left when she'd told him, but had decided to return.

It would be a difficult lie. Rafe would never abandon his baby. But he'd tell the lie convincingly for Brooke . . . who'd view as heroic his willingness to assume his paternal responsibilities, belated though such gallantry might be.

Rafe needed a less sympathetic lie. Okay. He'd hit his pregnant lover, become violent at her news. Maybe she'd even miscarried as a result. The violence had come naturally, he'd confess with a sociopath's non-chalance. Remember his forebears, those knife-wielding priests?

Rafe turned off Canterfield onto the Farm's cobblestone drive. Gilded with sunlight that first dawn, the road glistened with raindrops now — yet, here in this paradise, the man with the vanished heart and agonal soul felt hope.

Hope.

The grisly portrait of the long-ago past was washed away, and Rafe envisioned a shimmering tableau of the not-so-distant future.

He and Brooke would be in the stable, having fed the girls their teatime meals. They'd find a hayloft on this rainy afternoon, and he'd tell her the story of Rafael. And, as he talked, the horrific images would be banished, forever, for both of them. Brooke would see him as *him*, just him, untainted — no, made pure by their nine perfect days.

And if Brooke saw him as the man he was with her, he'd touch her, even though, for the last nine days, he'd vowed to wait. And wait.

But he'd need to touch her on this day, and she'd need him to. And they'd know with certainty, as they must, that Brooke

could feel his touch for what it was —
desire — and know what it could never be
— violent.

Brooke should have joined him in the
stable by three-thirty, and that assumed
she changed her school clothes first. Rafe
had convinced himself she'd be early, still
wearing her quetzal-feather green.

But Brooke wasn't there before three-
thirty. Or *by* three-thirty. And not by three-
thirty-one, thirty-two, thirty-three, or -four
. . . or -nine.

And not by three-forty-nine, when the
rain stopped.

At three-fifty-eight, in the rain-free
silence, the listener heard footsteps draw-
ing near.

8

She was delicate, the girl whose footsteps Rafe heard. Ethereal. Her eyes shone bright green against her translucent skin and her hair was cascading sunlight.

Lily had lost her hair, Brooke had told him. Not all of it, but substantial chunks, four Christmases ago.

Lily's hair had grown back as inexplicably as it had disappeared, and she hadn't cut it since. It would have reached her waist by now, had her health been unrestrained. But it had grown in rare spurts, as Lily herself did, and only when the autoantibodies permitted such growth.

"Hi. I'm Lily. You must be Rafe?"

"I am. Hi."

"I was looking for Brooke. Faye thought she'd be running late, because of the rain, and that she'd come straight here after school. Do you mind if I wait for her?"

Lily was the Forsythe daughter. This stable was hers. But she was asking his permission to stay. "Not at all. Would you like to help me feed the horses?"

"Yes. Thank you."

There wasn't anything for Lily to do. Rafe had already puréed the apples, warmed the oatmeal, and added to their respective buckets the vitamins, minerals and maple syrup each was to receive.

Lily followed as Rafe carried the buckets to the spot where the seniors awaited their tea.

Snow and Grace began slurping immediately. But Minnie was thinking about her meal. She was interested, sniffing, but uncommitted to venturing a taste.

Rafe would give her a few minutes to make the decision on her own before offering the syrupy concoction by hand.

Rafe watched Minnie. And Lily watched Minnie.

The silence was comfortable.

But here was the sister Brooke missed so much. . . .

"How was Switzerland?"

"Great. Thank you. The country was beautiful, and everyone was very nice. And —" Lily's voice became even softer "— for me, medically, it was wonderful. I feel good . . . strong . . . like new. Star Bright had better watch out."

"Star Bright?"

"Brooke. You know, from the child's

verse 'Star Light, Star Bright'?"

"I don't know it."

"Oh. Well, I guess it *is* a little-girl thing."

Rafe had learned a lexicon of new words from Star Bright. *Autoimmune. Hemolysis. Hypokalemia. Disseminated intravascular coagulopathy — DIC.*

He'd learned, as well, the correct definition of a word he'd thought he knew: *Aztec.*

And now from Lily . . . "Will you tell me the verse?"

"Sure! It goes like this: 'Star Light, Star Bright, first star I see tonight. I wish I may, I wish I might, have the wish I wish tonight.' "

"I like it."

"So do I. It was my mother's favorite, which made it Brooke's and mine. And it was perfect for us. Our names of course — Star Light for Lily, Star Bright for Brooke — as well as my light coloring and Brooke's incredibly bright mind. Then my mother died, and I became ill, and . . ."

Star Light and Star Bright had drifted apart.

Rafe had learned that sadness from Brooke. But, from Lily, he was learning something Brooke didn't know. Lily, too, felt responsible for the distance between them — was haunted, like Brooke, by an *if only*.

If only she'd been able to convince the traitorous antibodies to go away.

"And now," Rafe said, "you're good as new."

"I am," Lily murmured. "I really *am*."

And she'd just discovered that her father knew it, too.

She'd been in the kitchen when John returned from his inspection of the property, a search for standing water that might flood the buildings' lower floors.

He must have found such impromptu ponds, Lily decided when she glimpsed his scowl in the pelting rain. The frown vanished, however, by the time John entered the kitchen, and the report from his tour of the grounds was good.

Lily expected fatherly worry when she announced her plan to go to the stable in search of Brooke. She felt strong enough, she really did, and as for the rain — what rain? The downpour had diminished from torrential to virtually nonexistent in the scant moments her father had been inside, as if his scowl had sent it away.

John voiced no concern about her impending journey. He merely positioned her parka hood over her head, just as Carolyn would have, even though he knew Lily would sweep it away the instant she stepped outside.

The old Lily, that is. The girl whose mother was alive. The girl who'd enjoyed glorious health.

John might have been lost in a time warp. Except that he didn't seem lost at all. Even when he failed to remind her to be careful and said something quite surprising instead.

Have fun, Lily.

Have *fun.*

"Why does Star Bright need to watch out?" Rafe asked, returning to Lily's earlier remark as Minnie began to eat.

"Because one of these days, she won't be the only horsewoman on the Farm. I may have to ask her to teach me to ride again, though, *and* how to jump."

Rafe knew Lily hadn't ridden since her illness. It was far too dangerous for her fragile bones. But she was making a bold forecast now. She'd live to become a horse*woman,* and she'd be a dazzling equestrienne at that.

"Brooke will want to teach you."

"I hope so."

"I know so, Lily."

"You do?"

"I do."

"Will you teach me, too, Rafe?"

She'd been a rescuer once of broken and discarded things. Now Lily was asking if Rafe would help her with this most delicate of repairs. And, in her soft request, she was saying more: that only with his help could the rescue of shattered sisters succeed.

Rafe smiled at Star Light, believed in her glow. "Sure I will. Brooke and I will teach you together."

Brooke. Star Bright. Where the hell was she?

She was a mile away, only a mile at last. It would be a slow mile, as every sodden one had been, a journey of flooded roads and labyrinthine detours.

And of rain, which subsided when the lilac fences came into view.

Brooke was so eager to be home — to be with Rafe. She had so much to tell him.

She'd been wrong, unfair, about the Aztecs, and she knew why. Timing. Forest Ridge Academy's third-grade curriculum placed the history of Mexico in the fall semester, which meant it had begun just six weeks after Carolyn's death and only a few days after the hospitalization during which Lily, too, had nearly died.

It had been a terrifying time. No wonder Aztec warriors had haunted Brooke's dreams, grabbing Lily even as Brooke watched — her vigil not good enough — taking her away in the blackness of night.

Brooke had feared the Aztecs. Hated them. And, she realized during her Monday morning drive to school, she'd made them symbols of all that had been lost. Stolen.

Maybe — probably — in her grief and fear, she had even made *them* the thieves.

Not surprisingly, she'd exaggerated the bad and ignored the good. Not that she'd remembered any good. But she'd decided to find some in the school library, during second-period study hall and again at lunch. Something *good* to tell Rafe.

It was an easy search. Most Aztecs *had* been farmers. And there *had* been poets. And musicians and architects. And weavers and engineers.

The Aztecs had been passionate about flowers. And mosaics. Nahua mosaic artists worked in turquoise, amethyst, gold — and feathers, discarded plumes rescued from the ground, not stolen, never stolen, from birds.

Aztecs tied the knot, literally, when they wed, the bride's blouse to her groom's nuptial cloak. They were young, those wedding celebrants, the bride just sixteen, the groom twenty or twenty-one. By Rafe's age — and hers — Rafe's forebears would have been welcoming, with special poems, the first of their many children.

Would Brooke tell Rafe that his ancestors had been, at their respective ages, already married? Maybe.

May. Be.

She'd definitely ask him to teach her to say in his musical language, *Who needs diamonds when you have the stars?* And, *Who needs pearls when you have the moon?*

Brooke was supposed to deliver the valedictory address at her graduation in June, an assignment that had been worrying her — a lot. She had nothing of value, much less inspiration, to impart to the classmates she scarcely knew. She imagined those classmates would agree.

But she'd found a Nahuatl poem, a nineteenth-century translation by a Scotsman, and if she could recite that to her classmates . . .

The rain no longer fell. But new ponds would have appeared in Rhapsody's pasture. She and Rafe would be inside the stable, cocooned within the cherished scents of horse and hay, and she'd tell him what she'd learned, all the goodness and joy, and why she'd been so unfair, and he'd forgive her and they'd be back where they were before he'd withdrawn.

And maybe, from that place, they could even go forward. Maybe, maybe, they would touch.

There hadn't been, in their nine perfect days, even an accidental caress. Rafe had kept a polite distance.

But had he ever wondered, as she so often had, how his skin touching hers might feel? And had he wanted, sometimes desperately, to know?

Maybe today, as they reached for the same piece of straw — *Who needs gold when you have a stable full of straw?* — it would happen by accident, and . . .

Brooke turned off Canterfield at four. She'd join Rafe right away. Yes, in the green that was royal to the ancient Aztecs . . . and magical to the modern one.

Brooke's plans changed when she approached the mansion. Her mother's west-wing suite was illuminated. So, too, was the east-wing bedroom where Carolyn had died and John still slept.

Lily's bedroom was dark, though, as lightless as Brooke's bedroom six windows away. It was supposed to have been a temporary separation seven years ago. Just until Lily was fully recovered. It had, of course, become a permanent one.

A flicker of motion, her mother's gliding silhouette, drew Brooke's gaze back to the west wing. She saw John, too, in his study on the floor below.

John wasn't moving. He stood, head bent, as if studying a document on his desk. And yet . . . his stillness seemed ominous. Utter and absolute. Like Carolyn had been. Like death had been.

John and Marla were home five days ahead of even their most optimistic plans. And Lily's bedroom was black. And Marla's gliding shadow wasn't a reassurance. Her mother never walked any other way.

But . . . *no.* There were other explanations. Logical ones. John would've checked in with Curtis Franklin on his return. And, given their busy practice, a complex legal issue — or two — would surely have arisen while John was away.

John was pondering that. And her mother was unpacking. And Lily would be in the kitchen enjoying a reunion visit with Faye.

Brooke would see Faye and Lily. Soon. She'd sped past the stable and was parking her car.

The kitchen was bright in the storm-darkened twilight. Faye was alone. And unhearing above the water running in the sink.

"Faye?"

"Brooke! You're home. Good."

"Is Lily?"

"What, home? You bet. She's at the stable looking for you."

"So she's all right?"

"More than all right. I get the distinct impression from John that she's well on her way to being cured."

"Oh, Faye." New and wondrous logic explained John's motionless silhouette. He was praying. Giving thanks. And speaking to his beloved Carolyn. *Our baby's fine, my love. Our little girl is fine.* "I'm going to the stable."

"Brooke?"

"Yes?"

"In the interests of happiness all around, I wonder if you should scoot upstairs first? To wish your mother welcome home?"

"Good idea, Faye. Thank you. I do believe I will!"

9

The door to Marla's suite was wide open. Brooke stepped out of her shoes and into the sitting room.

During the era of Forsythe men, a constant stream of dignitaries had enjoyed rooms such as this. Beginning with Charlotte, the guest list became more selective. Just because someone happened to be a president, first lady, chief justice or king didn't mean . . . And Charlotte's daughter, Emma, being Emma, never invited any strangers at all.

Marla's suite was cream, mauve, grand. And bright, even on a stormy day. Yet, for Brooke, the suite felt shadowed, as it always did, veiled.

There were secrets here. Secrets . . . even though in the sitting room, they were hidden in plain view.

During the years of Lily's illness, the alcove beside the fireplace had become a library of medical texts. A copy of *Stedman's Medical Dictionary* sat on the shelves, too, beside the most current edition of the *Physicians' Desk Reference* — the *PDR*.

Every relevant page was bookmarked — by Marla — for John, for Brooke, for Faye. And for Lily, if, when, she ever wanted to read about the symptoms she was living. The procedures she was enduring.

Until such time, the books were here, in plain view yet somehow hidden. Like Lily's illness . . . This was what truly shadowed the room.

But the veil would soon be gone. The darkness was dissipating even now, with just the knowledge that Lily was on her way to being cured.

And the other secret in the west-wing suite, the one hidden in the nightstand beside her mother's bed? Inconsequential by comparison. So what if Brooke felt its shadowy presence every time she walked into the suite? Her discomfort, her worry, was *nothing* compared to the agony of a bone marrow biopsy or the constant fear that your body would betray you forever.

Brooke was smiling as she approached the open bedroom door, her footfalls soundless on the carpet. In the moments before Marla realized she was there, Brooke simply stared at her mother.

Marla Blair was beautiful. Morning,

noon, night. With makeup or without. With sleep or without. And after a transatlantic flight, her clothes were unrumpled and she looked refreshed.

Hidden in plain view. That was Marla. She could hide her exhaustion, conceal her fear. She'd done so throughout Lily's illness, holding all of them together with her steadfast optimism — which now had been proven correct.

If a positive attitude was the best medicine, then it was Marla who'd made Lily well.

"*There* you are!" Marla abandoned a stack of neatly folded clothes, laundered in Switzerland before the trip home, and greeted Brooke with an enthusiastic hug.

Brooke towered over her mother and outweighed her by many — many — pounds. The mother-daughter coloring was identical, skin, hair, eyes, although the freckles were Brooke's alone. And, of course, they didn't look alike.

"I'm so glad you're home, Brooke." Marla released her and looked . . . up. "I was beginning to worry."

"I'm fine. Safe and sound. I'm glad you're home, too."

"I'm glad to *be* home. And oh, do I have news."

"Lily's doing well?" Brooke had no intention of spoiling the revelation that was her mother's to make.

"Wonderfully well. So well that being a bridesmaid will be pure fun for her, not fatiguing in the least."

"Being a bridesmaid?"

"With you. At the marriage of *your* mother and *her* father."

"You and John?"

"Would you please not look so shocked?"

"It's just that —"

"John and I are too old for romance? Forty-three may seem decrepit to you now. But I assure you it won't when you're there. And forty-six — well, John's better in every way than when he and I dated twenty-five years ago."

"You and John dated?"

"In college. Long before either of us met Carolyn. I was a freshman. John was a senior. It was Curtis who introduced us. He and I were about ninety minutes into a *disastrous* blind date. John and Curtis were friends, and John and I clicked."

"But it was all right when it ended?"

"Perfectly! For both of us. All of us. Curtis is, as you know, a dear, *dear* friend, and John and I were very old news by the

102

time he and Carolyn fell in love." Marla's expression sobered. "John misses Carolyn, Brooke, and he'll love her forever. We all will. But she'd be happy about John and me. She'd want him to be less lonely, less alone — don't you think?"

"Yes. I do." Carolyn would want happiness for John. For them all. And, on this day of such joyous news, Carolyn would want every veil to be lifted, every secret exposed. The one in the sitting room.

And the one in the bedroom, too.

Brooke's gaze took a meandering route to the nightstand, from her rain-rumpled skirt to the snowy-white carpet to Marla's bedroom slippers tucked beneath the dust ruffle.

"What on *earth* are you thinking?" Marla finally asked.

"I was wondering if you still have the gun."

"For heaven's sake, Brooke! Are you still obsessing about that old thing?"

"I'm not obsessing."

"But you're remembering it, which is far more than I've done for years. I do still have it. But you know what? John would obsess, too, if he knew. So how about, as a wedding present to you and John, I simply get rid of it?"

"That would be *great*."

"Consider it done. And speaking of wedding presents you might like, how does Brooke Rutledge sound to you?"

"John wants to adopt me?"

"Of course! Wants to and is going to."

"That's so nice of him."

"It's what he wants," Marla repeated. Her eyes strayed around the room, an unfocused journey as her mind traveled to very specific thoughts, then fixed on her daughter. "And, Brooke, it's important for Lily's future and the future of the Farm."

"I don't understand."

"The time may come when the Farm and its responsibilities will fall to you."

The bedroom veil, which had been lifting, fell again. "The Farm is *Lily's*. And she's doing wonderfully well, you said so yourself. And Faye got the distinct impression from John that she's on her way to becoming cured."

"She did? Well, that's *definitely* our hope. And if John wants to call it a cure, why not? He's waited long enough for this day."

"But isn't it a cure?"

"Not technically. Since we still don't know what she had, the doctors are reluctant to say it's truly gone. 'Permanent remission,' they're calling it. But as long as nothing happens to upset the delicate balance she's finally achieved, for all intents and purposes it *is* a cure."

"What could upset the balance?"

"Any number of things, the most certain of which would be pregnancy."

"Because of Charlotte and Emma? All the difficulties they had?"

"What they went through would be a significant stress on Lily. On anyone. But their multiple miscarriages were probably a sign of the times, a much less sophisticated era in obstetrics, and not genetic at all. Just as we learned last year from Lily's gynecologist that Carolyn's ruptured ectopic *doesn't* increase the likelihood that Lily would have the same thing."

"Carolyn's ruptured ectopic?"

"That's why she died, Brooke. She hemorrhaged internally. I thought you knew. I assumed Lily would have told you."

Star Light and Star Bright don't talk much these days . . . these years. Yet on this stormy afternoon Lily had gone to the stable to find her. "No. She didn't."

"She probably didn't want to remind you of Carolyn's death. Bring up all that sadness. I didn't mean to, either."

"I'm okay." *Oh, Carolyn.* "So Lily *could* have a completely normal pregnancy. . . ."

"Yes. She could. But it would mean taking a terrible risk. All sorts of immunologic changes need to happen in a normal pregnancy, the most important of which is a natural immunosuppression. That's a delicate balance in itself. The mother's immune system needs to be suppressed just enough that the baby won't be seen as foreign, but not so much that either mother or baby has increased susceptibility to infection. Since no one knows what Lily's illness has been, except that it's *something* autoimmune, it's impossible to predict how her immune system would react. But everyone's worried that it could be . . . catastrophic. For Lily, her baby or both."

"So she should never have children."

"No, Brooke. She never should. It's simply too dangerous. But she'd take the risk, you know she would, if the future of the Farm depended solely on her."

Just as, since 1879, it had depended on the other Forsythe women — Forsythe mothers. Lily was born to be a mother, and a grandmother, and the mistress of Fox-Haven Farm. That was what Carolyn would have wanted — *oh, Carolyn* — and what John would want, too.

Did want. That was what Brooke had seen in his study. What his deathly still

106

shadow meant.

"I don't think John should adopt me."

"What?"

"And I don't think he really wants to."

"Yes, he does."

"But there's no reason! The doctors could find a definite diagnosis for Lily any day. They'd know how to take care of her during a pregnancy then, even if they discovered that what she had couldn't be cured. If John adopted me now, it would feel like he was giving up on finding a diagnosis — and a cure — for Lily. Giving up on Lily herself. Don't you think so?"

"No. I really don't. And neither does John. It wouldn't stop the search for answers. Lily knows that. But it would be a relief to her, one less worry, to know that in the event a *true* cure is never found, the Farm would remain within the family."

"But I'm not a Forsythe."

Marla smiled. "Only if you're a stickler for genes, which Carolyn never was. She loved me as a sister and you as a daughter. The Farm is your home, Brooke. You love it as much as Lily does. Don't you?"

"Yes." And what her mother was saying was true: No one would give up on Lily, ever. So why did the room feel even darker?

"Good. Besides, according to Lorraine, you've already begun doing a little property management. You fired Jared, I hear, and hired someone new named Rafe?"

"I didn't exactly fire Jared, and it was Lorraine who hired Rafe."

"And is he working out so far?"

He. Rafe. With whom Brooke felt like a ballerina, this man she wanted so desperately to touch, and because of whom she'd decided not to go to college this fall. Her life was here, with Rafe — of whom her mother would *not* approve. Brooke didn't want the thought. But there it was. And it was true. Marla would be particularly disapproving of the mestizo cowboy as a match for her daughter if the Farm fell to Brooke.

Which it never would. A diagnosis would be made. A cure would be found.

And the woman who should be a mother *would* be.

But only, the shadows in the ever-smaller bedroom warned her, if John didn't adopt her — if there was no hint, however slight, that anyone believed Lily could ever be replaced.

There was a perfect way to render the adoption issue moot, an obstacle her mother would be extremely loath to overcome.

"You'd need to contact my biological father, wouldn't you? To ask him to legally relinquish his parental rights?"

"In theory. Yes. But I don't know who he is."

Her absentee father hadn't been worth knowing, Marla had told Brooke the one time the subject had come up. Which meant, Brooke had always assumed, that it had been a relationship her mother regretted, an embarrassing lapse in judgment — and in taste. A mestizo cowboy, perhaps?

But now . . . Did Marla really have so many lovers, she had no idea which one had fathered her child? "You don't?"

"No." Marla sat with surprising heaviness on her bed and stared for several moments at her nylon-stockinged feet. When she looked up, Brooke saw the exhaustion that had, until then, been concealed. "He's the reason I have the gun. I bought it, too late, because of him."

"Because he —"

"Attacked me. Raped me."

"Oh, *no!* I'm so *sorry.*"

A faint smile touched Marla's tired face. "You're hardly responsible. And if it hadn't happened, I'd never have had you. I won't deny it was traumatic. But I dealt with it, got over it, long ago." She glanced at the nightstand where the gun purchased too late was kept. "It happened in my own bed, Brooke, in the colonial near Embassy Row."

Brooke knew very little about the Georgetown house where her mother had lived before moving to the Farm. It had been a minor footnote to the stories Marla and Carolyn had told. *No wonder.*

"Did you live there alone?"

"No. There were six of us, five physicians — residents at Swedish — and me. And no, it wasn't one of my three male housemates who attacked me. We were close friends, *trusted* friends. All six of us. Friends," Marla repeated quietly, "who decided it would be fun to have a party that New Year's Eve. It wasn't a wild party. Gatherings of sleep-deprived interns and residents never were. I was very tired, too, that night and went to bed before midnight. The next thing I knew . . . well. I was raped. He was a guest of a guest, I've always imagined. A date, husband, brother, friend. Probably someone in town for the holidays."

"But what if he wasn't a guest of a guest? What if he's *still* a doctor at SMC?"

"I seriously doubt he's a doctor anywhere, Brooke. And certainly not at Swedish. Yes, there are despicable doctors. Faye's ex-husband is a case in point. And maybe there are even psychopathic ones. But SMC recruits the best of the best. A psychopath wouldn't have the credentials, either personal or academic, to practice there."

"You've spent so much time at Swedish in the past seven years. That must have been awfully difficult for you."

"Not difficult at all!" Marla's tiredness vanished. "It's felt comfortable. Like going home. I loved visiting my stranded-in-the-hospital housemates. My SMC memories are good ones. It's been easy for me to return. But you see why John can't ever know about that New Year's Eve."

"He doesn't know?"

"No one does, Brooke. Except you and me. I never even told Carolyn. John would worry if he knew, and he's had enough worries, real ones, to last a lifetime. Okay? As *your* wedding present to me?"

"Yes. Okay."

"Thank you." Marla shook her head in faint disbelief. "We've touched on some rather serious topics, haven't we? I hadn't intended to. Jet lag, I suppose. But I have one more. Don't worry! It's not *that* bad.

111

Or maybe it is."

"What?"

"I know I'm not the world's greatest mother."

"But you are!"

"For Lily, maybe, but not for you."

"I'm *fine*."

"Because of you, not me. You've always been so grown-up. Maybe, now that Lily's doing so well, we'll be able to spend some time together before you're off to Vassar."

I'm not going to Vassar.

"Would you like that?"

She would. Had always wanted to. "Yes."

"Good. So would I. Well, Faye's making a fabulous dinner to be savored soon. I'm going to shower and get a little dressy first."

"Should I?"

"Get a little dressy? Not unless you have an overwhelming urge to do so. Tonight's about celebrating who we are and the family we'll be." Marla rose from her bed, glided over to Brooke, and moved an unruly tendril away from Brooke's eyes. "You, my lovely tomboy, may wear your most comfortable jeans."

She'd change later from her school clothes to jeans.

All that mattered right now was getting to the stable — to Rafe — as quickly as she could. The shortest route took her down the stairs and out the front door without even a ten-second detour to retrieve a coat.

She could have used one. The wind was as cold as the revelations that swirled within.

Carolyn, oh, Carolyn had hemorrhaged to death. And it had been a precious little life, a baby that would have been so wanted, that caused her to die.

Marla had probably hemorrhaged, too, the night Brooke became the product of a man's violence, a woman's terror and the lack of a murder weapon nearby.

The night she'd inherited her mother's brains and her father's brawn.

My lovely tomboy. Brooke had been happy to be called a tomboy, especially as affectionately as Marla always said it. But she hadn't *felt* like a tomboy for the past nine days. Hadn't been one. But what if Rafe saw her as the tomboy she'd been and not the ballerina she'd become? What if that was the reason he kept a polite distance between them?

Lily should never have children. Brooke almost welcomed the remembered revelation, hated as it was, because it came with a punishing gust that, for the moment, blew away her thoughts about Rafe.

Almost welcomed it . . . then did. Because by changing one little word, the revelation lost its chill. She felt warm now, despite the icy wind.

Lily should never *bear* children. And wouldn't have to. Brooke would provide safe haven for Lily's babies. The solution was so obvious. A less jet-lagged Marla would have tumbled to it. Brooke would have, too, if everything hadn't felt so veiled.

The veils were gone now. It didn't even matter whether Lily's illness ever had a name. Or a cure. The permanent remission would keep the Forsythe mother-to-be wonderfully well forever.

Brooke was tempted to let Marla know right away. And could. Her mother's shadow hadn't yet glided away.

But there was a second shadow in the brightly lit bedroom. John's.

Brooke *could* tell them both. And yet . . . the pull to the stable — to Rafe — was stronger.

Rafe, who would see her for the ballerina she was, and Lily, with whom there'd be closeness again.

Brooke smiled into the lashing wind as

she ran toward the stable. She felt graceful as she ran. She could even turn cartwheels if she chose to, perfect ones like Lily's.

The sound, loud and sharp, thundered when the stable door was mere dancing steps away. Another sound exploded within instants of the first.

Brooke spun toward the bedroom from which the sounds had come — and where both silhouettes had disappeared.

Brooke saw Faye running toward the west wing, and now Brooke was running, and Rafe was beside her, and then in front of her, and Lily, who hadn't run in years, was running, too. . . .

Rafe told them all to wait in the foyer while he went upstairs.

None of them did.

So they saw, all of them, what lay on the snow-white carpet.

And Brooke's heart, as it was breaking, whispered softly: *Who needs rubies when you have so much blood?*

10

FoxHaven Farm

Wednesday, April 11

Present Day

Rafe looked from the greenhouse clock —
3:00 — to the pasture beside the pond. It
had been Rhapsody's pasture during those
nine perfect days. And the equine girls' pasture. And their pasture, hers and his.

Assuming her flight was on time, Brooke
would reach the Farm within the hour. By
four. Teatime once for rescued horses and,
twelve years ago, a time of devastation for
Star Light and Star Bright.

Brooke hadn't screamed at the sight of
her mother and Lily's father lying dead on
the bedroom floor. She'd merely stared at
the carnage, a vision hauntingly reminiscent of what Rafe had seen in the library
earlier that day.

Lily hadn't screamed, either. But she'd

collapsed, and then clung to Rafe, as his sisters had, needing him, trusting him. He'd carried her from the blood-spattered bedroom to the ambulance that arrived, sirens shrieking. He'd ridden with her — still clinging to him all the way — to SMC. Only when she was sedated and sleeping in a familiar hospital bed had he left her side to find Brooke . . . who was long gone.

A limousine had come for her within an hour of Elise Blair's next-of-kin notification that her daughter was dead. Elise's orphaned granddaughter had been driven to Dulles, where one of Elise's protective ex-husbands had met her and flown with her to LA.

It was Curtis Franklin who told Rafe about Brooke. John's friend and partner had been in the mansion throughout the night, solemnly hosting the crime-scene investigators, the coroner, the towns-people, the press.

Curtis remained Rafe's source of infor-mation about Brooke over the ensuing twelve years, his only source until the Internet.

Rafe gleaned slightly more data on-line than the bare-bones facts the attorney knew. Brooke was an archeologist. A Ph.D. She had an adjunct faculty appointment at

Berkeley, where she'd earned her degree, but according to an alumni website, Dr. Blair had forsaken the ivory tower for the dust and dirt of the dig.

Dust, dirt and sand. Brooke's specialty was Egypt. She was a "wizard" — a quote from a colleague — at interpreting hieroglyphics, notably the pyramid texts, and had "immeasurably advanced" the understanding of the ancient Egyptian "fascination with the stars."

Rafe learned about Brooke's steel magnolia grandmother, too, from Curtis. At the behest of Elise Blair, a wrongful-death lawsuit was filed against John's estate.

It didn't matter that the forensics were clear: Marla had fired first, a kill-shot to John's heart, and in the scant seconds before his death, he'd turned the gun on her.

But John was the aggressor, the lawsuit contended. He'd frightened Marla. Threatened her. Marla had acted in self-defense.

That theory was the most logical — and lucrative — for the plaintiff's attorneys to choose. And although the notion of a threatening John Rutledge would have been dismissed out of hand before the events of that afternoon, so too would any inkling of the horror that had indisputably occurred.

No one in town believed it was terror of John that had prompted Marla to shoot. Indeed it was only after the murder-by-intruder hope was dashed that the people of Forsythe even considered the possibility that either Marla or John had so much as touched the gun.

Once considered, the idea that the deaths were accidental drew wide appeal. Marla was showing John the gun. She didn't know it was loaded, even though the registration confirmed it was hers. The weapon fired at point-blank range, propelling the fatal bullet into John.

There were two schools of thought on what happened next. Marla's death was equally accidental, the first contended. As John was recoiling from the lethal blast, his fingers, still touching the gun Marla had been showing him, squeezed the trigger reflexively. The second school of thought conceded that a dying John might have lashed out, as even the gentlest of wounded animals could, but he was not in any way to blame.

Both John and Marla had been beloved in life. They remained so, both of them, in death. It had been a moment of madness, those who couldn't *quite* buy the accident theory insisted. A trivial disagreement that escalated beyond all reason, fueled by some metaphysical phenomenon invoked by the storm. Full-moon lunacy was well described, as was the hysteria that came with high tide. It was hardly a stretch to imagine cosmic factors responsible for "rainstorm rage."

No one in Forsythe subscribed to the self-defense argument proffered by Elise's attorneys, nor would they have, regardless of how persuasively the Bel Air legal team presented its case.

But the California attorneys never had the chance to be persuasive. As executor of John's estate and trustee of Lily's several fortunes — Emma's, Carolyn's, John's — until she turned twenty-one, Curtis was empowered to settle the lawsuit without mentioning it to Lily, or anyone, ever.

But Curtis did mention the legal action to the blue-eyed stranger to whom Lily clung emotionally long after the April killings. Rafe concurred with Curtis's plan to settle without informing Lily. Curtis felt quite certain that Brooke's grandmother had made a similar decision to keep Brooke in the dark.

The lawsuit was the only significant

issue Curtis had even considered with-holding from Lily until Brooke's request six weeks ago to visit the Farm.

Marla's mansion possessions had been shipped to Bel Air within a month of her death. But the contents of the cottage — Marla's private retreat after moving her office into town — had not.

By the time Faye offered to ship the cottage items, Elise Blair was already so overwhelmed with the mansion mementos that the matter of sending anything more was placed on indefinite hold.

The cottage itself was also placed on hold, a careful hibernation maintained by Lorraine. She'd purchased The Lilac Cottage company through a lease-to-buy agreement with Elise and, by adhering to Marla's standards of excellence — including disclosing potential problems in the nicest possible way — had kept her legacy alive.

Brooke told Curtis she'd like to go through her mother's things in the cottage, if that was okay.

Curtis discussed her request, first, with Rafe.

Rafe had known exactly how Lily would reply: Of course it was okay.

But, as Rafe returned his gaze to the

greenhouse clock on this Wednesday afternoon, he wondered if it really was.

He was about to find out.

The archeologist was planning a five-night FoxHaven stay, beginning soon. Assuming her plane was on time.

The United non-stop from San Francisco to Dulles was on time, and Brooke's luggage reached baggage claim before she did, and the courtesy bus whisked her from curb to rental-car lot without delay, and the Wednesday afternoon traffic on US-50 was so light that in mere moments she'd be turning left onto Canterfield and a mile beyond that she'd make the right turn onto the Farm.

The only glitch, really, was her heart.

It was stumbling. Gracelessly. Her brain, however, whirred.

Why was she doing this again? a pushy cluster of gray cells wanted to know.

Because, as those cells well knew, she couldn't move forward without first going back. She was stalled on a personal — yes, emotional — level, despite apparent success in other areas of her life.

She'd succeeded brilliantly in school. No surprise there. There'd even been success when she'd given the "real" world a try —

although, arguably, that was where the "apparent" proviso might well be applied.

Could rendezvous with ancient pharaohs truly be classified as *real?*

Brooke was now racing to her rendezvous with a far less ancient past. And notwithstanding endless brain-to-heart conversations, during which she'd believed all potential issues had been amply explored, at this moment she felt totally unprepared for what lay within the lilac fences dead ahead.

What? No, who.

Lily and Rafe.

Lily and Rafe.

The little Brooke knew, she'd learned from Curtis. Her mother's disastrous blind date, then dear, *dear* friend, had been kind to Brooke from her first frantic call — to make certain Lily had survived the trauma of the deaths — to yesterday's, when Brooke had inquired about any last-minute wishes that she cancel her plans.

Lily's emergency admission on that fatal April evening had been her last. She'd been healthy ever since.

But stalled, too? As unable as Brooke to truly move on?

Brooke hoped not. But she didn't know. Asking Curtis felt awkward, and she'd never really considered approaching either Rafe or Faye.

Faye had moved to Chicago when Lily was twenty. Curtis had even told Brooke why. Faye's estranged stepdaughter, Jen, had called out of the blue and their relationship had grown close again. Faye, Jen and Jen's family were frequent FoxHaven guests, and mother and daughter ran a very successful wedding-cake business in the Windy City.

Brooke never asked about Rafe. Never needed to. Whenever she asked Curtis about Lily, she heard as well about Rafe.

Rafe and Lily — who *wasn't* stalled, Brooke discovered when she saw the magnificent tile mosaic at the very entrance of the Farm.

Not only had Lily returned to her art, she'd rescued Carolyn's Christmas gift, the surprise the girls had been working on before Carolyn died.

The girls' artistic collaboration would have been a tiny version of the mosaic Lily had made, and a painted one. But Lily had finished the project faithfully, exactly as they'd so excitedly planned. . . .

Noble Spirits, Brooke's favorite Craft House paint-by-number kit was titled. Before her collaboration with Lily, she'd completed four cantering-horse tableaux, all identical, except for sequential improvements in her technique.

Brooke had always viewed the designated colors as etched in stone. So, too, their assigned places within the lines. She'd been sure the slightest departure would jeopardize the result — the art — that even she could achieve.

Lily had no qualms about deviating from the *Noble Spirits* blueprint and voiced enthusiastic reasons to do so. If Brooke used the deeper of the already provided golds — number 6, not number 5 — on the forelock and tail, the cantering horse would look exactly like Carolyn's beloved Meg.

And if Brooke painted the stable white trimmed with lilac, instead of rust trimmed with brown, Meg could be cantering on the Farm. True, the FoxHaven shade of lilac wasn't included in the kit — no lilac at all. But they could mix pink, blue and cream . . .

It was at that point, when Lily shifted from what Brooke could do — which Brooke knew she could not — to what *they* could do, that Carolyn's Christmas gift was born.

Lily decided to add lilacs to the painted

landscape, too. Carolyn's lilacs — the ones Lily believed her flower-artist mother *would* create.

And here they were, on the mosaic at the entrance of the Farm, the FoxHaven lilacs that might have been. Carolyn hadn't decided which pink would be best for her "Emma." So many shades would do. It was left to Lily to choose, and her choice had been extraordinary, a blend of peach and rose. And the "Charles" that blossomed on Lily's mosaic? The exact blue, that favorite blue, dabbed into Carolyn's journal on the last afternoon Carolyn's girls would ever have with her.

Lily had finished their gift, had journeyed beyond the shattered past to the happiness that had come before. She'd rescued the remnants of that happiness, the broken chips and splintered shards, and created from the rubble this image of beauty, of remembrance.

And of Meg.

FoxHaven's Nutmeg Lady would be twenty-four. Would be, or would have been.

Brooke had never asked Curtis about the horses. Marla's kind friend mightn't have known the answer offhand. But he'd have found out for Marla's daughter.

126

And then what?

Brooke would have hurt more, ached even more.

As she was hurting, aching, now.

"Onward," she whispered to Lily's mosaic.

Onward to the past.

11

The past was the present, Brooke discovered as she drove along the cobblestone drive. Here was spring as it had always been on the Farm. Glorious with promise. Unchanging, yet ever new.

And in the pasture beyond the paddock . . . Meg.

Her mane was burnished gold in the teatime sun, and Rhapsody's lustrous coat gleamed black. And in this suddenly blurred yet joyous marriage of present and past, Brooke saw a roan filly and an ebony colt.

Meg's grandbabies. The children of Rafe's Rhapsody and Brooke's Fleur.

Who wasn't there. Her Fleur.

She would've been only fifteen. Brooke prayed her lovely girl hadn't suffered. And that she hadn't been afraid.

She wouldn't have been. Rafe would have been with her, touching, comforting —

But Rafe hadn't needed to escort Fleur to a final, loving peace. She was trotting into the paddock, jaunty and alert, and searching, searching, until Brooke stepped out of her car and was found.

Fleur welcomed her with velvet kisses, moist nibbles to Brooke's caress, and nodding in her happy way as Brooke's hands traveled from lips to jaw to eyes to ears.

The greeting was familiar. The way their reunions had always been. And when the separation had been especially long, from dusk till dawn, or all day at school, Brooke would hug the powerful neck.

She hugged now and whispered, "Sweet girl, sweet girl, sweet —"

"She remembers you."

The voice was quiet. Familiar.

His.

Face the past. Confront its every shadow. Especially the twilight shadow that was Rafe, the memory that was more substantial, surely, than the man from which it was cast.

Rafe should *not* loom larger than life. Brooke's brain had made that obvious observation many times. Nor should Rafe cast a shadow beyond the actual time they'd shared: nine perfect days, a night of diamond stars and phantom Aztecs, a stormy afternoon of death.

Should not.

But did.

Which was all the more reason to face the past, the reality, him.

Onward . . . to Rafe.

Who was still larger than life.

Fiercer. Harsher. Stronger.

Even more stunningly male.

His blue eyes glittered darker, pierced deeper, and as on that first morning twelve years ago, they wanted — what?

Brooke had stepped away from him then. One startled step. Such retreat was blocked now. But the obstacle was a comforting one.

Brooke swayed against the warm muscled wall. Fleur acknowledged the renewed contact with her happy nod.

"She's missed you." *I've missed you.*

Rafe's thought came without warning. And with memories of a girl on the very brink of womanhood, a winter flower awakening to spring.

Before him stood the woman that nascent flower had become. Elegant. And snowy-white. The archaeologist must have taken to wearing wide-brimmed hats beneath the equatorial sun and gloves, perhaps snow-white too, when she dug in the desert sand.

Her freckles were gone, deprived of the sunlight that sustained them, and her auburn hair, once an unruly mane, was very short, an expert layering that prohibited even a hint of her natural curl.

Brooke wasn't the wildflower he'd imagined she would be. And the cultivated blossom she'd become had been pruned too severely. The kind of overzealous slashing that stunted, not encouraged, growth.

But she was still *his* Brooke. Her tailored blue suit, although remarkably unrumpled from her transcontinental flight, was covered with bright roan, proof of her unrestrained embrace of Fleur. And her stylish heels and fine mesh stockings were caked with dirt.

Still his Brooke, the one he'd missed and —

The chill of other memories froze Rafe's thought and laced his voice.

"So. Brooke. You're back."

"Yes."

"Why?"

"To go through my mother's things."

"We could have shipped them to you."

We. Lily and Rafe. "Yes. I know."

"But?"

"But I thought I'd learn more by going through them here, in the cottage, just the way she left them. . . ."

"Learn more about what?"

"Her."

"Why she shot John, you mean."

"No. I — *no.*"

"But isn't that what you do, Dr. Blair? Don't you dig and keep digging until all the answers are found?"

"When there's reason to believe there *are* answers."

"Which you don't think is the case here?"

"None that we can ever know."

"You don't subscribe to the accident theory."

"No. Do you? Does Lily?"

"No."

It was a single *no.* Rafe was answering for both of them.

Brooke looked away, had to, toward the mansion — from which, at any moment, Lily would appear.

"She's away for a few days."

Brooke fixed her gaze on the bedroom where shadows had glided in lamplight before dying on snow. "Until Monday morning when I'm en route to Egypt?"

"Based on what you told Curtis, she got the impression you'd rather she wasn't here."

"I just didn't want her to feel she had to be."

"Brooke?"

She didn't look at him. Couldn't. His coldness surprised her. Hurt her.

Yes, she'd expected distance from Rafe. And she'd prepared for politeness without warmth. But she hadn't anticipated this brusque interrogation with its knife-sharp edge. Even though she *should* have. Rafe's scrutiny of her was for Lily's sake. Brooke glanced from crime scene to cottage — where she wanted to run. *Again.* "Yes?"

"Tell me something true."

The knife pierced deeper with the cruel reminder of their past. *Everything I've told you is true!* she'd exclaimed that long-ago day.

Brooke couldn't be so emphatic any-more. She hadn't lied to him . . . yet. But she'd danced to the very edge of truth — so gracelessly, perhaps, that Rafe had detected her clumsy teetering.

Rafe was demanding a truth from her. Any truth. Her choice.

Brooke faced him. And chose to plunge the dagger the rest of the way. Into her own heart.

"You and Lily are married."

"That would be my truth and Lily's, not yours. Wouldn't it?"

"Yes. Of course."

"You're here for closure, aren't you? For

want of a better word."

"Yes."

"Then tell me what happened that afternoon."

"Well. Let's see. My mother shot John and John shot her."

"I meant, Brooke, what happened between us. Why you ran away from me. Was it that I reminded you a little too much of an Aztec priest?"

"*What?*"

"I know you didn't run until we'd gone back downstairs. But by then I'd already knelt beside them in the bedroom. For anyone who'd seen images of the Aztec ritual, it might have looked as if I'd caused the carnage myself."

"No, Rafe! *No.* I was grateful you went to them, touched them, tried to find any hope of life. Did you really believe —"

"That you were repulsed by my Aztec roots? I let myself believe that for a while. It was easier to blame my brutal forebears than face the truth and blame myself."

"What truth?"

"That you didn't trust me enough to let me help you. I'll give you a little more truth, in the interest of closure and clarity and any lingering curiosity you may have.

It was a big deal to me at the time."

"I'm sorry."

"Don't be. I recovered. It was presumptuous of me to expect your trust. We barely knew each other."

"But I did trust you."

"Which makes what you did all the more intriguing. Why not tell me, Brooke? What can it possibly matter now?"

It shouldn't matter now. Wasn't supposed to. In fact, if her goal was to diminish the twilight shadow to its — his — proper size, what better way than to expose it to the glaring light of her confessions?

No better way. But Brooke didn't want him to vanish. Not yet. She needed more time with the man who'd been troubled that she might not have trusted him and whose scrutiny had become far less sharp.

She told him a truth, but not a revealing one. "I was in shock."

"I know. But your actions were purposeful. You might not have thought them through at the time, but there were reasons for the decisions you made. It would surprise me if you hadn't at some point during the past twelve years at least attempted to analyze what those reasons were."

At some point? *Constantly.* "I suppose."

"I suppose, too. And you have to agree such retrospective analysis has some merit, given that it's the cornerstone of your career. Besides, Dr. Blair, you have an eyewitness. Me. Why don't I walk through the events as I remember them?"

"Do I have a choice?"

"You already made it, Brooke — you decided to return." He paused. "I have to start with the memories in the bedroom, I'm afraid, when I was kneeling beside your mother and John. I was looking at them, so I can only tell you what I heard. Faye, calling 911. You, silent. Lily, whispering *no, no, no,* until the new sound, the cry she made as she collapsed. We all rushed to her. You got there first."

"But she *reached* for you."

"Only because you yielded to me, Brooke. You moved away from Lily so I could get closer to her. We heard the sirens almost immediately after that. You didn't say anything, but you ran out of the bedroom. To meet the paramedics, I assume, and bring them up?"

"Yes. But I didn't need to. By the time they entered the foyer, you were carrying Lily down the stairs."

"There didn't seem any reason to wait in

the bedroom. Tell me what you remember next."

"Lily wasn't gasping the way she had been, and she was quite a bit more alert. It was because of you, whatever you'd said to her. When the paramedics took her from you, she got worse right away . . . until you touched her, comforted her again. You remember that, don't you?"

"I remember it, Brooke, but I can't explain it. I've wondered if it's because just before we heard the shots, Lily and I were in the stable, feeding the horses. It was a nice memory. By reaching for me, she — her subconscious — may have been trying to return to that memory, and, more importantly, to erase what happened afterward. Whatever the reason, she was better when I was nearby. I had to go with her to the hospital. I had no other choice."

"I know. I wanted you to go with her."

"And I know that. But what I don't know, Brooke, is why *you* didn't come with us. You could have — I asked you to. You heard my question . . . even though you wouldn't look at me."

"That's why you wondered if I was remembering you in the bedroom, seeing you as an Aztec priest."

"It wasn't much of a leap. Until today,

the last words we exchanged were the night before the deaths, when we talked about my brutal and sadistic ancestors. In any event, for reasons I'm hoping to hear, you wouldn't look at me. You heard my question, shook your head and ran away. To the stable?"

"No. The cottage. It was locked, but I stood on the porch." *Until you and Lily were gone.*

"So we agree on the essential facts, and we know I didn't remind you too much of an Aztec priest, and we even know that you trusted me. So what was it, Brooke? Why did you run away?"

Because I didn't belong on the Farm any longer. Not with you. Not with Lily. Not with my dreams.

And because nothing on the Farm belonged to me.

"Brooke?"

"I watched you carry Lily down the stairs, the way you held her, and she held you. It looked so . . . right."

"And you decided that would be an opportune moment to do a little match-making between your fifteen-year-old sister and me? And declined to come to the hospital with us so we'd have more time alone? You're going to have to do a

138

lot better than that, Brooke."

"Maybe it . . . bothered me."

"Seeing me hold Lily."

"Yes."

"Even though it was you who'd put her in my arms? I'm not buying that, either. Not as the reason you ran. But —" his voice became more fierce . . . and more gentle "— I do like it. Assuming it's true, it makes me think you may have wanted me as much as I wanted you."

"You wanted me?"

"All day, every day. And all night."

"I couldn't tell."

"You weren't supposed to. I thought you would've been willing."

"And that would have been bad?"

"Not for me. But for you. For us. Too much, too soon. At least that's what I'd decided before . . . that day. I was planning to tell you then. Show you, if you wanted me to."

Brooke's sole source of support chose that precise moment to decide that a drink of water was in order — and without warning ambled away. Brooke lurched, wobbled and would have been caught by Rafe if she hadn't quickly recovered on her own.

Quickly, and with astonishing grace.

Horses always gave her grace . . . even when wandering away.

"Are you all right?"

"Sure. Thanks." Brooke smiled at the loudly gulping Fleur. "She's never had the world's longest attention span."

"Are you all right overall, Brooke? Healthy? You're so thin, you can't have much reserve."

"I'm fine! I feel better not being the hulky, bulky tomboy you knew."

"I never knew a hulky, bulky tomboy. I wanted you, remember? Around the clock. Lily and I aren't married, Brooke. And we've never been lovers. We're friends. No more, and no less. So think about it."

She'd recovered physically. She was even standing on her own. But . . . *I wanted you.* He'd said it twice. Past tense. Or was it? "Think about what?"

"You know what. Us. It's safe. I'm safe. I promise I won't even get you pregnant."

"You couldn't . . . can't."

His smile was slow and easy. "Is that a challenge?"

"I'm on the Pill."

"Now maybe I'm the one who's bothered."

"What? Oh. No. I'm not taking it for contraception. It's just that my periods are so heavy it's more practical — why am I telling you this?"

"Because," he said softly, "you want me to know."

12

The cottage was like an ancient tomb. Airless. But Brooke wasn't breathing anyway.

Rafe had wanted her twelve years ago.

And he wanted her now.

Desperately? The way she wanted him? No. In fact, if he hadn't told her, she wouldn't have known it now any more than she'd known it then.

As long as she'd happened by the Farm, his casual invitation implied, why not?

It was what consenting adults did, in the real world, where Brooke Blair spent almost no time.

She wasn't a virgin, however, not since six weeks after John and Marla's deaths. She'd lost weight during those impossible weeks, every one of the many, many pounds that had separated her from Marla. When she'd reached that weight, where she'd been ever since, she'd donated her auburn ponytail to Locks of Love.

Then she'd needed to be touched. To know how it would feel. It wasn't difficult to find an accomplice. But she didn't like the touching. Hated it. Her accomplice wasn't Rafe. She didn't balk, didn't struggle, didn't flee — wouldn't permit herself to. But as a consenting adult, she'd never consented again.

Now Rafe had asked, so casually, if she'd like to be touched by him. There'd been desire once, and curiosity still.

So why not?

Rafe hadn't anticipated his reaction to seeing her. Not even close.

He'd been celibate since leaving Texas. Twelve years. Because of Lily in the beginning. She'd needed him close by, mere seconds away, a need for proximity with which he'd been happy to comply.

It had been years since Lily had needed such constancy. Years. And still he'd remained abstinent. Chosen to.

By the time he was twenty-two, he'd had enough sex to last a lifetime. Enough intimacy with loneliness. Too much.

But was that the real reason? Or was it Brooke?

Maybe. Yes. *Hell.*

He'd simply decided not to acknowledge how much he missed her . . . and that there'd been a time — denied but not truly forgotten — when he'd believed there could be intimacy without loneliness . . . with her.

Brooke made herself breathe. And with the expertise derived from years of practice, she compartmentalized all but the task at hand: to survey the cottage and settle in.

Only in the morning would she begin to explore the artifacts of her mother's life.

Archaeologist Brooke Blair was a master at such explorations, and so disciplined that she permitted nothing to lure her from her methodical approach. She identified the epicenter of the excavation first, the place where the dearest treasures were kept, but saved its examination until last.

Brooke had been known to study shards of pottery for days on end, even when a bejeweled sarcophagus lay in plain view.

From the cottage door, Brooke assessed what lay in plain view here: the comfy sofa, the plush carpet, the porcelain lamps abloom with spring. The decor was Carolyn's, not Marla's.

Emotion gushed from a compartment the archeologist, who was also a daughter, couldn't possibly seal. The *Mom* mom's heart prints were here. *She* was here. And the other mother, Brooke's real one?

Brooke's gaze fell on the *Entrepreneur* mom's rolltop desk. Marla had loved that desk, and they'd had such fun, both mothers, both daughters, searching for it. All four knew the moment it was found. Made of white pine, it was at once feminine and functional: spacious drawers, expansive desktop, cubbyholes . . . and it locked and unlocked with an ornate brass key.

Marla's desk had been delivered to the cottage that very day. Two months later, the daughter desks arrived, smaller but otherwise identical to Marla's. They could use their cubbyholes as Marla planned to, as an easy way to organize. Or, Carolyn had suggested, they could be used for wishes, to be written down and tucked away — a guarantee, it seemed, that all such wishes would come true.

Brooke never composed a cubbyhole wish. She had no wishes until Carolyn died. And then? *Come back to us, Carolyn. Please.* And then: *Get well, Lily. Please get well.*

Brooke never committed to paper her anguished wishes. But they were engraved in her heart.

Were there cubbyhole wishes in her mother's desk? An impulse encouraged

Brooke to find out *now*.

Principles of archaeology aside, Brooke resisted the urge. She had learned, on that stormy afternoon, the lethal dangers of surrendering to impulse. Her mother had done so. Irrevocably. And whatever Marla's reason, in retrospect it couldn't possibly have been a rational one.

Brooke, too, had succumbed to impulse. She'd run from Rafe, and Lily. She hadn't known why at the time. But, in retrospect, the impulse had been rational.

Her life on the Farm was over. It had ended when the first gunshot thundered in the air. But she'd glimpsed how life would be, *and should be,* after she was gone. Lily and Rafe.

It was that glimpse, perhaps, that had made her surrender without a fight to the command to run.

Marla's impulse had been to kill. Brooke's had been to flee. It was reassuring, in a way. But the fact remained. She was her mother's daughter. She'd trained herself to block all impulses, no matter how urgent — or harmless — they were.

Brooke stood her ground at the cottage door. No exploring would be done until tomorrow and assuming the cottage held other artifacts, the rolltop desk would be opened last.

There *were* other artifacts. A scrapbook and a yearbook sat on the mantelpiece shelf. That was it. True, Elise had album upon album of what had been her daughter's full and vibrant girlhood.

But here was what Marla herself had chosen to keep.

And it wasn't much.

Like mother, like daughter. Again.

In discovering her mother, Brooke would be discovering herself. The realization came with surprising emotion, even though it was hardly a surprise. Nor should it have been.

Rafe had even alluded to it in the paddock. Uncovering the past to make sense of the present was the raison d'être of her chosen career.

Archeologists were grave robbers with reverence. And when it was a mother's grave, emotion as well as artifacts would be unearthed. Brooke wanted the emotion, welcomed it.

All the more reason, however, to get a good night's sleep.

Brooke wandered to the cottage kitchen. A bowl of foil-wrapped tea bags — Bigelow's Lemon Lift — sat near the stove and a Lilac Cottage mug stood beside the sink. Brooke felt quite sure her mother had used the cheery kitchen only for making tea. But Brooke could cook to her heart's content, or simply eat without any meal preparation at all.

Lily had stocked a buffet of options for her — a gracious hostess no matter who her guest.

FoxHaven's hostess-in-absentia had even left a note.

Dear Brooke,
    Feel free to wander in the mansion (Curtis says you have the keys). Also, please help yourself to any other food or supplies you need.
                                    Lily

Had Lily debated the *Dear?* And had the note itself taken more than one try?

Imponderables — to ponder nonetheless — after the good night's sleep that was hers for the taking in the bedroom Marla had never used.

Brooke had planned to live out of her suitcase. Habit, she tried to tell herself — but those incisive gray cells intervened. The real reason, and it was unacceptable, was that a ready-to-flee suitcase, like a loaded gun, could come in handy should an impulse strike.

She needed to unpack. Everything. Even her clothes for Egypt: her desert-wear, lightweight but concealing, and her pyramid-wear, heavy and warm.

Brooke's luggage contained more supplies than clothes. Sunblock. Tea — French Vanilla, not Lemon Lift — and a coil for heating water. Breakfast bars. Multicolored pens and Post-its. Miscellaneous medicaments advised for travel abroad.

And her period-preventing birth control pills always taken on a dig.

I promise I won't even get you pregnant.

But what if I want you to?

Brooke unpacked her birth control pills several stumbling heartbeats before removing the four thick notebooks impulsively packed — *Ha!* her brain countered. *Tell yourself something true.*

Okay. All right. There'd been nothing impulsive about packing the notebooks for Rafe.

Brooke set them on the vanity without so much as a glance at its silvery mirror. She looked at herself only when necessary, to confirm that her appearance was what it should be — painted within the lines and in color schemes designed by others.

Without her grandmother Elise, Brooke wouldn't have known such appearance experts existed. Elise had been unhappy about her granddaughter's short haircut. She'd wanted it shoulder-length. Marla-length. But Brooke hadn't budged. She couldn't bear to try — and fail — to look like Marla, to look in the mirror at all, as longer hair would require her to do. And it could never again be FoxHaven-length, either, the mane of the cantering girl she had been.

Brooke had relented on clothes, however. She wore the right ones. And on makeup. She wore very little, subtly applied. She wasn't an artist. Following a palette designed by those who knew was so much easier than trying to guess.

When no one was watching, Brooke Blair wore her tomboy jeans.

You were never a tomboy. I wanted you. All day, every day, and all night.

Rafe wanted her — casually — on this night. Perhaps he was waiting for her even now. Expecting her. Certain she would come. Confident she couldn't resist.

She was the one in pursuit of closure, after all. But being with Rafe was so much more to her than that.

Everything.

150

And yet . . . why not?

She had nothing more to lose. She couldn't possibly be more stalled or more lonely — all day every, every day, and all night.

13

Brooke went to him under cover of darkness. The carriage house door was open, an invitation to the balmy night breeze . . . and her.

Brooke heard Rafe's phone ring as she neared. He answered midway through the first ring, as if expecting the call. There was relief in his greeting.

"Lily." Then, after a brief silence, "So you're all tucked in? Safe and sound?"

Run, an impulse urged her. *Run and hide.*

Brooke wanted to succumb. But she fought the temptation with the truth. *Rafe cares about Lily. Face it. Feel it.*

Hear it. Listen to something true. Rafe could hardly disapprove.

Given a damaged wall of hieroglyphics, from which large pieces of carved story had been lost, Brooke had an uncanny knack for discerning the missing text.

Her interpretations were speculative, of course, and would have remained so had not subsequent discoveries on less — or differently — damaged walls proven them correct.

Not every interpretation had yet been confirmed. But Brooke's track record was so remarkable, her intuition so pure, that even the most skeptical of her colleagues presumed that unless and until there was convincing evidence to the contrary, Dr. Brooke Blair's decipherings were gospel.

Brooke had a gift when it came to the sagas of pharaohs chiseled in granite. And when it came to interpreting one side of a modern dialogue? When emotions swirled and the history-in-the-making was her own?

"How's your room?" Rafe's affection drifted on the warm night air. "Good. How about the view? . . . is that okay?"

Lily was at a hotel, Brooke deduced — as even a novice listener would. Her room was nice, apparently, although Lily would be unlikely to report otherwise.

There *was* something worrisome about the view. At least it worried Rafe — as if he thought it might be difficult for Lily. Brooke knew of only one such view: the D.C. hospital where Lily had endured such medically necessary pain, and where more than once Lily Forsythe Rutledge had almost died.

"Yes," Rafe was saying. "She's here . . . I'm not sure yet, Lily. I think so. I'll have a clearer picture when I talk to you tomorrow. . . . Friday or Saturday, I imagine. . . . Still Monday as far as I know."

They were discussing Lily's possible return to the Farm before Brooke's Monday morning departure for Egypt. Rafe was tending toward yes, it would be all right. He needed a little more time, though, to be certain, time for more inter-rogation — of her.

Run! Hide! As fast as you can and forever. It felt very wise, this unsolicited counsel from an impulse. As a matter of fact —

Don't you dare run away. Oh, and by the way, weren't you the one who made such a point of telling Curtis that Lily shouldn't feel she had to be around when you returned? And wasn't your reason then identical to Rafe's reason now? To protect Lily from all the painful emotions she might have if she saw you?

"You're in for the night?" Lily's pro-tector was asking. "Lily? Okay. Good . . . You, too."

That was it. The conversation was over. Lily had wished Rafe "Sweet dreams," per-haps. Or "Good night, Rafe. Sleep well."

154

Whatever nighttime farewell had prompted his soft "You, too" was familiar to both of them. Something they'd said to each other for the past twelve years.

Rafe and Lily.

Lily and Rafe.

Face it. She did.

Confront it. She had.

And now she could leave. Choice, not impulse. Walk, not flight. Considered decision, not frantic retreat.

Brooke wouldn't run. Nor would she hide.

She'd simply return to the cottage, make herself a cup of tea, wish herself sweet dreams, and get the good night's sleep so necessary for tomorrow's exploration of Marla's belongings — and Rafe's further examination of her.

On Friday or Saturday she'd see Lily. She wanted to, if Lily wanted to see her. And on Monday she'd leave. And that would be that. Closure. Clarity. Twilight shadows made life-size by the bright light of truth.

But.

Rafe and Lily were friends. No more, and no less. Wonderful friends. Caring and true.

But not lovers.

Trust. Not lust.

Rafe had given all but his lust to Lily; *that* he'd offered to her. It wasn't life or death for him. His heart wouldn't be torn from his chest.

It was just a little chemistry, a little curiosity, and a lot of closure, the sealing — forever — of a door left ajar from the past.

Brooke drew a breath and knocked.

Then needed the breath she had drawn, feeling she might never breathe again, for the desire she saw was unconcealed — and not casual in the least.

No wonder he'd hidden his longing from the seventeen-year-old innocent she'd been, the tomboy-ballerina who'd dreamed only of an accidental caress, a whispered kiss of skin on skin, in a hayloft on a rainy afternoon.

Rafe was twelve years older — fiercer, harsher — now than the man who'd worried his passion would be too much, too soon for a teenage girl . . . no matter how gentle he was, or how willing she might be.

And she was still that girl. Stalled there.

She was Brooke past, with fantasies of inadvertent touches, and he was Rafe present, with expectations of what consenting adults did in bed.

Realistic expectations. Based on experience. This sensual man had done it all, known it all, liked it all — and wanted it all.

With her . . . the woman he'd invited to be with him on this night.

"Brooke? Would you like to come in?"

His voice was soft. Husky. A voice she'd never heard. She didn't know this man. This Rafe. Didn't know him at all —

"We won't do anything you don't want to do."

— and knew him so well. The Rafe she had trusted for those nine perfect days.

"I'd like to come in. And I want to do everything."

Everything. Rafe drew a ragged breath. He'd been hoping she'd come, fearing she wouldn't, then telling himself it would be better for her, best for her, if she stayed away.

And now she was here, a snowy blossom mercilessly pruned, but Brooke. His Brooke. The lovely rescuer of tormented horses and tortured souls.

Rafe wanted her so much. Needed her beyond all reason.

His hands trembled a little as he touched her flushed cheeks. And his smile wobbled, a little, as he kissed her.

He'd been starving for her.

And she'd been starving for him.

And they'd already touched, long ago, in every way but this.

So tonight they touched skin to skin, discovering the silk of it, and the heat, and its many landscapes. Sounds accompanied their discoveries — a gasp of surprise, a moan of desire . . . and whispers that were songs.

Harsh, soft, deep, needy, Rafe whispered her name. Brooke, Brooke, *Brooke*.

Again and again.

And again.

And she whispered his.

But she was silent, in the darkness, when she rose from his bed and started to dress.

Rafe rose, too. Dressed, too.

In the darkness, as they dressed, it was the voice of the — apparently — successful Ph.D that said, "You don't need to walk me back to the cottage."

The voice that replied belonged to the cowboy who'd left the beds of his heiress lovers with a sense of relief. "Sure I do."

14

Lily's Excellent Adventure. She'd come up with the title before deciding on her itinerary. Even if her eventual plans had been a five-night stay at the Silver Fox Inn, which Harriet would have loved, it would've been an adventure for Lily.

But, like Brooke, she was journeying to her past, completing the journey started years ago.

Lily had already visited her FoxHaven past. The bedroom where a second Forsythe baby had cost Carolyn her life. The playroom, forsaken since that loss. The west-wing suite.

Lily had been fearful of what she would find in those mansion haunts — ghosts in their most menacing sense. But the

159

FoxHaven spirits were gentle, not sinister, even in Marla's room, where love had been slain.

The Swedish Medical Center ghosts were another matter, descended as they were from ghoulish memories, not loving ones. But Lily was determined to find peace with the lingering phantoms of lumbar punctures, marrow biopsies, arterial lines.

It was an easy trip, in miles, from Forsythe to D.C. The exit to Swedish Medical Center was well marked. And the recently opened Wind Chimes Hotel provided access to the hospital via a glass-enclosed sky-bridge.

From a twenty-second floor room such as hers, there was an aerial view of the center itself. Now, at daybreak, SMC glowed pink.

Had it always been such an unthreatening pastel? Maybe, probably, except in her memory. There the mammoth structure had been gray, the angriest hue of smoke, and it had been a living thing, a hideous creature of piercing fangs and grasping claws.

Lily's appointment with Dr. Rachel Davis wasn't until 11:00 a.m. Hours away. She'd see Dr. Davis in the center's new —

for Lily — Tessier Tower. Only after that would she roam the hospital areas she had known. She'd have the rest of the day then, and all night if she wanted. Or, should the memories prove too monstrous, the ghosts too intractable, she'd forge a swift truce with the unfriendly demons and take a tour of the White House instead.

Rafe knew about Lily's rendezvous with her SMC past. They'd discussed it at length. But even to him, the man to whom she'd typically revealed even her most inconsequential plans, Lily hadn't disclosed her monumental decision to see Dr. Davis.

She hadn't lied to Rafe. Never had and never would. She'd simply — no, not so simply — failed to mention the appointment she'd made.

Lily would tell Rafe. After. *If* there was reason to believe Lily's Excellent Adventure might, just might, become Lily's and Rafe's.

Brooke didn't sleep. Couldn't. Not even in the feathery comfort of the cottage bed — although it had been the imminent specter of sleep that had made her leave Rafe.

His invitation had been for sex, and

she'd been drifting into sleep, until she'd been jolted to wakefulness by a nightmarish vision of the future: dawn in his bedroom.

She was in his bed, in the vision, but Rafe was not. He stood over her, fully dressed, a little annoyed but mostly amazed. This was not what consenting adults did, especially casual ones, no matter how terrific the sex had been. He'd imagined she would know the rules, given her wanton and womanly performance in bed.

Some realistic corner of her hopelessly fantasizing brain had at least known there *were* rules and that she was undoubtedly violating them.

She'd left, as she supposed Rafe wanted her to, and when they'd reached the cottage door, the man who had invited her, so casually, to have sex — and who'd discovered her, so thoroughly, in darkness — smiled his slow and easy smile and said, *'Night.*

Brooke left her own bed, finally, exhausted from her tattered sleep. She made herself pause at the mirrored vanity. Then sit in its chair. Then look at the morning-after vestiges of the choice she had made.

"The seamy underbelly of lust," she murmured to the reflected image, its skin taut, eyes wreathed in purple, hair an auburn snarl. "Not a pretty sight."

Then why, some inner voice wanted to know, do I see a woman in love?

"Optical illusion."

Or delusion. Maybe she was seeing a crazy woman, jet-lagged — life-lagged — to the very edge of sanity.

But who had not yet gone over the brink. Nor would she. The meticulous excavator, whose ability to compartmentalize was absolute, would simply put all fantasies in an airless coffin tightly sealed.

Brooke needed to gather them first. They still floated and flew. They'd be entombed, however, by the time she finished her shower.

The delusions joined her in the steam. As, in the fragrant mist, did the memory of him, them, making love.

Having sex, Brooke amended sternly. To no avail. The memory remained vivid in her sudsy brain.

There were vulgar descriptions of what she and Rafe had done. Explicit ones. Brooke didn't want to lock them in the same compartment where the fantasies would dwell. But she'd have to unless . . .

The threat worked. In one fell swoop they leapt into their airtight compartment, which Brooke summarily sealed.

Dr. Brooke Blair stepped out of the shower, ready to dig. She began as she always did, no matter where on the planet she happened to be, with a cup of tea. She chose her mother's Lemon Lift on this FoxHaven morning, in Marla's Lilac Cottage mug.

As she savored the flavorful warmth, she wandered from kitchen to living room and present to past.

Marla's scrapbook was an archeologist's dream. And a daughter's. Mementos chosen by Marla herself.

Marla's academic achievements, from straight-A report cards to perfect SATs, were commemorated in frames and albums in Elise's mansion in Bel Air.

Marla's scrapbook celebrated the life between the accomplishments. Here was her mother as a girl. Being a girl. And becoming a woman.

She had many friends. Every player in the happy drama was identified, as were the events, from eight-year-old Carolee Swan's birthday party by the pool to Debra Lessing's Halloween trick-or-treat.

As grade school became junior high,

boys' names and photographs began to appear. Marla's girlfriends didn't vanish, however, never vanished, although Marla's boyfriends filled ever more space — along with ticket stubs from all the places they took her to, and snapshots of wet and frothy co-ed car washes, and more parties by Carolee's pool, and the many dances Marla attended during senior high.

The dances had names, engraved on tasseled programs. "Feelin' Groovy." "The Midnight Hour." "All Summer Long." "Crazy." Marla wrote her date's name beside each program, and recorded the names of all the other boys with whom she'd danced.

Marla's scrapbook mementos came to an abrupt and premature end on Valentine's Day of her senior year. Marla's date for "Heart and Soul" was Stephen Aames, the same boy with whom she'd attended every dance, movie, football game and party for the past two years.

Something had happened. Obviously. Every subsequent page was blank.

Even when the archive was an impersonal one, and examined as meticulously as always by Dr. Brooke Blair, she was forever astounded by the new — and often significant — observations she made on the second pass, the third . . . the tenth.

Brooke would go through her mother's scrapbook again. Many times. But she needed to go through the yearbook first. Would have, even if there hadn't been the worry about Stephen Aames. For his sake and her mother's, she hoped nothing tragic had happened to him.

The yearbook would tell her — and did so promptly. All graduating seniors were listed alphabetically on the inside cover. *Aames, Stephen* was the first.

Good. Nothing tragic. They'd simply broken up.

Brooke had no more experience with yearbooks than with tasseled dance programs, co-ed car washes or dinner dates before the ballet. And even if she'd completed her senior year at Forest Ridge, her yearbook would've been as unlike Marla's as a scrapbook of Brooke's teen years would have been, compared to her mother's.

Marla's Savannah High classmates had written on every page, entries ranging from *Love ya!* to serious and sometimes groveling reflections on what their friendship with Marla had meant.

Marla wrote in her yearbook, too. *Ha!* in turquoise ink beside the assertion from a girl never pictured in Marla's scrapbook that she was truly *Marvelous Marla.* And *Love ya, too!* in fuchsia for her friend Carolee. Marla recorded reactions, in fact, to virtually every yearbook entry.

She color-coded her commentary, the way Brooke encrypted her archeological notes. It would take Brooke a few passes to decipher her mother's code. Even Marla's system for coloring the usual array of smiling — and frowning — faces was complex.

A page entitled "Favorite Maxims" preceded the formal photographic display of graduating seniors. It was unclear precisely how the sayings had been selected, much less whether these "favorites" had been solicited only from certain members of the senior class.

But Marla Blair had two.

A secret is a lie.

When you have nothing to hide, hide nothing.

Had Marla lived by the wisdom she'd shared with her classmates? As a business-woman, yes. Definitely. Her honesty-is-the-only-approach policy, dispensed with Marla's charm, had been the cornerstone of The Lilac Cottage's success.

But Marla had hidden the secret of the

rape. Had lived that lie.

Had she died because of it? Killed because of it, too?

15

It was a while before Brooke turned to the photo gallery of graduating seniors. Once again, Stephen Aames was first.

Brooke already knew that his senior portrait wouldn't be framed in black.

But the photograph *was* framed, in red, by hand, with a heart. Marla had traced and retraced the romantic symbol, until very little of Stephen's face remained. Then she'd drawn a slash across his eyes, his nose, what was left of his mouth.

It didn't take a hieroglyphics whiz to decipher ♥. Hate, not love. Hatred, where love had been.

The archeologist would have lingered on the impassioned glyph of teenage love — lust? — gone awry. But the daughter needed to move on. The next page bore reminders of the heart. So did the next. Deep impressions and slivers of ink were evident, in fact, until midway through the alphabetical *B*s.

Marla Blair's senior portrait was unmarred, and familiar. It sat, in a sterling-silver frame, on Elise's baby grand. The accomplishments listed beneath Marla's yearbook photo were familiar, too, except for the one awarded by her classmates. *Most likely to succeed.*

Had Marla succeeded?

Oh, yes. Rape survivor, entrepreneur, single mom, beloved best friend, devoted second mother to Lily, helpmate and fiancée to John.

Marla had succeeded brilliantly, if one discounted the occasional madness to which she'd succumbed, the impulse to deface a boyfriend's image with such fury that her tracings tore the page . . . and the other impulse, the final one, to fire a bullet into the heart of the man she was planning to wed.

Smiles abounded in the doctors' office on Tessier Tower's eighteenth floor.

Even the fish in the mirrored aquarium seemed to swim with glee.

And why not?

With rare exceptions, devastating as such exceptions could be, Dr. Rachel Davis and her colleagues had chosen a most happy specialty.

A smiling nurse — Fran — escorted Lily from the waiting room. Rachel wanted to

170

talk with Lily first, Fran explained, after which Fran would show Lily to an exam room, check her vital signs, and depending on how soon Rachel would be joining them, draw blood for whatever tests had been ordered.

Rachel Davis was smiling, too. And organized and prepared.

"This is volume five of your medical records." She gestured to the slender file on her desk. "It contains your last SMC admission, a summary from the Geneva clinic, and since volumes one through four are missing, copies of various consultation reports submitted by physicians who cared for you over the years."

"The first four volumes are missing?"

"Misfiled, I would guess. That's not as rare as it should be, I'm afraid, especially when multiple volumes are involved. The good news, in your case, is that it's more of a frustration than a problem. What I have provides an excellent overview. Your physicians made their reports particularly complete — because, I gather from Dr. Hart, the earlier volumes had been missing for a while."

Dr. Hart. He was a ghost, a ghoul, from Lily's yet-to-be traveled past.

"Lily?"

"I was remembering the bone marrow biopsies."

"He hated having to do them on you. I know that for a fact. When I saw he'd been one of your doctors, I called him to clarify a few points. He was in London when your father died and didn't learn of his death until he'd returned. The only reason he didn't get in touch with you then was because he knew you viewed him as fearsome, not comforting. He's really a very nice man, not to mention a terrific doctor. He asked me to give you his best and to tell you how delighted he is that you're doing so well."

"Is he surprised?"

"Not at all. Autoimmune processes can remit as mysteriously as they appear. He'd love to take a look at your records, though. Because the earlier volumes were missing, he was never able to review them the way he would've liked — all at once and in proper order."

"He'd want to review them now?"

"Absolutely. A diagnosis that was elusive twelve years ago might be crystal-clear today. Many so-called new diseases are really newly recognized ones. It's a bit like the 'overnight' successes you hear about, people who've struggled for years in virtual

172

anonymity and then suddenly, or so it seems, hit it big. In the medical context, diseases may exist in relative obscurity until a critical mass of case reports is reached — or an outbreak occurs. AIDS, Toxic Shock and Legionnaires' Disease are recent examples of diseases that occurred as isolated curiosities for years before making their epidemiologic splash. The medical literature is filled with others."

"Does Dr. Hart have a specific diagnosis in mind?"

"Not that I know of. And there may not be one that's recognizable yet. But you had *something*. And if your blood studies look as good as you do, we may well be in the position of presuming that whatever *it* was is gone. Having a definitive diagnosis would simply make that presumption a certainty. I've asked the folks in Medical Records to search one more time for your missing files. Should they magically appear, Dr. Hart will gladly review them."

"That would be a lot of work for him."

"A lot of time, maybe. But not a lot of work. He'd like to review your records. Wants to. And sadly, he has the time. His wife Joanna died a year ago. They'd been together almost thirty years, just the two of them, no children, and not even a wide circle of friends. They had each other, and that was enough. And now . . . he keeps as busy as he can. But he can't be on call every night and every weekend. In any event, with his input I've compiled a battery of tests we need to do. Those results, coupled with the exam I'll do today, should tell us a lot. Okay?"

"Yes. Okay. Thank you." Lily started to stand.

"Whoa," Rachel said. "Let's pretend, and I honestly don't think it's a stretch, that your exam and your labs are all fine. Maybe we should spend a few minutes discussing the primary reason you're here. . . ."

The knock was soft. But Brooke was startled nonetheless, caught between where she'd been — staring yet again at the heart that framed Stephen Aames — and where she was: the cottage on the Farm. Wearing a wristwatch that read two.

In the afternoon, the ambient light told her. But it might've been two at night, as lost as she'd been in her mother's past.

Two. In the afternoon. And knocking softly at the door?

Rafe. Awareness dawned, exquisitely, and the compartment of fantasies opened wide.

Brooke might have ached from the hours spent cross-legged on the floor. Except for turning pages, she hadn't moved.

Instead she sang, her body did, carols from every place he'd touched her.

Everywhere.

Did Rafe want more touching, after all?

Brooke had her answer when she opened the door.

His curiosity was sated. He'd had his fill.

Rafe was here because he had to be. To assess her, for Lily.

"Rafe. Hi."

"Hi."

Rafe's greeting was as subdued as hers. He ached for what was lost, even as he raged at his foolishness in believing it could ever have been found.

The hell of it was, he *had* found it. The intimacy without loneliness. But when Brooke left his bed, Rafe wished he never had.

He'd thought about telling her how he ached. And raged. And why: that, unlike Brooke, he couldn't have torn himself from the peace he had felt. Could not. But he decided against telling her. It was his problem alone that it hadn't been impossible for *her* to leave.

"I thought I'd take these guys for a walk

before it starts to rain. You're welcome to join us."

These guys were the equine family of five. The horses wore their healthy coats and nothing else. They'd come of their own accord, upon invitation from Rafe, for a leisurely stroll on this cloudless afternoon.

"It's going to rain?"

"It is." Rafe had, it seemed, a lingering bond with the God of Rain. *Trust me, Brooke.* He almost spoke the aching words aloud. He looked at her instead, the woman who hadn't wanted to stay with him for dreams. Really looked. And saw pain, he thought. Pain. Too. "Are you okay?"

"Of course! It's just that this is more difficult than I'd thought it would be."

"This?"

It sounded like *us* to Brooke. As if Rafe wanted her to confirm the disappointing truth he already knew. The girl he'd wanted too much, too soon, had been revealed for the woman she'd become. Too little, too late.

"Going through my mother's things, even after all these years and despite the fact that we weren't ever very close."

"Maybe this isn't a good time for you to take a break."

There'd never be a better time to be appraised by the distant blue eyes. Or a worse one. "Actually, it's fine. May I join you?"

"It's the reason we're here. Do you have a jacket?"

"Yes."

"I think you should get it."

Their stroll didn't begin even after Brooke had retrieved her windbreaker. There were reunions first. With Fleur again. Lots of velvet kisses to bestow. And continued touching, Fleur's chin on Brooke's shoulder, as Brooke greeted Meg.

The Nutmeg Lady's twenty-four-year-old eyes, so placid and wise, reminded Brooke of the other elderly eyes she had loved.

Patient Grace.

Gentle Snow.

And Minnie. Oh, Minnie. Her funny, lovely Minnie-Min.

"They died peacefully," Rafe said.

Because he, her Rafe, wouldn't let the beloved creatures die any other way. Her Rafe. With whom, had the world been different, she would have loved the dying horses, too.

"That must have been so difficult for you."

"It's always difficult to say goodbye."

His stark gaze was impossible to read. And yet . . . he seemed a little ravaged to her. And not wanting her stare.

Brooke averted her eyes, to the stallion she had saved.

"He looks . . . friendly. Friendlier, anyway."

Rhapsody knew he was being talked about. He snorted and watched without watching.

"He's very friendly, despite the reputation he feels he needs to maintain." A reputation that couldn't withstand the affection in Rafe's voice. Rhapsody whinnied. "He's also quite the family man."

"Madly in love with Fleur?" Brooke asked, as she would've asked the Rafe with whom she'd worried about the tormented horse for those nine perfect days. "And the kids?"

"Madly," that Rafe replied. And smiled. "He takes fatherhood very seriously."

His smile faded. Her Rafe went away. Brooke gazed at the frisky teenagers nearby. The youngsters wanted to get the show on the road.

"His children are very well behaved — whoever they are."

"She's Lark. Skylark's Lilac Song. And

he's Shadow. Knight Shadow's Serenade."

"Beautiful names for beautiful babies."

"Lily named them."

Lily. Lily. Face it.

"Do you ride much, Brooke?"

"Not at all."

"Want to?"

"Yes."

"Then we will. Before you leave."

We will. They'd made that promise twelve years ago. But it had been shattered by that stormy day.

Now Rafe was making the promise again. And it was more solemn than twelve years ago.

Not a beginning but an end. Just one more item on the list of things that needed to be done. Just another door that needed to be closed.

Before you leave felt to Brooke, to her heart, like *So you can leave.*

16

They were strolling to a place they no longer belonged. A time when desire had been born, but had yet to disappoint, and bold confessions came gift-wrapped in trust.

But they were saved before reaching the pasture by a building forsaken long before their nine perfect days — since Carolyn's death — but which had been reclaimed sometime in the past twelve years.

The glassy walls, dirt-splattered during the abandonment, sparkled now, and the once-darkened greenhouse lights were aglow.

"I've become a breeder of lilacs."

"You have?"

"I have." Rafe didn't pause a beat before offering her, them, a place without memories of that April. "Want to see?"

"Yes." *Please.*

It would be another season before the seedlings beneath the sunny lights would flower. But there were blooms within the greenhouse, photographic images that would blossom on Rafe's computer screen just for her.

"We have two hybrids," Rafe explained as he made a selection from a box of CDs, "that are ready to go."

"To be sold?"

"Yes. Canterfield Nursery will ship them for planting this fall."

"Daughter lilacs," Brooke murmured. "That's what Carolyn called the hybrids she hoped to create."

"She did create them, Brooke. Both hybrids come from the seeds she pollinated before her death. The seeds," Rafe added softly, "you collected after she died."

Brooke watched as the fingers that had touched her so intimately retrieved three envelopes from a desk drawer.

"Recognize these?"

She did, of course. "Charlotte" X "James" in her handwriting, and "Charlotte" X "Rochester," and "James" X "Mr. Lincoln."

Her handwriting had never been attractive. Wasn't now. But it had been especially round and clumsy at age ten. It hadn't mattered then. She'd tried to make her writing prettier, though, that day a week after Carolyn's death. Tried so hard . . . and failed. But that hadn't mattered, either. Carolyn had shimmered nearby, so proud of her for remembering, despite her grief, to gather the seeds.

"Brooke?"

They were in a new place for them. But the voice was the one she had known in the pasture beside the pond. It belonged to the man who encouraged her to tell her own stories, the man she trusted to listen and to care.

Trust . . . not lust.

Brooke looked up from the envelopes as she'd looked up from the sun-gilded blades of grass and saw the same — same — blue eyes.

"I thought Lily and I would plant the seeds on my birthday, as Carolyn and Lily and I had planned to do. But Lily became ill."

"And?"

"Well." She shrugged, and confessed, "I decided that if I planted them and they died, Lily would die. But if I *didn't* plant them, she'd be fine."

"What if you planted them and they survived?"

"I didn't really consider that possibility. It wasn't a very confident time. Or a very rational one. Maybe if Lily had planted the seeds. . . . Did she?"

"No. I did." Rafe inserted the CD and clicked on a numbered .jpg file.

A lilac, in the identical, *impossible,* peach and rose Lily had chosen for "Emma" on her *Noble Spirits* mosaic, filled the screen.

"This is 'Emma,' " Rafe said.

"She's *so* Emma. Delicate, yet bold. What color is she?"

"Coral."

"That's a new color for lilacs."

"It is. But it's official. The Lilac Society's already given their okay. And that's Emma, too, isn't it? The iconoclast among the traditional?"

They were her words, more or less, spoken to him on the sun-warmed grass in the pasture by the pond. "You remember."

"Why wouldn't I?"

Rafe didn't wait for her answer. There wasn't one he wanted to hear. He clicked another file.

" 'Charles,' " she murmured, as a cobalt-meets-sapphire lilac blossomed on the screen. *No reason not to remember. In fact, you would remember. You believed you would want me then, all day, every day, and all night. But now . . .* Now she was here, and what he was showing her was extraordinary. *Onward.* "What exotic new color is the Lilac Society calling it?"

Rafe smiled. "Blue."

And she smiled. "Carolyn would be so thrilled. Maybe she is."

"I hope so."

"But . . ."

"Yes?"

"Well, you didn't just plant the seeds and a few years later give the Lilac Society a call."

"Actually, 'Emma' was about that easy."

"And 'Charles'?"

"Trickier. I needed to cross the 'James'-'Mr. Lincoln' hybrid with one I got by crossing 'Montaigne' with 'Dappled Dawn.' "

"So 'Charles' is a cross of four hybrids? Is there a scientific term for that?"

"A quadribrid."

"I remember Carolyn telling us, warning *one* of us in particular, that creating new lilacs was a project that might never succeed."

"And Lily's response?"

"After listening attentively and even agreeing, she would, within maybe a millisecond, start talking about all the lilacs Carolyn would create — soon. And now . . . I'm surprised Lily didn't help you plant the first batch of seeds." Brooke looked at the rows of seedlings yet to be.

"Does she now?"

"No. We decide together on the hybrids we want to introduce, and Lily chooses the names."

"But?"

Rafe was right beside her, close enough to touch. But not touching. Carefully not. And it was all right. They'd found, in this brightly blooming present, the comfortable companionship of the past.

They were friends. Again. No more . . . and no less.

It was Rafe who'd encouraged the confessions in the pasture. But in this newborn hybrid of present and past, it was the archeologist who was digging for a confession from him.

And got one.

"I think Lily's reluctant to be responsible for living things," he admitted in a low voice.

"In case she dies?"

"I think so. Yes."

"But isn't she fine?"

"She is. Just like she was before becoming ill."

"Is she afraid?"

"Of dying? No more than anyone else. But she worries about making long-term commitments."

So it was Rafe who made the commitments to the new generations of FoxHaven lilacs and horses. And Lily named them, treasured them, from afar.

And if Rafe wasn't here?

Creativity would still blossom on the Farm. But Lily's mosaics wouldn't grieve if she died. As Lily had grieved for her parents. And the colorful tiles sealed in grout would survive . . . as Carolyn and John had not.

"She wants the daughter lilacs, though, doesn't she? And the babies of Rhapsody and Fleur."

"Yes," Rafe said quietly. "She wants them very much."

"She's so lucky to have you."

"I'm not doing anything I don't want to do."

I know. It was a little precarious, this new hybrid of Brooke and Rafe. She tried a smile. Succeeded. "How did you learn to do all of this?"

Brooke expected a shrug.

Which she got . . . with another confession.

"My father was a farmer. A magician when it came to hybridizing maize. I've used his techniques."

"And created magic of your own."

Brooke hesitated. Then, "He'd be very proud of you."

Rafe drew a breath. "Maybe."

Seconds passed as Brooke waited for Rafe to decide whatever it was he was trying to decide.

She hoped for more words about his father. But he was staring at the sky, which now promised the rain he'd forecast without a cloud, wondering — most likely — how soon they should gather the horses.

"There's one more lilac I want to show you."

Rafe moved the cursor to another numbered .jpg, but hesitated before making the irrevocable click. The artist was reluctant, perhaps, to reveal too soon a work in progress.

"Are you familiar with 'Primrose'?"

"Yes." The Primrose lilac was yellow, the only one. Its blooms, although beautiful, were pale, butter-yellow not daffodil. "Why?"

Rafe clicked the file, and the answer came from the flower itself. *Because now there's another yellow lilac in town.*

And this lilac — Rafe's lilac — glowed with the perfect light of a smiling sun.

"Oh, Rafe . . ."

"That's the way it looks in spring. And

—" another click "— this is how it blooms in fall."

It was a darker sun that shone at Brooke now, a deeper gold, more solemn than the springtime sun, as if sensing the coming winter chill, yet defiant. And its leaves, green in spring, were the burnished hues of autumn.

Autumn.

"It blooms twice?"

Rafe smiled slightly. "My father worked very hard to keep us fed. He found ways of inducing the crops to yield year-round."

Rafe's father had kept his family fed, meaning alive, and now the farmer's son was keeping alive the wishes of the daughter who dared create only in tiles.

"You're happy with this lilac, aren't you, Rafe? Just the way it is?"

"I'm happy with it, Brooke. Just the way it is. But it needs a name. Any suggestions?"

"For a name? Me?"

"You."

"No. I mean, I'd have to think about it. I thought Lily chose the names."

"She does. She's thinking about it, too." Rafe looked again at the menacing sky. "We'd better go. The horses do pretty well with thunder as long as they're in the stable before it starts."

"There's going to be thunder?"

"There is."

Tlaloc will choose this day to roar.

17

The clouds above FoxHaven Farm were dove-gray. But to the east, over D.C., they glowered charcoal.

The brisk wind invigorated the horses. They liked the ruffling of their manes, and the potpourri of new scents that wafted their way. Still, they were happy to see Rafe. To see them both. If they'd been puppies, their tails would be wagging furiously — for him.

"Are you cold, Brooke?"

"A little."

"You need another jacket."

Rafe shed his and held it for her as she slipped it on. She felt his warmth, as if he and not his jacket had enveloped her.

Brooke shoved her fists into the pockets and found, in the left, Rafe's cellular phone. He carried it for Lily, she realized, in case Lily needed him, even from afar.

Lily trusted Rafe to be there for her. And, this afternoon, Lily's Rafe wasn't letting her down.

"I wonder if I'll pass the test."

Rafe heard the words and felt, *felt*, the despair. He'd been tested as a boy, had wondered if the time would ever come when he'd have passed all tests and been welcomed at last.

"What test, Brooke?"

"The one in which you're deciding whether it's all right for Lily to see me. I overheard your conversation with her, Rafe. I know you told her you needed a little more time to be certain."

"For you, Brooke, not because of you."

"I don't understand."

"I want to be sure it's all right for you to see Lily."

"Why wouldn't it be?"

"How about the fact that her father murdered your mother?"

"You think — Lily thinks? — I might blame her for that?"

"Aren't you thinking she might blame you for what your mother did?"

"Yes. And with good reason. My mother shot John, *killed* John, first."

"And that's your fault because?" Rafe waited. And heard only the hissing wind. "Okay. Why don't I tell you why Lily's able to convince herself she's at least partially responsible for what happened that day?"

"Please."

"Your mother had plans for The Lilac Cottage. The expansion throughout northern Virginia and into D.C. She abandoned those plans because of Lily's illness."

"My mother loved Lily! The only reason she kept working was so life would feel as normal as possible for Lily. That's why John worked, too. And when Lily's life couldn't be normal, my mother wanted to be at her bedside around the clock. She never resented being with Lily. Not for one second. I *know* that, Rafe. Doesn't Lily know it, too?"

"Most of the time, yes. But in an attempt to understand what happened that afternoon, she can't help considering the possibility that your mother had decided to leave the Farm, and maybe even Forsythe, and that when she told him, John responded with rage."

"Rage? That's not — I mean, that wasn't John."

"Nor by all accounts was it your mother. She'd been a rock, you told me, throughout Lily's illness. John's rock."

"But it wasn't as though John needed her to be. He was very strong."

"And under tremendous stress. You told me that, too. He hadn't had a chance to grieve for Carolyn before Lily became ill, and her illness was a constant worry after that."

"John wouldn't have snapped no matter how great the stress. And my mother wasn't planning to leave. She and John were getting married."

"Married?"

"Yes. I just assumed Lily knew."

"No. She didn't know."

"Well, she needs to." Brooke's left fist tingled as she uncurled it, sharp pricks of pain, but her fingers functioned well enough to grasp his phone. "Tell her now, Rafe. Please?"

Brooke's plea in Forsythe coincided with a clap of thunder over Washington.

Lily heard the boom, despite the insulated windows of the Wind Chimes Hotel, as she gazed at the scowling sky and thought about her day.

It had been, save for that one scowling moment, even better than she'd dared hope. . . .

Her physical exam had been entirely normal. The routine blood work would be back tomorrow morning. She'd check with Fran, and by her follow-up appointment next Thursday, the immunological studies would be complete and Rachel would have "run all the data by Dr. Hart."

She needed only to schedule the follow-up and she'd be on her way — back to her past.

The hospital ghosts would be friendly, she'd decided. Not a ghoul to be found. Even the most menacing phantoms in her memory would be as nice, in reality, as Dr. Hart.

Dr. Davis's receptionist had been busy with another patient. Lily detoured, happily, to the aquarium of gleeful fish.

The man must have entered the office as she'd walked the short distance to the mirrored tank. Her first image of him was a reflection. He was a doctor, at least dressed as one, in royal-blue scrubs beneath a bright white coat.

And he was angry.

Enraged.

As she spun from the mirrored image to the real man, Lily's thoughts spun as well. What qualified her to recognize anger, much less rage? Especially when it came packaged as this man's did, cold and contained. She had no experience with —

But she did. She'd seen such controlled fury once: her father's scowl at the pelting rain. Lily hadn't recognized John's rage for what it was. And the afternoon's subsequent events had trumped it in her memory . . . until now.

Armed with the remembrance of John's expression, Lily rushed back to the exam area.

"Fran!"

"Lily. Hi. Did you forget something?"

"No. I . . . there's a man in the waiting room. He looks terribly angry and I'm afraid he might be violent."

"I'm not terribly angry."

Lily turned toward the voice and caught a fleeting glimpse of what "terribly angry" might actually look like in the dark gray eyes — so fleeting, it had very likely been a mirage.

Lily did not, however, imagine his dismissiveness of her as his attention shifted to Fran.

"I need two minutes with Rachel, Fran, as soon as possible."

"She's just about finished in Exam Room B. I'll let her know."

"Thanks. I'll wait in her office."

He started to walk away. Then stopped. To issue a parting shot at Lily? No. His gaze settled on Fran's slightly bulging belly.

"This is new."

"Four and a half months." Fran touched her pregnant abdomen. "Cool, huh?"

"Very."

Then he was gone, without ever having looked at Lily again.

"Well," Lily murmured when he was out of sight. "That was embarrassing."

"Oh, don't worry about it! I can assure you he won't give it a second thought. And don't worry about Rachel, either. Even if he *was* angry — although, quite frankly, he didn't look particularly angry to me — it would be over a professional issue, not a personal one."

"You know him pretty well."

"Not really. I don't think anyone does. I do know he's gorgeous. How's that for a newsflash? And unmarried. *Not* that I'm in the market. He's also passionate about the innocents in his care."

"Innocents?"

"He's chief of pediatric surgery. We're the regional center for pediatric trauma. We see the worst of the worst. So it's a very important job. He was only thirty-five when it was offered to him a little over a year ago, and there was quite a bit of grumbling before he arrived. He was too young, of course. And, although nobody said it, maybe just a little too gorgeous.

Everyone imagined he'd be more interested in his social life than his professional one. Well, nobody's grumbling anymore — except for the people who are crazy enough to cross him."

"As I just did."

"No, you didn't. Do not, I repeat, worry about it."

Lily had worried about it. It was beyond insulting to suggest that anyone, much less a total stranger, might be violent. Not that he'd disputed his propensity for violence, or even her assertion that he was angry. He'd merely quibbled about the degree.

Fran was undoubtedly correct that he wouldn't give the incident a second thought. He had more important things to do.

Still, an apology was in order. *Operating Room* — not Dr. Something-or-other — had been embroidered on his white coat. But it would be easy enough to learn the name of the pediatrics surgery chief.

Or . . . she could leave the matter of her apology to fate.

Within the Pediatrics Pavilion, the surgical ward had been her SMC home, even when her admissions hadn't been surgical ones. The 7-North nurses knew her well, and she knew them, and it had been as good a place as any for her physicians from disparate specialties to meet.

She'd very likely see the surgeon in her travels. If not, the apology wasn't meant to be.

Lily hadn't seen him, which wasn't to say he hadn't also spent the afternoon on 7-North. But the thirty-six-year-old physician hadn't been where she was: immersed in the emotions of the past.

Lily had remembered her fear. But she'd forgotten her helplessness, the surrender she'd made — she'd had no choice — to every painful procedure she was required to endure. It had been a total capitulation.

But she had not surrendered to the illness itself. She'd battled, fiercely, the civil war that raged within. She'd given pep talks to the rag-tag army of cells that remained loyal to her, and pleaded with the heavily armed traitors to go away.

When Lily surfaced from the emotions to which she'd chosen to surrender, she saw a Pediatrics Pavilion that was quite different from the one she'd known.

The high-tech renovations were to be expected, but she was surprised by the art. It varied from ward to ward, quilts here, mobiles there, glass sculptures and papier mâché.

And on her ward . . . The 7-North foyer featured several large paintings. Expensive ones. Crafted by an artist whose work she knew — and had been known to like.

She might have liked these tableaux, had they been anywhere else. But in a place where sick and frightened children needed all the comfort they could get, the paintings were simply . . . wrong.

So wrong.

Lily, however, had a plan.

18

"Rafe? Please. Not in Lily's wildest imagination should she feel in any way responsible for what happened that day."

Rafe didn't look at the cell phone Brooke held out to him. He looked at her. Pale and cold, ferocious and fragile, Brooke wanted him to call Lily, to reassure Lily, *now.*

Brooke was holding the cell phone, but she was offering him far more: the chance to rescue the broken hearts of shattered sisters. It was Rafe's second such chance. Lily had made the same offer twelve years ago.

But not quite the same. Yes, like Lily, Brooke wanted his help. She even seemed to believe, as Lily had, that only with his help, only *if* he helped, would the rescue succeed.

But Lily had wanted both sisters to be rescued; she'd believed that both of them could be. Brooke seemed convinced only Lily could be saved.

Rafe would help. But it was a package

deal. Star Light . . . and Star Bright.

"It's not Lily's imagination I'm wondering about, Brooke. It's yours."

"Mine?"

"Just how wild is it?"

"Not wild at all."

That had been true, all her life, until last night. The girl who'd painted so carefully within the lines had become a woman who lived there . . . until last night. When she'd strayed. And the artist she'd become last night had painted daring landscapes of muscled flesh with her lips, her fingers —

"Brooke?"

"I told you. Not wild. At all."

"Yet you imagine that you're in some way to blame for what your mother did. And it's the reason, I think, the real one, that you ran away from me that day. True?"

So true.

The cell phone was still suspended in midair — which was beginning to feel like a gale force wind to her bloodless hand. Rafe wasn't going to call Lily. Not here. Not now. And she wasn't going to answer his question, not here, not now, even though the confession had to be made.

But . . . not . . . just . . . yet.

Brooke pocketed the phone and began to walk.

Neither spoke until, inside the stable, Brooke made another necessary confession.

"I was wrong about the Aztecs."

"You were dead right, Brooke. I have no doubt there's a revisionist version of the barbarism, some politically correct spin in which the amoral yet noble savages can't really be held accountable for their atrocities. I'm a little surprised you'd buy into it."

"I'm buying into truth, Rafe, not a spin."

"The glyphs don't lie."

"But they need to be interpreted correctly."

"Human sacrifice is pretty unambiguous."

"Yes, and I'm not saying it didn't happen. I think it's clear that it did."

"You think?"

"I know. It did. It had to, given what they believed."

"Meaning they didn't know any better? That's a little condescending, don't you think?"

"It would be, if it's what I meant. It wasn't a matter of knowing better, but of knowing different. The practice of nourishing the gods was at least a thousand years old, and probably four times that. The way the world was and had always been."

"Nourishing the gods? That's an interesting euphemism."

"It's not really a euphemism. Unlike virtually all other deities, the Aztec gods were mortal. Without sustenance, they would die. So would the Aztec sun. Four previous suns had already died. The Aztecs believed their sun, the Fifth Sun, would be the final one. When it perished, the world would fall into eternal blackness." Brooke paused, then said with sadness, "Darkness fell in broad daylight for the Aztecs, when Cortés arrived."

"Cortés," Rafe echoed. "My many times great-grandfather."

"Really?"

"So they said."

"Who said?"

"The elders in the village where I lived until I was fourteen."

Brooke started to say something. Stopped. Shrugged. But *wanted* to say it, Rafe thought.

"What?" he asked.

"There was a farming village in the mountains that was destroyed in a mudslide twenty years ago. The village is gone, but the site's become a mecca for archaeologists."

"Have you been there, Brooke?"

"Yes."

"Why?"

"Well, I knew an Aztec, after all. And the more I discovered how wrong I'd been about the Aztecs, the more fascinated I became with their civilization."

"So you've dug on the mountain?"

"No. That's not permitted. Never will be."

"Then why go there?"

"Because it's beautiful. Peaceful. A place to be, to *feel*. And to see —"

"The statue of Tlaloc."

"I'm not aware of any statue there."

"Sorry. I shouldn't have interrupted. And a place to see?"

"The maize. It's a unique hybrid created by a farmer with the help, the magic . . . or so the *folkloristas* say — of his blue-eyed son."

"The *folkloristas* have it wrong. The son watched and learned. The magic was the father's."

"But that's where you lived. You're the blue-eyed son."

"Guilty."

"No one knows you survived."

"Yes, they do. They just prefer to believe I didn't."

"What? *Why?* Because of Cortés?"

"Maybe."

"But you told me you were an Aztec, too. Which, presumably, the elders also knew."

"They said my other many times great-grandfather was Moctezuma."

"The Aztec of all Aztecs."

"For better or worse. And, Brooke, none of it may be true."

"You think the elders lied to you?"

Rafe considered for a moment. "No. I guess I don't. They just omitted critical pieces of data here and there."

"But . . ."

"But?"

"Your village was said to have been very like a sixteenth century — preConquest — village might have been."

"That's probably true. Why?"

"Because so much of what is known about the Aztecs comes from the friars who were sent to New Spain to convert the few who'd survived. Not surprisingly, there was a lot of revisionism involved. There had to be. The conquerors needed to create a record of a barbarism so grotesque that the destruction of an entire civilization was justified. It's believed that Aztec scribes were compelled to paint glyphs that conformed to that mandate, rather than the glyphs they painted before the conquistadors arrived. As a result, much of the pure Aztec lore was lost and what remains is largely a blend of native beliefs and Church doctrine."

"You think there might be pure Aztec lore in some of the bits and pieces the elders did decide to tell me."

"Don't you?"

"I don't know. They were well aware of the Conquest and the centuries since. Everything they told me was refracted through that prism and is likely to be revisionist, too."

"May I just ask you one little thing?"

She was lovely. His Brooke. And determined to find treasures — for him — in the mud.

His Brooke . . . who'd left him last night, been able to leave, and in a few days would be able to leave again. But until then . . .

"Sure, Brooke. Ask."

"Were you told about Aztlan?"

"The barren homeland to the north."

"And why the Aztecs migrated south?"

"Huitzilopochtli, the Hummingbird

God, told them to."

"And how they knew when they'd reached the place Huitzilopochtli wanted them to be?"

"They'd find an eagle perched on a prickly pear cactus."

"Did they?"

"Yes. They named their new home Tenochtitlan, 'the place of the prickly pear cactus.' "

"Which — this cactus — bears fruit that has an uncanny resemblance to a human heart. I imagine the elders never mentioned that."

"They steered pretty clear of anything even remotely related to the nourishment of the gods."

"It's undoubtedly a revisionist observation, anyway. Was there anything more about the eagle?"

"More? No."

"He wasn't clutching anything in his talons?"

"No."

"Or in his beak?"

"No. Okay, Dr. Blair. The eagle was supposed to be clutching what?"

"The same thing he's clutching on the modern-day Mexican flag. A snake. A symbol of evil to the friars."

"Snakes weren't considered evil by the Aztecs."

"I didn't think so. Quetzalcoatl, the Plumed Serpent, was the most beloved of all the gods . . . at least that's the modern spin."

"And the elders' spin."

"You said there was a statue of Tlaloc in your village?"

"In the forest. Last seen, it was being swallowed by the mud. I guess I've always imagined that sooner or later it would rise up again."

"Have you been back to the mountain?"

"No."

"Or read much about the Aztecs?"

"No."

"I have some notebooks I could show you. In fact, as luck would have it, I brought them with me."

"Why?"

"To show them to you, *give* them to you if you'd like them."

"I meant," Rafe said softly, "why do you have notebooks on the Aztecs?"

"I told you. The more I learned about them, the more fascinated I became."

"And you knew an Aztec . . . after all."

19

Rafe wanted to see Brooke's notebooks — very much. He'd call Lily first, they decided.

Brooke was welcome to listen to his side of the conversation. But she had baking to do in the cottage.

Rafe had told her where the raspberry scones would be, in a cake box in the freezer, and that Faye had made them during her most recent summertime visit with Jen and Jen's family. The children gathered the berries, with Lily and Jen, and whatever remained after raspberry toast promptly became filling for scones.

Had Lily remembered their raspberry-toast breakfast the day Carolyn died?

Probably, Brooke thought as she placed the frozen scones on a cookie sheet. *Of course.* But maybe she remembered all the other days more.

The oven pinged, signaling that preheating was complete. By the time Rafe arrived, the fragrance of warm raspberries perfumed the air.

"Lily's fine."

"Her visit to the haunted halls of SMC went well?"

"Very. But even better was what you wanted me to tell her."

"Oh, good! Thank you."

"I'm just the messenger, Brooke. And I have a return message for you. Lily would like you to immediately purge from your wild imagination whatever it is that makes you feel responsible for their deaths."

"Without knowing what the 'whatever' is?"

"And without ever needing to know."

"But . . ."

"Lily's not to blame, but you are? And neither your mother nor John bears any responsibility at all?"

"I don't blame either of them. I wonder why that is."

"I don't know, but Lily feels the same way." As had the orphaned Rafael. He hadn't blamed the elders for what they'd neglected to reveal. He'd blamed himself for failing to hear their omissions in the silence. "Maybe it's what survivors do, especially when the rest of their family has perished."

"I guess so," Brook said. *I know so.* "Is

Lily coming home?"

"She'll be here Saturday morning. Early. She's spending tonight, probably all night, working on an idea she has for a Pediatrics Pavilion mosaic. She's showing it to a Dr. Hart, one of the pediatricians from her past, tomorrow at eleven."

"After which she needs to catch up on her sleep before making the drive."

"Which she promises to do."

"Thank you, Rafe. Again."

"Anytime. Are you in the mood for a fire?"

"Yes. Please. Would you like some hot chocolate? *Is* that something you like?"

"Hot chocolate? Yes. Why?"

"*Chocolatl* was a favorite of Aztec nobility. They drank it cold — and thick and frothy — through straws of gold. Did you?"

"Drink it that way? Yes. But without the gold."

Tlaloc's rain clouds sobbed.

Rafe's fire glowed.

And Brooke's Aztec research sat between them on the carpeted floor. The colors of the four notebooks had been specially chosen: quetzal-feather green, mosaic-art turquoise, seashell-palace pink, and the

211

gold of the hybrid maize created by a certain farmer . . . a certain father.

Each notebook was devoted to a specific aspect of Aztec life. Green, not surprisingly, was myths and lore. Turquoise was poetry and the arts. Architecture and engineering were bound in pink. And, in gold, the Spanish Conquest and ensuing five hundred years.

Within each notebook, different colored inks indicated the various discrepancies Brooke had found, and Post-its of many colors linked related topics from one notebook to the next, and the sections underlined in aqua were derived from the *Florentine Codex,* and — Brooke stopped midway through her explanation.

"That would be great."

"What would?"

"If we went through the notebooks together. The only drawback is that helping me dig into my past takes you away from your digging into yours."

"I'm done for the day. I need to put a little distance between what I've looked at so far and what I'm planning to do tomorrow."

So they explored the Aztec civilization together, and without consulting Brooke's notebooks at all.

She knew the stories of the Nahua as she knew the sagas of the Farm: by heart.

She told him, among so many things, a little more about the nourishment of the sun. She wanted him to understand. It was a sacred honor. Aztec warriors often volunteered.

"It was like plucking a petal from a rose."

"Except that the rose survives the plucking."

"So did those who kept the sun alive. They ascended to the Palace of the Sun, the highest of the thirteen levels of heaven, and spent eternity in that shining paradise. All the levels of heaven were . . . well, heavenly, and each was customized for its eternal guests. Milk Tree Heaven was for babies, and for those drowned or struck by lightning, there was the Heaven of Rain. I think it's my favorite of all the heavens, although it should actually be called the Heaven of Rainbows because — Rafe? What is it?"

"Nothing." *Let my sisters, oh please, my sisters, live forever in the shining clouds.* "No," he said softly, "that's not true . . . I'd forgotten about the rainbows, Brooke. I'm glad you reminded me. Tell me more."

The Aztec afterlife was determined

solely by the way a person died. No matter how exemplary that person's life on earth, unless death occurred in one of the designated ways, the Aztec soul went to hell. The descent to the underworld was a trial in itself, a journey with such obstacles as the Wind of Knives.

"That's evocative," Rafe said.

"Isn't it? And it makes me wonder what it *felt* like to be an Aztec."

"Felt like?"

"Yes. What the *world* felt like. Was it terrifying? It could have been *very* terrifying. The gods, as legends, are enchanting. But if you believed they were real, you could have spent every minute of your life worrying that a petulant god would wreak havoc. And there was the constant concern that the sun would set and never rise again. And the odds were excellent that you'd spend eternity in hell, no matter how honorably you lived. It should've been a prescription for hedonism. But even the revisionist record is clear. The Aztecs worked hard and conducted their lives with great dignity. They believed in love, children, marriage. And music, and poetry, and flowers. There *was* joy in their world. But did it surpass the fear? Did they awaken, ever, with a sense of hope?"

The boy named Rafael had awakened with hope every morning as he'd greeted the triumphant sun. Hope that he would pass the elders' tests and be permitted to farm beside his hard-working father and tell stories to his joyful sisters. . . . "Except for the elders, no one in my village knew about the ancient gods. Or that the sun might die. Or that there were levels of heaven and hell. But the elders knew and were fearful. When I found the statue of Tlaloc, it was as if I'd found the Rain God himself — or *was* him."

"Tlaloc, not Cortés?"

"Who knows? Was the conquistador as fearsome as a god?"

"Yes . . . but only because he was mistaken for one."

Omens of doom had haunted the emperor Moctezuma long before Hernán Cortés planted the flag of Spain on the beach at Veracruz. Sacred temples burned to ash, and talking stones forecast Moctezuma's downfall, and phantom women wept and wailed. Lake Texcoco churned, and in the mirrored crests of lake birds, a conquering army could be seen.

Moctezuma finally understood the omens when news reached him of Cortés's ships — floating temples on the sea — and

215

of the fair-skinned conquistador himself: Quetzalcoatl had returned.

Quetzalcoatl . . . the god of flowers . . . who disguised himself at times as a fair-skinned man. He'd been tricked by a rival god and forced to leave in disgrace on a raft of serpents. But Quetzalcoatl had vowed to return and had even specified the date: the year 1-Reed, which, by extraordinary coincidence, was the European year 1519, when Cortés arrived.

"Moctezuma welcomed Cortés with wariness. But as a god. It must have been confusing to the Spaniard. Who did they expect him to be? And what if he let them down? Any misgivings Cortés might have had were forgotten, however, when he saw the mountains of gold in the emperor's palace. By the time Moctezuma and his people realized their mistake, the empire was lost."

Welcomed with wariness.

Who did they expect him to be?

By the time the elders realized their mistake, it was too late.

"Rafe? What is it?"

"Cortés was fair-skinned."

"Yes. And his lieutenant, Alvarado, had blue eyes. That's what you're wondering, isn't it? If the elders believed you were

Cortés incarnate, coming to destroy what little was left of the empire?"

"They wanted to take me from Veracruz to Mexico City, to retrace Cortés's march from the sea. I told them I didn't want to go, that the village was my home and that I thought they should begin sharing the stories of the gods with the other villagers. You wondered about joy, Brooke. I saw it then."

"They believed you were Quetzalcoatl."

"I think so. Yes. For one glorious moment that's exactly what they believed."

"Maybe you *are* Quetzalcoatl."

"Brooke."

"He is the god of flowers, Rafe."

"I found the statue of Tlaloc, Brooke, and the elders' joy turned to terror. The rains came and the mountain crumbled. They must have believed I was Quetzalcoatl, then realized — too late — their mistake. That I was Tlaloc instead."

"The elders weren't mistaken." It sounded like a statement of scientific fact. "Quetzalcoatl's return just coincided with a rainstorm. It *happens*."

"Your too-wild imagination." A lovely imagination for him . . . and a tormenting one for her. "Talk to me, Brooke. Tell me why you believe you're in any way responsible for the deaths." *And why you ran away.*

Then let me tell you, Star Bright, why you could not possibly be to blame.

20

"My mother wanted John to adopt me. He may have gone to her bedroom that afternoon to tell her *no*. I know it sounds crazy to suggest she shot him because of that . . . but what she did *was* crazy."

"For which you're hardly to blame."

"Except that my mother had forgotten about the gun. I reminded her of it just moments before she shot John. He had no idea she had it. She didn't want him to know. That's why the accident theory doesn't work. She'd never have shown it to him. She was going to get rid of it as a wedding present to us both."

"You didn't put the gun in your mother's hand, Brooke. You didn't even put it in her bedroom."

"But I put in her *mind,* Rafe. She was exhausted, jet-lagged — and just to tip the balance toward that fatal instant of madness, I managed to get her talking about my father. Remember I said I didn't know him? Well, neither did she. . . ."

Brooke told him about the rape, and the rapist.

"My mother was adamant he wasn't a doctor. But I wonder if that could be part of the reason she didn't want me to visit Lily in the hospital. She never really explained, just said it was for the best. Maybe she wasn't completely certain he wasn't both a psychopath and a physician, after all. If so, he might have seen himself, and her, in me. That's a little farfetched, isn't it? Revisionism fueled by wishful thinking."

"Wishing for what, Brooke?"

"An alternative to the real reason she asked me to stay away — because that's what Lily wanted."

With the exception of the eagle-clutching-snake quandary, Rafe added no new perspective on the Aztec stories Brooke had told him. She was the expert on his past.

But when it came to the story of Star Light and Star Bright, the expert was Rafe. "Lily wanted you to visit her, Brooke. I know that for a fact."

"Did she think I didn't want to?"

"She understood. She felt she'd let you down by being so ill."

"I was the one who watched her go into

septic shock. I *wanted* to be with her at the hospital. She needs to know that."

"She already does. I've told her, Brooke, over the years. I'll tell her again, if you like, as well as whatever else —"

"Everything. Please. The gun. The rape. The adoption. And there's one more *what if.* I was on my way to the stable, after I'd just finished talking to my mother about the gun and the rape. I saw John in her bedroom, and for a moment I considered going back to tell him he didn't need to adopt me. That it was okay if he'd changed his mind. But I —"

"Wanted to get to the stable."

"Yes." *To you.*

"That's not a crime, Brooke. Nothing you did is. You're wrong, though, about John. He hadn't changed his mind about adopting you. We found a note in his study. It hadn't been there while he was in Switzerland, so it's clear he wrote it shortly before he died. Your name was on it with an arrow pointing to Curtis's."

"Meaning John had planned to speak with Curtis about me?"

"He tried to that afternoon. But Curtis was at a deposition in D.C. We didn't know why John wanted to talk to him about you. But we do now. It was about

221

the adoption, Brooke. You know it must have been. Don't you?"

"Yes. I guess I do."

"We don't know what happened that afternoon, Brooke. We'll never know. But no one put that gun in your mother's hand but your mother. And she's the one who pulled the trigger. You believe that, don't you?"

"You mean rationally? And from the vantage point of a grown woman, not a devastated girl? Yes. But it's hard not to replay it. Rewrite it."

"I know. If only I hadn't found the statue in the forest, my family wouldn't have died."

"You can't possibly believe you had anything to do with the rainstorm!"

"And you," he said softly, "can't possibly believe you had anything to do with their deaths. Okay?"

"Okay."

She smiled. Tried to. She was so exhausted.

"Time for you to go to bed, Brooke. To sleep."

"Alone?" The word was an impulse. A wish from her heart.

"I thought that was what you preferred."

"No."

"But you left last night."

"I didn't know you wanted me to stay."

"Oh, Brooke."

"You did?"

"I did. I wanted to sleep with you, Brooke. Dream with you. I still want to. . . . Beginning tonight. If that appeals to you."

"Yes," she whispered. *Oh, yes.*

21

It rained all night in the nation's capital, a splashing that sounded like music against a certain hotel-room window where an all-night mosaicking marathon was underway.

It sounded to Lily like a march, à la John Phillip Sousa, and it matched her energetic mood perfectly.

Parade music to mosaic by.

To live by.

Lily had never stayed up all night working on a mosaic. Stayed up all night, *period*. Rest, like nutrition and pep talks to her ever-more-healthy cells, had been sacrosanct.

But nothing on this rainy night was going to rain on her parade — until her marching thoughts ceased at the memory of the surgeon with the storm-gray eyes.

Assuming there was interest in her proposal to make mosaics for 7-North, he would see her mosaics every day.

Her mosaics . . . made of candy.

She'd been en route to her hotel room, to search the Yellow Pages for craft stores nearby, when she hit on the idea of candy. There were problems with using candy, but they were easily resolved.

Every sugary piece would be glued and grouted, impossible for even the most determined young fingers to pry free, and she'd apply a clear acrylic coat over the entire mosaic. The candy itself would be sealed, too. Cake-lady Faye would have a technique.

Lily found the raw materials for tonight's sample mosaics in the hotel gift shop. There was even a little rescuing involved. Easter candies, in their springtime pastels, were destined to be discarded soon.

Clear nail polish would work as a stand-in sealer, and from the Wind Chimes business center she purchased posterboard and glue. On the real thing, she'd use grouts of many colors. For the mock-ups, colorful paper would do . . . was doing very nicely. Marching forward artistically despite thoughts about the scalpel-wielding pediatrician. Would he like her M&M birds and butterscotch moons? Or her peppermint castle in a gumdrop sky?

Probably not.

Undoubtedly not.

Well, too bad. Lily believed — no, she *knew* — the mosaics would make sick and frightened children smile.

It didn't matter if the surgeon couldn't see the images as his patients would, if he couldn't remember what it was like to be a boy.

Which he couldn't. The realization hit with the jolt of crashing cymbals.

And just as decisively as Lily had deemed him angry and dangerous, she knew the reason why: The chief of pediatric surgery had never been a boy.

He'd created a mosaic, too, on this rainy night. There'd been no raindrop music in his studio. No music in the operating room at all.

Silence had reigned as he pieced together the shattered fragments of a battered child. The broken boy would survive.

And would he flourish?

The surgeon worried, how he worried, about his young patient's heart. Physically, it had been untouched. But it had been damaged — ravaged — by violence.

I think he might be violent. The words had stayed with him, a weighted shadow, as had the memory of her fear.

He'd seen it in the aquarium mirror and had been moving forward to help her when he'd realized that what she feared was him.

Her fear hadn't vanished. It had merely been eclipsed by her courage to act.

They were on the same side in the war against violence.

And yet: *I think he might be violent.* It bothered him immensely. Because the assertion was false?

No. Worse. Because it was true.

He *was* violent. But only with himself. He pushed himself to exhaustion, then pushed some more. He ran endless miles along the Potomac, harder, faster, harder still, and when he needed to be within *stat* distance of the hospital, he punched a weighted bag in his Wind Chimes Towers condo.

His limbs were powerful. His heart was strong. The heart of an athlete . . . and of a broken boy. The chips and shards were there, in the surgeon's heart, piercing slivers too sharp to touch, too imbedded to remove, too colorless to see.

Or so he'd thought until today.

Within the cottage in Forsythe, the splashing rain sounded like a Nahuatl lullaby. Rafe heard the music as he felt the precise moment when Brooke trusted him to protect her on the vulnerable journey from wakefulness to dreams.

Rafe wanted to join her in those dreams. But he was dreaming already. What could be better than holding her while she slept?

Nothing . . . except to surrender, too.

To trust her, too.

By the time he awakened, the sun had already conquered the forces of darkness.

Brooke stirred a little when he did. It was morning, he whispered to her. He was going to check on the horses. She should keep sleeping, keep dreaming.

Which she did until 10:45.

Still dressed for dreams, she wandered into a living room warmed by flames and perfumed by scones.

Rafe rose to greet her. To touch her.

"Good morning."

"Good morning. I've never slept this late. Or this well."

"Neither have I."

"Is the stable crowd happy?"

"Happier since the rain relented enough to give them a little time outside. After that, I spoke with Lily."

"Did she finish what she'd hoped to?"

"She did. And likes the results. She sounded wide-awake despite no sleep."

"She'd better not be driving home until tomorrow."

"She's not. She knows she's running on

just enough adrenaline to carry her through the meeting she has scheduled fifteen minutes from now."

"Did you tell her . . . ?"

"Everything. Her response was immediate, Brooke, and ferocious. Not by any stretch of the wildest imagination was anything that happened your fault."

"That's nice of her."

"Truthful of her. She also said that your mother and John had seemed particularly close in Switzerland, so it's likely they *were* planning to marry."

"Which makes what happened all the more inexplicable."

"So it's all the luckier we're not trying to explain it. Are we?"

"No. We're not."

"Nor is Lily."

"Thank you, Rafe. Again."

"You're welcome, Brooke. Again."

Rafe led her to their fire-warm excavation site. Her Aztec research was there, and scones and hot chocolate and . . .

Brooke knelt beside the glyphs of the gods. The last of the Aztec scribes had died in the early 1600s, and with them the sacred art of picture-writing. Or so the world thought.

"You drew these. This morning?"

He nodded. "One of my earliest lessons."

"They're beautiful, Rafe. *Amazing*." She greeted each enchanting — if difficult — deity by name. "Hello, Tlaloc, you villain of the piece. And Huitzilopochtli, fierce as always. And the mischievous Smoking Mirror."

When Brooke came to the final glyph, Quetzalcoatl, she looked from the god of flowers to the blue-eyed artist.

"And," she added, "a self-portrait. May I keep these?"

"I made them for you."

She started to thank him, but was stopped by his smile. The thank-you wasn't necessary. None of her thank-yous had been.

"This feels like Christmas morning when Lily and I were girls. We'd come downstairs in our nightgowns and robes, and, with a fire and breakfast nearby, we'd sit on the living-room carpet and open gifts." Brooke cast a frown at Marla's white-pine desk. "That may be where the analogy breaks down."

"You're worried about opening the desk. Why?"

"Because of what I learned that afternoon, I suppose. That she had secrets. The rape, of course . . . and the fact that she was capable of aiming a gun and pulling the trigger. As her daughter that scares me."

"There's not a chance in hell you'd ever have a gun, much less use it."

"But —"

"Any more than I'm likely to arm myself with an obsidian knife and carve open a chest."

"This is a slightly more modern family history. Twelve years, not —"

Rafe stopped her with gentle fingers on her lips.

"I have a suggestion for our Christmas in April. We begin with scones and chocolate. Sustenance for the dig. Then we open the rolltop desk. We'll view it as a gift. And then," he said softly, "and for the rest of the day, we make love."

Make love.

22

The Wind Chimes-SMC sky bridge provided Lily with rainproof transit to Dr. Peter Hart's seventh-floor Peds Pavilion office.

Lily had scheduled her appointment over the phone, with Dr. Hart's secretary, Edith. She hadn't mentioned the mosaics, only that she'd been a patient of his and wanted to say hello.

Edith was as pleasant in person as over the phone. Sixty-something and sprightly, she took the top half of Lily's bulky bundle and started to rave.

"These are fabulous! What are they for?"

"Thanks. For 7-North. If anyone's interested. I thought I'd show them to Dr. Hart first. If he thinks the idea's worth pursuing, maybe he could point me toward whomever I should meet with next."

"He'd point you toward himself, and he will be very interested. Follow me."

Edith led the way to a spacious office — the widowed hematologist's office — that was as stark as his life must be since the loss of his Joanna.

"Peter's not here yet."

"I'm early."

"A few minutes." Edith put her armful of mosaics on an oval table and gestured for Lily to do the same. "He, on the other hand, is running more than a few minutes late."

"That's fine. I'm not in any hurry."

"Good. This does give us the opportunity to properly display these works of art before he arrives. You really didn't know he's unhappy with the paintings on 7-North?"

"No. I really didn't."

"Well, he is. They're wrong for the ward, he says. For any ward in the Peds Pavilion."

"I agree."

"He's going to love these, however. Mark my words. And your timing couldn't be more perfect. He's already put the center's administrators on notice that the 7-North paintings have to go. He wasn't involved in selecting the art. Who'd have thought he'd need to be? Not that he'd have to worry about being involved with you creating the art. But he'd like to be, I think, if you didn't mind."

Dr. Hart couldn't be on call every night

and every weekend, Rachel had said. Which meant that some nights and weekends must be particularly lonely for him. Lily had discovered that she was quite capable of marching energetically past her usual bedtime, and her weekends were always free.

"I wouldn't mind at all."

"Great. So." Edith scanned the dreary office. "We could put a couple on the windowsill. And the X-ray viewing box might work. The radiograph clips shouldn't cause any damage."

"It doesn't matter if they do. These are just mock-ups to give Dr. Hart an idea of what I have in mind."

"He'll want you to call him Peter, and you'd better not be planning to throw these away."

"They're a renewable resource."

"Which you enjoy renewing?"

"Which I love renewing."

"I'd be careful who I said that to." Edith's warning came with a smile. "There are enough barren walls at SMC to keep you busy forever."

Maybe I have forever. But maybe sometime soon I'll be busy — forever — on the Farm ...

The time had come, this Christmas in

234

April, to open Marla's desk.

Brooke unlocked it with a simple twist of the ornate key on Marla's key-ring, a memento shipped within weeks of Marla's death to Elise's home in Bel Air. Brooke hesitated before opening the desk. Would she find a treasure trove? An empty coffin?

A Pandora's box?

Onward. She drew a breath, lifted. The wooden curtain rolled up and away.

And?

Four things came into view. Three — jewelry box, memo pad, pen — on the desktop, and the fourth, an envelope, tucked in a cubbyhole. Here was the very epicenter of her dig. To be explored last. She needed, first, to examine the floor-to-desktop drawers.

The left-hand drawers contained the artifacts of the entrepreneur, a predictable array of office supplies . . . and colored Post-its and pens. Her mother had chosen a bolder palette than Brooke's, just as Marla had preferred the zing of Lemon Lift to the mellowness of French Vanilla.

But the broad strokes were the same.

Brooke was smiling when she opened the desk's single, deep right-hand drawer . . . and found a stack of notebooks so similar to those she'd created for Rafe that she looked toward the fire to confirm that his were still there.

"I am my mother's daughter, aren't I?"

Rafe was standing behind her. He kissed her auburn head and reminded her gently, "Nothing wrong with that, Brooke."

Nothing wrong with anything, she thought, *as long as you're here.*

"I wonder what horribly maligned civilization *she* was studying." Brooke lifted the four thick volumes to her lap. "Oh! These are Lily's medical records. I wonder why she had them . . . To take to Switzerland, I suppose, for the doctors there to review . . . Or maybe not."

"Why?"

"Lily's SMC nephrologist would have sent a comprehensive summary to his Swiss colleagues. And —" Brooke touched Marla's orderly rows of bold-palette Post-its "— this seems to be a review my mother did herself. Judging by what she's written on the Post-its, she was cross-referencing symptoms — and possible diagnoses — from one admission to the next."

In the same way Brooke had cross-referenced Aztec facts — and possible theories — for Rafe.

"I wonder if she found any clues to whatever it was that Lily had. . . ."

23

Peter Hart didn't like being late. But it came with the territory — patient care — which was the way he'd chosen to spend his life.

Peter had never regretted the decision. He was nevertheless sorry to have kept his eleven-o'clock appointment waiting until almost noon, especially since Edith had to leave by eleven-thirty to be on time for the grandparents' luncheon at her grandson's elementary school.

Peter apologized as he entered his office.

"Sorry I'm so late."

"It's fine!" Lily rose from the chair where she'd been sitting since Edith left, and turned, smiling, toward the voice. *"You."*

"You," Peter echoed. And missed, in a way that astonished him, the smile that had so swiftly disappeared.

"I'm here to see Dr. Hart."

"I'm afraid you're seeing him."

Lily looked from gray eyes that seemed a little sad to the bright white coat he wore.

Like yesterday's coat, it covered surgical scrubs. But today's embroidery read *Peter Hart M.D.*

"I've made a mistake. I thought I'd scheduled an appointment with a different Dr. Hart."

"There are several on staff. Do you know the first name?"

"No. I was his patient as a girl. I didn't see another Hart on the directory at the Pavilion entrance, but I obviously just missed it."

"I'm the only Hart in Peds."

"I *know* he's still here. A pediatric hematologist?"

"There's a Robert Hart in hematology. But he's an internist."

Meaning he took care of adults. "That must be him, though. A terrific physician and a very nice man?"

"Both."

Lily believed she heard affection in his quiet voice. And pride. "Is he your father?"

She believed wrong. The gray eyes darkened.

So did his voice.

"No."

"Well," she murmured. "I'm very sorry for what I said yesterday, and for the confusion today."

There needed to be another sentence. A ladylike farewell. *It was lovely seeing you again. I look forward to next time.* Or even as a last resort: *Have a nice day.*

But Lily had already managed what she could.

All she could.

She fled gracefully — but she fled.

"My mother clearly put a lot of thought into trying to connect the perplexing dots." Brooke stared at the medical records in her lap. "And she was so bright she might have uncovered something that could lead to the certainty that Lily's illness is gone. Someone should look at these — don't you think?"

"I do. Someone should. Beginning with you." Rafe glanced at the slender fingers that had been touching the Post-its but had yet to open a file. "You want to, don't you?"

"Yes. For whatever insights I might glean about my mother. Medically, I'd have nothing to add."

"I thought you'd read everything there was to read too," Rafe told her softly as he reprised her exact words of twelve years ago. "I'm not suggesting you should be the only one to take a look. I'm simply unwilling to dismiss out of hand any ideas you might have."

"Thank you."

He smiled at the brilliant woman who didn't need to thank him for anything. "You're welcome."

"I'd need to get Lily's permission first."

"You know she'd say yes."

"I do. Because of you. But I'll ask her myself, when I see her tomorrow."

Brooke returned Lily's medical records to the drawer and retrieved the envelope from the cubbyhole.

It was thick, as if filled with wishes.

The envelope itself contained a wish come true for the mother who'd told her girls about cubbyhole wishes in the first place: the invitation to Carolyn's wedding.

Inside the invitation and protected by its thick parchment were photographs — not wishes, but treasures nonetheless.

The first was dated November eighth of Marla's freshman year in college, four years before either she or John met Carolyn.

But here they were, Marla and John, enjoying each other's company — and in love? If a stranger had happened upon this photograph, the answer would have been a resounding *yes*. But from ancient glyphs to modern albums, familiarity with the story was essential to its correct interpretation.

A dorm-room snapshot of the roommates who became best friends was next, followed by a photograph taken at Carolyn's wedding to John. Here was how love looked on John Rutledge. There was no need to compare this image of Carolyn's husband with the one taken on a date during Marla's freshman year.

There *was* no comparison.

John loved Carolyn. And Carolyn loved John. And if maid of honor Marla had ever been *in* love with John, the "in" had been replaced by her love for her best friend — and her happiness for that best friend's groom.

Twenty months elapsed in the photographs Marla had saved, from lilac-blossom wedding to snowy Christmas Eve. A wreath adorned the Georgetown colonial's wedgewood-blue door, and on the mansion's front steps, in varying degrees of exhaustion and a variety of dress, stood the six housemates.

Two wore jeans, parkas and were ashen with fatigue. They weren't doctoring on this December day, but had undoubtedly been doing so for the past twenty-four hours. The three who were making the

Christmas Eve trek to SMC wore white beneath their winter coats . . . and slightly weary smiles — in anticipation of the long hours that lay ahead.

The sixth housemate, the MBA, was dressed stylishly. And seasonally. Charcoal-gray coat. Ink-black books. And just for fun, and with a flamboyance that worked, a scarf of knitted snowflakes. Marla seemed to be en route to work, too, perhaps a half-day at the property management company followed by last-minute shopping in the afternoon.

Marla hadn't written her housemates' names on the Christmas Eve photo. Like Carolyn and John, these friends would never be forgotten. And, like Carolyn and John, the SMC physicians would have hated what fate held in store for Marla just one week later.

Marla's New Year's Eve rape was unforeseeable on that snowy day. And she hadn't saved, in her cubbyhole envelope, any snapshots of the party itself, the get-together of her ever-tired housemates and their medical friends that should have been so safe.

The next photo was dated January fourth. Marla and another woman, pretty and blond, were seated at a kitchen table.

At first glance, Brooke thought the other woman was Carolyn. Hoped she would be.

But she was unfamiliar. Not Carolyn. Not a housemate. A rape counselor, one might have guessed; their conversation appeared serious. Intense.

Marla had never told anyone, however, about the rape.

"She looks okay, doesn't she? Okay *enough*," Brooke clarified, "five days after the rape. Not looking, at least, as if she desperately wished she'd had the gun."

"Maybe she already sensed you inside her."

That was implausible, of course. As scientifically unlikely as a golden lilac, much less one that blossomed in spring and in fall.

But it was the flower magician telling her this was possible: that her mother might have sensed such a tiny bud.

Brooke believed it. Believed him.

But, as she saw moments later, he had it wrong.

The "okay enough" in the immediate aftermath of the rape had, in retrospect, been shock — the survival instinct that allowed the victim to go through the motions until the trauma could be faced.

By Valentine's Day, Marla's blocked

memories had been unblocked. The photograph was a self-portrait. The camera was probably sitting on Marla's nightstand, where, on New Year's Eve, there hadn't been the desperately wished-for gun.

Brooke had never seen the physical resemblance between her mother and herself. There hadn't been any between the reclusive tomboy and the vivacious entrepreneur.

But in grief they might have been twins. Complete with severely cropped auburn hair and ashen skin, Marla looked as Brooke had six weeks after Marla's death.

When you have nothing to hide, the girl most likely to succeed had advised, *hide nothing*.

And *A secret is a lie*.

Marla hid nothing in her self-portrait, not even the gun she'd kept secret from everyone — except her daughter — until the day she died.

Marla revealed the weapon to the camera, but didn't aim it in any specific way.

Her archeologist daughter nonetheless interpreted the Valentine's Day glyph. With comparable ease Marla could have fired a bullet into the psychopath's heart . . . her own temple . . . or her six-week pregnant womb.

24

Lily was halfway across the Wind Chimes sky bridge when she decided to return to SMC — not, of course, to the Peds Pavilion office she'd so recently fled.

She and the surgeon were through. Her fault, not his.

It had not been her finest hour. True, she'd managed an apology. Barely. And, although purely by mistake, she'd had an appointment with the exact person she needed to see regarding her mosaics — Peter Hart.

She should have acknowledged the lucky coincidence and seized the opportunity to discuss her idea. And if he'd been dismissive, disdainful, so be it.

At least she would've given her art a chance. Herself a chance.

Peter Hart a chance.

Other than being impossible to read — so why did she keep thinking she could? — he'd been perfectly civil. She'd even imagined emotion. Sadness. Why? And fondness. Why not?

The more relevant question was why she'd asked him if he was Robert Hart's son. She knew he wasn't. The widowed hematologist had no children.

Where the question had come from, she couldn't guess. The same misguided place, no doubt, that had sent her dashing to report a would-be murderer on the loose and had her imagining turbulent emotions in the very still waters of his dark gray eyes.

Even if Peter Hart liked the mosaics adorning his bleak office, even if he loved them, she just couldn't see them working together.

She'd been cloistered her entire life. The few men she'd known had known all about her, had cloistered her, too. She was discovering, on her Excellent Adventure, just how removed from the real world her life at FoxHaven Farm had been.

Not ready for prime time. But not planning, either, to beat a hasty retreat. She was going to see the other Dr. Hart. Her adrenaline had gotten a second surge during the awkward moments with Peter.

Robert Hart was easy to find once she knew where to look. Internal Medicine was housed in the center's Asquith Tower. The directory at the Tower entrance informed her his office was AT11-801. Asquith Tower. Eleventh floor. Room 801.

The nice hematologist who'd bored large holes in her delicate bones wasn't in the office at AT11-801. He was standing in the hallway just outside.

At least Lily assumed it was he. From her hospital-bed — and sick child — vantage point, she'd scarcely noticed what her many doctors looked like.

She'd known their names, though. And their voices. And the painful procedures that came with each. Dr. Newman, arterial blood gas. Dr. Maitlin, spinal tap. Dr. Farley, endoscopy. Dr. Rivers, cerebral arteriogram.

Dr. Hart, bone marrow biopsy.

The man who stood outside AT11-801 was listening, not speaking. A young woman, probably a medical student, was sharing a potpourri of eager thoughts as he glanced through the handful of lab reports she'd brought for him to read.

He was able to do both. Listen attentively and scan the data. *Just like her father.*

A wave of loss swept through Lily. She missed her father so much. Loved him so much. Would have said — so much — to him if only she'd known, as he'd lifted the hood of her parka and told her to have fun,

fun, that she'd never see him alive again.

The physician in the hallway was the age her father would have been. Mid-fifties. Only the reading glasses he wore gave the slightest clue to his age.

Another wave of longing flooded her as Lily recalled her father's sheepish smile when he'd first started wearing such glasses. And his delight when he'd discovered the inexpensive drugstore ones worked perfectly.

John Rutledge became a true believer in the wonders of simple magnification. He'd converted Faye to reading glasses, and Marla and Curtis, too.

"Lily?"

The voice was Dr. Hart's. Definitely. But for a wondrous moment the face she saw was John's, the smiling eyes over the half-lenses propped on his nose.

"Dr. Hart. Hi. I don't want to interrupt."

"It's okay!" the young woman insisted. "I'm late for a clinic. Thanks for the curb-side consult, Dr. Hart."

"Any time, Julie."

Robert Hart walked toward Lily. She met him halfway.

"You look wonderful, Lily."

"Thank you. I *feel* wonderful. And, so

far, the lab results are normal."

"Seeing you and knowing you've been symptom-free for a dozen years, I'm not surprised. Please come in."

A sense of home, not starkness, greeted her. A home away from the home he'd shared with his Joanna. Her touches were here. Still. Why would he ever put them away?

Joanna herself was here, in a silver-framed wedding portrait Robert wanted Lily to see.

Joanna and Robert, the engraving read. The date was May, two years before Lily was born. And the setting, beneath a trellis of lilacs, was one Lily knew well.

"You were married on the Farm."

"We were. Thanks to your parents, who made the offer, and Marla, who asked them to."

He'd known Marla, he explained, because, along with four other SMC residents, they'd shared a house in Georgetown. Marla and Joanna became very close in the months before Marla's move to the Farm, and upon learning that Joanna and Robert were getting married, she'd arranged a dinner with her Fox-Haven friends and her Georgetown ones, during which the offer of nuptials amid the lilacs was made.

"It was the only way to get married, your mother insisted. And your father agreed. They were right. It was." Robert gazed at the wedding photo for a moment, then at the orphaned daughter nearby. "I never saw your mother again, Lily. I wish I had. She was very lovely. But we moved to Boston after the wedding. Joanna had Hodgkin's lymphoma and, since our families were in Boston, we decided to continue her therapy there. Only Joanna was certain she'd go into remission . . . which she did. She had twenty-nine good years. We remained in Boston for the first ten, then returned to D.C. I rejoined the SMC faculty about a week before you became ill. Neither your father nor Marla knew I was in town until I showed up at your bedside."

"They didn't ask you to see me?"

"Not initially. Your doctors did. I've always specialized in adult hematology. My research, however, has been in disseminated intravascular coagulopathy. DIC. It affects patients of all ages and is triggered by a variety of underlying processes — trauma, tumors and, as in your case, septic shock."

"Once triggered it stays around?"

"Occasionally. Usually, though, with treatment of the underlying cause, the DIC goes away. Which yours did. Even though every so often, for the next seven years, I'd come by and do a bone marrow biopsy."

"Not because of your research."

"I'm glad you know that without asking. You had other hematologic abnormalities that necessitated repeated looks at your marrow. I remained involved because your father — and your doctors and Marla — wanted me to be. I hated doing the biopsies, Lily. They hurt. There's no way to get around it."

"And no other way to get the information."

"I'm afraid not. But I am sorry."

"I'm not. How else would you have known what medications I needed?" *The miracle drugs that kept me alive until the traitorous antibodies were forced to surrender.*

Lily smiled at the man who'd lost his beloved wife, as her own father had lost Carolyn. The man who, in emotional ways, lovely ways, reminded her of John.

"Would you like to visit the Farm?"

"Oh. I . . . yes. Thank you, Lily. I would."

"Is there a good time? A best time?"

"Best would be when I'm not attending.

That would mean the remainder of this month, and again in June, and then not until September."

He couldn't be on call all the time, Rachel Davis had said. But he was taking July and August, the summer vacation months, when his colleagues with wives and children liked to get away.

"Could you come this weekend?"

"I could." Robert's expression became thoughtful as the journey to his past suddenly loomed near. "Yes. This weekend would be just fine — except that you're not sure, are you?"

"I'm sure it would be lovely for Brooke to meet you, since you and Marla were good friends. She'll want to. I'm just not certain about her plans for this weekend, so I'd better check with her first."

"Talk to me, Brooke."

"She must have felt like this the afternoon she shot John. She must have flashed back to this place of despair. John would never have done anything to hurt her. Or frighten her. But something must have tripped the memory. I just want to put my arms around her and tell her it's going to be all right."

"Isn't that what you're doing?"

It was what Rafe was doing with Marla's daughter, embracing her even though they didn't touch.

"Yes," Brooke murmured. "Yes."

She held the disturbing photo a little longer, then set it gently aside. With trepidation, she glanced at the next. Which was fine. Happy. A wedding photo taken ten weeks later on the Farm.

The groom was one of Marla's physician housemates. Tuxedoed in his wedding photo, he'd been in jeans on Christmas Eve, off-call but sleep-deprived. His bride was the blonde who'd been talking so intently to Marla five days after the rape. She'd looked healthy in early January. But by May, at her wedding, she appeared quite frail . . . and very much in love.

Marla was Marla again. Her auburn hair, ten weeks longer, was a lustrous halo around her smiling face. She was glowing, in fact — aglow, perhaps, with the bloom of pregnancy.

Or perhaps not. "She can't be five months pregnant here."

"She doesn't look it," Rafe agreed. "But it happens. Lorraine was almost six months pregnant before anyone — including Harriet — could tell. We know you were born four months after this photo was taken, don't we? Pretty definitively?"

Very definitively. The just-born photographs, with processing dates, were mounted in Elise's albums. And Brooke had a copy of the birth certificate itself.

"Yes. We do."

The next and final photograph added more documentary proof. Taken in late August, two weeks before Brooke was born, it showed a clearly pregnant Marla admiring a mauve-and-cream bassinet in her FoxHaven suite.

"She looks very happy on the verge of having you."

"I hope she was."

"I know she was." Rafe smiled at her, and saw her exhaustion despite their wonderful night's sleep. "Maybe we should take a scone-and-chocolate break."

"Probably. But I'd like to finish. There's not that much left."

Brooke returned the envelope to its cubbyhole, then looked at the items on the desktop.

The pen and memo pad were standard-issue Lilac Cottage office supplies. But there was nothing standard about the carelessness with which they'd been left: the pen tip exposed, the memo pad askew, as if Marla had jotted down something urgent, then left to deal with it.

Nothing was written on the memo pad. Brooke's practiced fingers detected indentations, however, as she skimmed its top page. She could do a rubbing for completeness's sake, to learn what Lilac Cottage crisis had been the businesswoman's last.

An archeologist would have made the tracing then and there. The daughter had a more pressing priority. She wanted to explore the final item, the jewelry box, and be done with it.

Brooke dreaded opening the box. She hated that jewels, not Lily's medical records, had been what Marla treasured most. She was also somewhat surprised Marla even had more jewels. Every gemstone she'd ever seen her mother wear, as well as a fortune in others, had been in Marla's west-wing suite.

There might be girlhood trinkets in the box, costume jewelry worn when washing cars or partying at the pool. Or perhaps the mother, so dazzling in so many ways, had been as artistically challenged as Brooke. Maybe she, like Brooke, had thrilled at the illusion of creativity that could be hers if she followed the careful instructions in jewelry-making kits.

Brooke hoped for home-made bracelets. What she found was so much more.

Many, many pills. They were carefully arranged in their velvet compartments, as carefully as Marla's most cherished gems, in tidy clusters of color and shape.

"Lily's pills. The extra ones for Faye. The doctors always prescribed a few more than Lily needed, so Faye could practice hiding them in the shakes."

There were only pills in the jewelry box — until, in the bottom drawer, Brooke found a bottle of over-the-counter eyedrops.

"That's odd," she said. "Lily never had any trouble with her eyes. She *might* have developed problems at some point. She was at risk for Sjogren's syndrome. I suppose my mother had them on hand just in case."

Just like Marla had saved these extra pills. In case. But maybe there was another reason Marla had saved them.

Maybe the woman who loved gemstones recognized Lily's pills for the treasures they were.

Who needs diamonds when you can save Star Light?

25

"Who's Brooke?" Robert asked.

"Marla's daughter."

"I had no idea Marla had a daughter."

"There's no reason you would." And a very good reason, Lily realized, he wouldn't. Like Carolyn and John, Robert would have worried had he known about the New Year's Eve rape. "Brooke didn't visit me in the hospital. And since she was so healthy, Marla wouldn't have talked about her when I was ill."

"Does she live on the Farm?"

"No. In fact, this is the first time she's returned since the shootings. And the first time we've spoken."

"So this is a reunion weekend?"

"Yes."

"Will it be difficult for you?"

"No." *Thanks to Rafe.* "It will be good."

"The two of you may have more than enough going on this weekend."

"We may. But it would be nice for Brooke to meet you."

"And nice for me to meet her. If not this

visit, perhaps the next. Let me give you my pager number." Robert looked through his reading glasses as he jotted it down. "It's the best way to reach me day or night."

"Okay." Lily put the number in her purse. "Well. I should be going."

"I'm delighted you stopped by, Lily."

"I am, too. Admittedly, I took a fairly circuitous route. I made an appointment with another Dr. Hart. The one in pediatrics."

"Peter."

Robert's voice softened as he said the name. And Peter's had hardened when he'd said Robert's.

Yet there was a sameness in their emotions, Lily thought. Something turbulent and deep.

"What's the story with Lily Rutledge?"

"Peter." Rachel Davis acknowledged the familiar voice before looking up from the progress note she was writing.

She was making her midday rounds on a ward where the pediatric surgeon had no reason to be. But he'd tracked her down, as Peter Hart did whenever there was something he wanted, and now he was shutting the door to create privacy in the doctors' write-up room. "Did Fran tell you her name?"

"No. Don't worry. No confidentiality was breached. Lily gave it to me herself, via Edith, when she scheduled an appointment with me today."

"An appointment? To apologize, I suppose, for seeing what no one else could — the storm beneath the calm."

"She did apologize, but that wasn't the primary reason for the appointment."

"You've already seen her?"

"Yes. And it was awkward. She thought she'd be seeing Robert. She'd been his patient, she said."

"And?"

"That could mean she had, or has, malignancy-associated DIC."

"You know I can't tell you anything about Lily's medical history. Just as I know you wouldn't request her records to find out."

"That's right. I wouldn't. And I don't care about details, Rachel. I just want to know if she's all right."

"Why?"

"She brought in some mosaics she's done. Ideas, extraordinary ones, for 7-North. Before discussing the project with her further, I just wanted to be sure that she was —"

"Oh, Peter."

"She *is* ill."

"No. It's not that."

"Then what, Rachel? Please tell me."

"Okay. Here goes. If you have to have her mosaics, Peter, if you must display *her* art on *your* ward, it would be best if someone other than you oversaw the project."

"Best for Lily?"

"Best for Lily."

"Because?"

"Because of what I can tell you about Lily. The facts in the public domain. They're not medical, but they are relevant. Lily's mother died when she was eight. Seven years later her father was shot, murdered, in their home. Lily saw his body within minutes of his death. Given that history, in response to your earlier question, she's remarkably all right."

"So the answer to *because* is that it would be best for Lily not to be subjected to me after everything she's been through."

"That's cutting to the chase. 'Subjected' is wrong, Peter. I'm just not sure that Lily needs the . . . confusion of you."

"Confusion?"

Rachel sighed. "You want me to explain?"

"Please. I can take it."

"I know. Okay. Remember during your internship when a certain third-year medical student spent six weeks as your constant shadow?"

"You know I do."

"What you don't know is that in the process of my learning so much — medically — from you, I also thought we'd become friends."

"We had. Did you want — ?"

"More? Yes. I'm not talking about sex. Although I won't deny I thought about it. I think you did, too."

"Often. But you were involved with one of your classmates. Scott."

"You remember his name. That's really impressive."

"Not really. Or did you think I wasn't listening?"

"No. I knew you were listening, and that you were interested in what I had to say. That's what you do, Peter. It's one of your many gifts. You engage completely with whoever happens to be on your radar screen. Except for your patients, however, it's out of sight, out of mind. It hadn't occurred to me that our 'friendship' would end the instant my clerkship did. I was accustomed to maintaining friendships with house officers with whom I'd spent far less quality time than I'd spent with you. It *was* quality time."

"I thought so, too. But I never followed up, did I?"

"Nope. You never did. And now, ten years later, here we both are at SMC."

"You've been more distant."

Rachel smiled. "I got the message the first time. I take friendship seriously and you don't."

"It's not personal."

"That's what so interesting. It's *not* personal. It took me about five minutes to discover I wasn't alone in being surprised by the abruptness with which your relationships ended — and that included women who'd been your lovers. It's who you are. Who you've chosen to be."

"I'm sorry, Rachel."

"I know! And I knew you would be, which is why I've never mentioned it before. It's okay with me, Peter. I understand the rules." Rachel paused. Shrugged. "Maybe it would be perfectly fine for Lily to work with you on a project you're both passionate about — and then never hear from you again once the project was through. But I think, I worry, that it wouldn't be."

"I'm so proud of her."

Brooke had closed the rolltop desk and was standing to face him when she spoke of the mother whose most precious treasures had been the gems of modern medicine that had saved Lily's life.

"She should have been proud of you."

"She was, Rafe. She even said so, sort of, the day she died. How grown-up I was. For a tomboy."

"You were hardly a tomboy."

"I think the boys of my age would have begged to disagree."

"Their loss."

"What is it, Rafe? Is something wrong?"

"No. I just wanted to be sure our April Christmas was what you hoped it would be."

"It is so far."

Rafe smiled, touched her face. "Now what shall we do?"

"Didn't you say something about . . . ?"

"Scones? Yes, I believe I did."

"Wasn't there something else?"

"Yes," Rafe said softly. "I want to make love to you, Brooke. I need to."

"I want that, need that, too."

"But we also need to talk, don't we? To tell each other everything that's true?"

"Yes," she whispered. "Could we do both?"

Talk. Make love. Make love. Talk.

Lust and trust.

Love and truth.

And the chatter of the fire, the lullaby of the rain, the sound of a telephone.

It wasn't a cell phone in a jacket pocket that sounded, but a phone on an end-table nearby.

"I didn't realize it was connected," Brooke said.

"Neither did I."

Which meant it was Lily who'd made sure her guest would have the convenience of a phone. Maybe Lily had even hoped for this moment, when she'd be the one calling the cottage, because talking to Brooke would be all right now. It would be easy, thanks to Rafe. . . .

"Lily!"

"Brooke? It's Lorraine."

"Oh, Lorraine. Hi."

"Hi. I'm trying to find Rafe. He's not answering any of the other phones, including his cell phone, and I really need —"

"Has something happened to Lily?"

"No, Brooke, nothing like that. It's my daughter's horse. She's trapped in a sink-hole. The only way to get her out is to lift her out. They're bringing in a crane, but it'll take a while. She's stunned now. Bewildered. But she's going to get panicky. Rafe knows her pretty well. I was hoping he'd be willing to keep her calm."

"I'm sure he will be, Lorraine. And he's right here."

Rafe's conversation with Lorraine was brief. Based on the two questions he asked — How's Sarah? Where's Tom? — Brooke decided that Sarah was Lorraine's daughter and Tom was Lorraine's airline-pilot husband — who, Brooke sensed, wasn't home.

"I'm on my way, Lorraine." Rafe replaced the receiver and looked at her. "I need to do this."

"Of course you do! You're especially worried about Sarah, aren't you?"

"She reminds me of a girl I used to know." Rafe smiled at that girl. "A younger version. She's only eleven. But she's very serious, very responsible, and is no doubt blaming herself that Daphne got out, that somehow she wasn't vigilant enough — you know how that is."

"Yes. I do. Fortunately, Daphne's going to be fine, thanks to you. It'll take me one minute to change."

"I want you to stay here, Brooke. Take care of our horses. Talk to them. Comfort them. Remind them that thunder and lightning aren't really so bad."

"You *cannot* be standing in water if there's lightning!" But that was where he'd be. In the sinkhole with the panicky filly, whispering to her as the rain pooled at their feet. "Rafe?"

"I'll be okay, Brooke. I promise."

"But —"

"I promise."

Rafe touched her worried face and smiled.

"I'll be back, Brooke."

"For scones."

"For you."

26

Talk to the horses, Rafe had told her. *Comfort them.*

"Hey, guys," Brooke greeted them as she opened their stall doors. "You know what? It's still too rainy to go outside, and the specter of sinkholes isn't a happy one. But what if we just mill around inside for a while? Stretch our legs, have a bite to eat?"

That was agreeable to the agreeable horses. They were untroubled by the loudly splashing rain overhead and the roar of thunder in the distance.

"I wanted to go with him. But you just know he wouldn't have let me stay in the sinkhole with him. And he didn't want me standing in the rain. He wanted me warm and safe, just like he wanted all of you warm and safe. He takes pretty good care of us, doesn't he?" Brooke asked the lovingly tended animals. "And we love him, don't we? I love him." She turned to Rhapsody. "What do you think of that?"

The black stallion looked neither alarmed nor surprised. In fact, he seemed to approve. And as she touched his powerful jaw, he didn't withdraw from the caress, not physically, not invisibly. Not at all.

"Time for bed," she announced eventually. "More napping, more dreaming, on this rainy cozy day."

She'd nap and dream, as well. As she waited for Rafe's return.

Brooke saw the gold-toned Range Rover the moment she left the stable, a terrestrial sun on this storm-darkened day. The mansion lights glimmered, as did the smiling woman who approached her in the pouring rain.

Lily was as tall as Brooke — no, taller. Freed from the imprisoning antibodies, her cells had grown exuberantly.

Gloriously.

Lily's delicate features were framed in a shining cloud of curls, and her graceful limbs were sleek and strong.

The springtime daughter had blossomed in sunglow, while the autumnal one had faded, wilted, in night-dark tombs.

Both Brooke and Lily had believed their reunion would be easy, easier, thanks to Rafe, unimpeded by the doubts he'd helped each of them reveal.

And it *was* easy, so unencumbered with

extraneous emotions that the pure ones simply flowed. Their watery words came in sputters.

You look . . . *so do* . . . you, too.

It's so . . . *wonderful to* . . . I know.

The sentences didn't need to be finished. Both knew the missing words. Finally the younger sister, the taller and healthier one, suggested the shortest drenching dash. "To the cottage?"

"To the cottage."

"Scones? Hot chocolate? Tea?" Brooke asked when they'd draped wet jackets on the coat tree by the door. "Or any of the other goodies you left for me?"

"Hot chocolate. Please." Lily selected the drink of an Aztec princess, then wondered about the Aztec prince. "I didn't see Rafe's truck."

Brooke's explanation accompanied them to the kitchen. Lily responded with worry and fondness for all concerned. And she added a tidbit about Daphne.

Lorraine and Rafe had agreed that, when the time came for Daphne to foal, Shadow would be the sire. The decision made, they'd told Sarah — who was thrilled.

"I hope it's okay that I'm home early," Lily said as they returned to the living room with their brimming mugs.

"It's wonderful, Lily! Except it means you drove after no sleep, in a storm, during the Friday-afternoon rush."

"You sound just like Rafe. Or maybe I should say that for the past twelve years, he's sounded just like you. I'm *fine,* Brooke. I drove very cautiously. Besides, I'm wide awake. Energized."

Lily floated gracefully onto the sofa Carolyn had chosen. Brooke joined her. It felt to her as if Carolyn was holding them both.

"They loved your mosaics?"

" 'They' was just 'he,' and my guess would be that if and when he notices the mosaics cluttering his spartan office, his reaction will not be love. We had an encounter yesterday, you see, an incident in which, based on a fleeting glimpse, I diagnosed him as a would-be murderer."

"And he knew your diagnosis?"

"Oh, yes!"

"Well, I think it was quite bold of you to schedule a meeting with him."

"It would've been bold had I known I was doing it. It was a mistake. The Dr. Hart I wanted was Robert, not Peter. I'd assumed he was a pediatrician, since he'd been the hematologist involved in my care."

"The one who did all the bone marrow biopsies?"

"I really believe they hurt him more than they hurt me. Robert Hart is a very nice man. I saw him too, finally, after the Peter Hart fiasco." Lily stared briefly at her hot chocolate. "The nice Dr. Hart was one of your mother's housemates in Georgetown. In fact, thanks to your mother, he was married in the garden here."

"Was his bride ill?"

"Yes. How did you know?"

"I found a photograph in the rolltop desk."

"She was undergoing therapy, ultimately very successfully, for Hodgkin's lymphoma. She — Joanna — died a year ago. He's lonely without her. Of course. Sad. He's also a closet archeologist. He offered to dig through my medical records if the four missing volumes are ever found."

Without a word, Brooke crossed to the rolltop desk, retrieved the charts and presented them to Lily. "They are found."

"Brooke," Lily murmured as she set the stack in her lap. "This is *wonderful.* I don't think anyone believed all four volumes would be recovered, much less reunited. I can just see your mother chatting with the clerks in Medical Records, expressing such confidence in them that they wanted to search for the misfiled charts one more time and *find* them. She was probably planning to make copies before returning the originals."

"You really don't hate her."

"*No*, Brooke. I thought — didn't Rafe tell you that?"

"Yes. He did. But —"

"Do you hate my father?"

"Not ever, Lily. Not for an instant."

Instants passed. A lifetime.

Eventually Lily lifted the flap of the top chart.

The first few pages were administrative. Lily's vital statistics, insurance carrier, legal next of kin. A consent form was there, too, signed by John. The attorney permitted his daughter to be seen without tinkering with the hold-harmless clause. He didn't care about reserving his right to sue. He cared only about the life of his child.

Finally Lily came to the record of her final admission before the deaths, the ten-day emergency hospitalization during which her referral to the clinic in Geneva was arranged.

" 'History of present illness,' " she read. " 'Thin, tremulous, chronically-ill appearing white female, age 15, in acute distress. T 36.9. BP 64 palp. HR 170, with frequent ectopy. RR 28. Party dress soiled with V and D.' "

Party dress. Dance dress. The dinner dance was a tradition shared by the upper classes of Forest Ridge Academy — all girls — and its all-boys counterpart, Ashcroft School. It was the first "Spring Fling" for either Lily or Brooke, and Brooke had only gone because of Lily.

The Ashcroft boys had flocked to Lily during the social hour before dinner. Yes, she'd promised, she would dance with every one of them — despite the dizziness she'd been experiencing for the past several weeks.

Lily hadn't mentioned the dizziness to anyone. Or the weakness. Or the muscle spasms. She'd only missed eight school days since January and, until she truly had no choice, didn't want to miss any more.

Besides, she'd brought one of Faye's shakes to the dance. It would calm her stomach, she'd be able to eat, and, thus fortified, she'd be able to dance.

She did feel better after drinking the shake. Much better — until she vomited. The vomiting came with no warning, as did the diarrhea — "fulminant and explosive," her medical record read.

"You held me while I vomited, Brooke. Became as covered as I was in 'V' and 'D.' That was a pretty incredible thing for you to do."

"No, it wasn't. You'd have done the same for me if the situation had been reversed."

"I'd like to think so."

"There's not a doubt in my mind."

"Well. The situation wasn't reversed, and if you hadn't been there . . ."

"The ambulance would have arrived just as quickly."

"Yes, Brooke. But I'm not sure I would have survived."

"Of course you would have!"

"No. My electrolytes were really off. Dangerously off. I'd been denying my symptoms for a while. And when you were holding me, my heart was fluttering and missing beat after beat. I was in trouble, Brooke. I knew it vaguely then and realized it clearly later. If you hadn't been there telling me to fight, *making* me, I don't think I would have."

"Lily . . ."

"It's true. Do you remember what you kept saying? 'You're going to be fine, Lily. You're going to be well. This is *never* going to happen again.' "

274

"I can't believe I said that."

"But you did. Over and over. And, Brooke, you were right. Have you looked through these charts?"

"No. I wanted to get your permission first."

"You have it, Brooke. Of course!"

"The more important examiner would be Dr. Hart."

"Who *could* come this weekend. He'd like to, in fact. On the other hand, I could give him the charts next week."

"This weekend's fine with me. More than fine. It feels right. Like . . ."

"Closure?"

"Yes."

"Closure of the past," Lily mused, "and commencement of the future."

"Let's do it, Lily."

"All right. I'll invite him . . . soon."

"The adrenaline's wearing off?"

"Beginning to. But there's something else, someone else, I'd like to talk to you about first. Rafe."

27

Nature had dug the grave very deep, and with walls that crumbled when anyone neared its sodden edge.

Worried rescuers did near the edge. It was necessary, from time to time, to see how badly man and horse were doing, how much deeper the water, how much colder Rafe had become.

The second crane had yet to arrive, and it had taken longer than it should have to determine that two would be required. The only way to save Daphne would be to pluck her straight up. They'd known that from the start. But because the heavy equipment couldn't get as close to the hole as they'd hoped, both cranes, reaching from different angles and working precisely in tandem, would be needed.

Even then a happy outcome was in doubt.

Rafe could be rescued. Probably. A team of men at grave's edge could — probably — pull him out. As long as the walls didn't give way entirely.

Rafe refused to be rescued. Yet. Daphne's calm was precarious, and her situation would be disastrous if he left her. Rafe's refusal to be rescued became increasingly adamant. He threatened to unbuckle his harness if they tried. So the rescuers waited, watching the water level rise and worrying, as Rafe became ever more unyielding, that his temperature was dropping dangerously low.

It *was* low, Rafe knew. His thoughts had been drifting for a while. But he could pull them back on command. If he chose. Which for the moment he didn't. It took energy to control his thoughts, precious energy he needed to conserve.

So Rafe permitted his thoughts to drift. Maybe he even needed them to, emotionally, for not surprisingly, they wandered back to a mountain of mud.

The mud that had devoured his family had been warm. Tropical. A balmy death, a heated grave.

And the mud on this northern Virginia day was icy, heavier perhaps than its tropical counterpart and not unlike the tons upon tons of cement that entombed a civilization — all but its screams.

Rafe heard the screams in the bone-chilling rain. Listened to them. Until the remembered cries cost too much, and even his soul began to shiver.

Rafe redirected his thoughts then, shepherded them to where he wanted to be, would be, once Daphne was safe — in the fire-warm cottage with Brooke.

Rafe conjured the image clearly. Yet still he shivered.

Why?

Because of something he knew, yet didn't quite know, a vague suspicion he'd recognized even before his mind chilled and his thoughts began to drift.

It had been unearthed on this Christmas in April. Partially unearthed. The exhumation wasn't complete, its long-buried corpse not fully disgorged. But it *would* be.

Rafe needed to see the moldering remains.

The foggy yet foreboding knowledge had to do with Brooke, a decaying revelation that would make her heart scream and scream if she ever knew.

Which she wouldn't. He'd see it first, examine it, then bury it beneath tons upon tons of . . . love.

"Rafe?" Brooke repeated.

"What do you think of him?"

I love him. "Think of him, Lily?"

"You knew him for a week or so twelve years ago, and you've obviously talked to him quite a bit over the past two days. Admittedly, that's not a lot of time, but do you like him?"

"Yes. Of course. Why wouldn't I?"

"No reason at all. I *want* you to like him."

Brooke saw Lily's radiance, felt its piercing truth. "You're in love with him."

"I was. *Madly,* and for quite a while. He was my Prince Charming, the fairy-tale hero who rode in on his midnight-black charger and rescued me from my grief — after, that is, I awakened from my slumber. I slept, almost around the clock, for a very long time after the deaths. Slept and grew. Faye fed me every time I opened my eyes and Rafe talked to me. Comforted me. It was only when I truly awakened that I realized I was in love."

"Did Rafe know?"

"Yes! It wasn't subtle. *I* wasn't subtle. And just for good measure I confessed all."

"What did he say?"

"He was pretty terrific. He was *way* too old for me, he said. Even though I was seventeen at the time. And eighteen and then nineteen. Still, he insisted it was a teenage crush and that my selection of him was basically by default. Aside from Curtis, he was the only man I ever saw."

"What did you say?"

"All sorts of bold things. Remember the Lily who believed everything was possible and was quite persistent in those beliefs? Well, she rematerialized in a very big way once the evil antibodies relinquished their grip. I believed I was in love with him. I *was*. I still believe it. It was wonderful, painful and completely unrequited. Rafe could have left the Farm. He was known in Forsythe by then. Respected and liked. Anyone would have welcomed him happily. But he stayed. We weathered the storm of my infatuation together and came out of it close friends. Best friends."

"You still love him."

"Always. But in a more, I don't know, enduring way. A *real* way. The madness, thank heaven, is gone."

"And he loves you," Brooke managed to say. Somehow.

"In the same way I love him. Love. Not *in* love. Although there were times, I think, when Rafe was a little in love with me."

"How could he not be?"

"Easily." Lily shrugged. "Sometimes I think about how much my parents would've liked him. Loved him. How grateful they would've felt that he's been here for me."

John and Carolyn *would* have loved Rafe. Unlike Marla. Brooke didn't want the thought. But it came swiftly, chillingly, as it had twelve years before. Marla had met the half-breed cowboy only in death, when Rafe had searched her bloodied body for the softest breath, the faintest heartbeat.

And if he'd brought Marla Blair back to life? Even then she wouldn't have approved of him. Not one bit.

"Rafe wants to be here," Brooke murmured at last. It wasn't a flash of insight, merely a reiteration of what Rafe himself had said. *I'm not doing anything I don't want to do.*

"Yes. He does. I know that now. I asked him directly a few years ago. I should've asked him long before then. But I was afraid to. I felt so safe knowing he was nearby. Pretty selfish, huh?"

"Pretty understandable. And he'd have told you, don't you think, if he'd wanted to leave?"

"He would have and he didn't. So here we are, twelve years later. Can you believe there've only been two days — the past two — in all those years that we haven't seen each other at all . . . much less a lot?

I'm *really* glad you like him, Brooke."

"I do." Brooke smiled, *smiled,* as Marla had been able to smile no matter how she ached, how she worried, how she feared. *When you have nothing to hide, hide nothing.* And when you have something to hide? Marla's daughter knew the answer. *Hide it well.*

Lily smiled, too, and yawned. "I do believe the adrenaline is abandoning me. I'd better call Dr. Hart and go to sleep. Have you spent any time in the mansion?"

"Not yet."

"Do you want to?"

"Yes. I think I need to see her bedroom."

Lily nodded solemnly. "And, if you like, my studio?"

"I'd definitely like to see that."

"Great. Shall we say breakfast at a leisurely nine?"

"Perfect."

They walked together to the cottage door. Lily slipped into her jacket, gave Brooke a hug, reached for the doorknob. Then she turned to face Brooke again.

"I saw an obstetrician yesterday. No, I'm not pregnant. But I want to be. Hope to be."

"Lily —"

"I know. There are risks. Which is the

reason I saw Dr. Davis. She specializes in high-risk pregnancies. So far, the only certain risk is for an ectopic."

"I thought that wasn't an inherited risk."

"It's not. I'm at risk because of my own medical history. The adhesions left from the infection and the surgeries. But the ectopic risk can be eliminated entirely with in vitro fertilization — which is what I'd be doing anyway. I'm not . . . involved with anyone." Lily leaned against the solid door as Brooke had leaned against the warm wall of Fleur. "Then there's the uncertain risk."

"Your illness."

"Yes. Dr. Davis is running a battery of tests, many of which are already back and fine, and with Dr. Hart reviewing the records this weekend, we'll soon know everything that can be known. The best hope is that, in retrospect, they'll be able to figure out what I had."

"At which point they'll tell you it's gone."

"That would be . . . lovely. Otherwise, the worry would remain that it's quiescent and could flare up with pregnancy." Lily's hand tightened on the door knob. "I'm willing to risk that."

"But you wouldn't have to. You could

have your baby without taking any risks at all."

"You mean a surrogate. Dr. Davis and I discussed that possibility. But even though custody wouldn't be an issue, since the maternal DNA would be mine, I can't imagine asking anyone to have *my* baby, not *hers*."

"You wouldn't be asking just anyone, Lily. In fact, you wouldn't even have to ask. Standing before you is a very willing volunteer."

"Brooke! That's so —"

Closure, commencement, celebration. "Something I'd very much like to do."

"But . . ."

"Really."

"Thank you."

"So, yes? Unless we know with absolute certainty that it's gone?"

"Yes." Lily shook her head. "I hadn't even thought about asking you to be a surrogate, Brooke. At least," she added quietly, "not before the baby's born. I had been hoping, though, that if anything ever happened to me, you'd be willing to be there for her. Or him."

"Nothing is going to happen to you."

"But something could, Brooke. Something always can."

As they both knew all too well. And now Lily was asking her to do what Marla had done when Carolyn died, to love her baby as a friend would.

As a sister would.

As a mother would.

"Of course I'd be there for your baby, Lily. *Of course.*"

"And for Rafe."

"Rafe?"

"He'd need you, too."

"I don't understand." But she did. Oh, she did.

"I'm going to ask him to be the baby's father. . . ."

28

The phone awakened Lily from a very deep sleep.

"Rafe," she answered it dreamily.

"It's Peter Hart, Lily."

"Dr. Hart."

"Peter."

"Peter."

"I'm sorry for waking you." *For not being Rafe.*

Lily's bedside clock read nine-fifteen. In the evening. "It's early. Most of the world would still be awake."

"Most of the world didn't spend last night making candy mosaics. They're wonderful."

"Thank you."

"Edith said you'd be willing to make some for 7-North?"

She needed to sit up and turn on the light. But whatever adrenaline would have been required for such action was as sleepy as she.

"Lily? Are you still there?"

Lily managed a single syllable. "Yes."

"Barely? And not so willing, after all?"

"Edith said you'd want to be involved in the project?"

Want? Yes. But . . .

"It's not necessary, Lily. It's just a matter of logistics, to make sure you have everything you need. Edith would be more than happy to oversee those details. It sounds as though that's what you'd prefer."

"Wouldn't you? I mean, thanks to me, our two previous . . . encounters have been —"

Lily doesn't need the confusion of you. The memory of Rachel's words wasn't necessary. Peter was hearing the same message loud and clear — well, soft and dreamy — from Lily herself.

"Confusing?" he suggested.

"Oh. Well, I . . . oh, dear."

"Time to go back to sleep?"

"I guess. I'm sorry."

"That's my line."

"Sorry!"

Peter heard her smile. "Don't mention it. Are you going to remember I called?"

And Lily heard his. "How will I know?"

Rafe returned to the Farm at ten-thirty. He'd hosed himself off before leaving Lorraine's. He couldn't get more cold or wet, only less muddy, having already declined all grateful offers of hot shower, dry clothes, food, *anything*.

The second crane had arrived in time. Rafe and Daphne had been plucked safely from the sinkhole and placed onto sodden but stable earth.

The happy ending was a good omen, Rafe kept telling himself on the drive back to the Farm. Brooke would not yet have discovered what he feared.

The corpse had been almost fully unearthed, despite his foggy brain, and it was ghastly.

But, he kept telling himself, it might just be a hideous figment of his chilled imagination.

He'd find out while she slept, would do the final excavation then.

Later . . . or sooner.

Brooke's car was gone.

And Lily's was in the carport.

Lily was home — and asleep, if the pattern of mansion lights signaled what it had signaled for the past twelve years.

So where was Brooke?

The cottage living room provided no clues and only a little reassurance. The glyphs he'd drawn for her were there. The bedroom offered no clues, either, but was more reassuring: her clothes in the closet, her suitcase on the floor, her passport on the dresser.

Brooke hadn't left. She'd simply gone out — why? where? — into the rain-slick night.

Rafe didn't like it. Hated it.

But he would put her worrisome absence to its most productive use by proving that his forebodings had been pure mirage — pure nightmare, the kind of illusion that made perfect sense in the neverland of sleep, but was revealed for the implausible jumble it was the moment you woke up.

Rafe was ready to wake up.

He returned to the living room and opened the rolltop desk. The desktop appeared untouched since he'd seen it last. The jewelry box was closed. The envelope was nestled in its cubbyhole. The memo pad and pen remained askew.

Rafe skimmed his fingers over the memo pad, detecting the depressions but unable to read them, then held it to the light.

The illuminated shadows were what he had feared.

Were there other explanations? Maybe. He'd sure as hell search for them. And if the nightmare was real?

He'd move heaven and earth to make

certain Brooke never knew. He tore off sheet after sheet until not even the slightest indentation remained, then turned his attention to the right-hand drawer.

Empty. Lily's medical records were missing. In the mansion, he hoped, *hoped* . . . or with Brooke — somewhere — on this perilous night.

Speculation was pointless. Especially when there might be a note for him in the kitchen — no.

Or in the carriage house. No.

Brooke hadn't returned from her late-night errand by the time he stepped out of his hurried shower. Nor did she return while he dressed — or during the phone call he made.

And she was gone for another restless, pacing hour after that.

And when, at midnight, she finally appeared, she was such a different Brooke from the one he'd left hours before. True, the wind howled and the rain pelted. Hours before, neither would have prevented her from joining him in the sink-hole with Daphne.

But the storm provided cover for her now, a reason to scarcely look at him as she stepped from the car, rushed to the trunk and retrieved the cardboard box, labeled

Kinko's-Chantilly, which she would not, *would not,* permit him to carry into the cottage for her.

The wind and rain remained outside.

But the storm came in.

"Brooke?"

Without his help, although his hands hovered near, she set the carton down and removed her coat. "How's Daphne?"

"Safe." Rafe followed as Brooke carried the carton to the carpeted floor. "How are you?"

"Fine." Brooke knelt beside the box, opened it, withdrew Lily's medical records, the copies she'd made of them and two twelve-packs of Liquid Paper. "Lily's home."

Rafe knelt, too. "I noticed."

"Have you spoken to her?"

"No. Brooke?"

Her slender fingers pressed through the cellophane seal on the first of the twelve-packs. "Yes?"

"What's wrong?"

"Nothing."

"Except that your reunion with Lily didn't go as well as you hoped."

She glanced up, briefly, from the row of Liquid Paper bottles she was arranging neatly on the floor. "Yes, it *did.* Thanks to

291

you. It was wonderful to see Lily. She's wonderful, isn't she? So lovely, so beautiful, so —"

"Tell me what's wrong."

"Nothing! Everything's *fine*."

"You went through the desk again."

"What? No."

"But you've copied Lily's medical records."

"Oh, yes. Well, that's because Dr. Robert Hart — Lily's hematologist *and* the groom in the wedding photo — will be here in the morning to review them."

"In the morning? Why?"

"For the reason we discussed, to see if a definitive and reassuring diagnosis can be made."

"What's the emergency?"

Brooke looked up from her new task, tidying the stacks of copied files. "I can't believe you're asking that! The sooner Lily knows what she had — *and* that she's free of it — the better."

But not better for you. "It's been a long day, Brooke. Let's go to bed."

His voice was in bed with her already, caressing her with the promise of dreams that could not be.

Brooke's voice was in the desert, already. Where she needed to be. She did so well in the parched land of ancient pharaohs.

"I can't," the renowned Egyptologist replied. "I have to get Lily's records ready for Dr. Hart. It turns out that in addition to writing on the Post-its, my mother made comments on the pages themselves, like in her high-school yearbook, assessments of diagnostic speculations made by Lily's various doctors. I'm interested in my mother's comments, but since they're opinion, not fact, I'm going to delete them from the originals. It's the most scientifically honest thing to do. I'm not destroying archival evidence, merely her analysis of it. You look like you don't agree."

Oh, but I do. "I agree — with that. What I'm having trouble with is your assertion that everything's fine. That *you're* fine. What aren't you telling me?"

"Nothing."

"Brooke? Remember how we were going to spend the rest of this day? Talking, making love and telling each other every truth?"

"Yes, of course." *And there's something quite wonderful. But it's Lily's truth to tell. Lily's baby to have. Lily's . . . and yours.* "But everything's changed."

"Define 'everything.' "

"Lily's home."

"And?"

"And we had our time, Rafe. Our closure." *And, for us, there can't be more. Neither commencement nor celebration.*

"And that's it? All you want?"

"Yes."

"Which is what you would've told me whether or not Lily came home a day earlier than planned?"

"Yes."

"I don't believe you." His voice was gentle. And he smiled. "But okay. For now. I'll help you delete your mother's comments."

"No, thank you. I'd like to read them as I go along."

"You made copies."

"Yes, but not color copies. Her comments are color-coded. If possible, I'd like to figure out the code before deleting it."

"You want me to leave." His smile already had.

"Yes. Please."

29

Peter had no conscious memories of his infancy, when his cries of hunger were smothered by his father's massive hand. Nor did he remember the shouting at him, the swearing at him, that preceded the near-lethal suffocations. Or the cigarette ash that fell on him even when he *was* fed. Or the smoke that was nearly as asphyxiating as the smothering.

Peter had no idea that he walked at an age when most babies only crawled, or that he never truly toddled. Like a child of war and famine, his thin legs were guided not by the wonders of discovery, but the instinct merely to survive.

Peter couldn't possibly recall as a retrievable memory the time his mother kicked him for eating food meant for the dogs, or when his father threw him against the brick fireplace with such force his ribs cracked.

Only his heart remembered the sound of his small bones breaking. Only his soul knew the pain. And only in his spirit dwelled the memory that he hadn't dared to cry.

Pediatric surgeon Peter Hart eventually read his ward-of-the-state files. His childhood had, undoubtedly, influenced who he'd become. But it wasn't the whole answer, Peter knew. His records confirmed that, too.

On the scale of child abuse, his own treatment, albeit appalling, had not been extreme. His neglect had been whimsical, not systematic. His parents couldn't be bothered with methodical abuse, hadn't cared enough to be bothered.

Their son was an annoyance, ignored as much as possible and swatted away when the irritation grew too great.

Peter had become less of a nuisance with each passing day. By the time he was four, when his parents abandoned him, he could feed himself, bathe himself, dress himself. But he was still the child he'd been since birth, the kind of child parents could leave without a backward glance. Months delinquent on their rent, Peter's parents fled in the middle of the night. They took their killer dogs with them, but not their boy.

He was found a week later, bathed and dressed but starving. There was no food. A week after that, he spent his first day in school. In paradise. He loved school, excelled at it — so much so that at age nine the boy from the public orphanage was awarded an academic scholarship to a private school.

Peter made a friend at this school for the elite sons and grandsons of Boston. His first friend. And, arguably, his last.

Samuel Lancaster Tremaine was an adored grandson, and a well-traveled one. His grandfather had served for almost three decades, regardless of what party controlled the White House, as an ambassador-at-large.

Sam's childhood had been lived abroad — Paris, Vienna, Prague — and in the company of grown-ups. And with his violin.

Sam and Peter were an unlikely duo. Little Lord Fauntleroy and Huck Finn. But they shared an essential bond: neither had ever been just a boy.

With his grandparents' smiling but wary permission, Sam invited his new friend to spend the Christmas holidays at their home. The Tremaines' wariness was justified. They'd read Peter's files, taken note of the recurrent refrain. The boy was brilliant but not social, unable to form relationships in the foster homes to which he'd

been sent . . . and from which he'd invariably returned.

Nothing bad had ever happened. But the
subtext was there. Some fundamental flaw
made him unadoptable. The question was:
How dangerous, how violent, was the
defect?

Sam perceived no imperfections in his
friend. But he detected enough reticence
on his grandparents' part that he didn't
share with them what he'd shared with
Peter: that if the holiday visit worked out,
which it would, he was going to ask if
Peter could live with them permanently.

Peter knew it would never happen. Not
for the boy who'd been a pariah in his own
home.

Peter saw love, in Sam's home, for the
first time in his life. Sam's love for his
grandparents, and theirs for him — a love
so bountiful it spilled, as kindness, to
Sam's never-loved friend.

The Tremaines were grateful, too. Until
Peter, their violinist grandson had played
card games for fun. Bridge. And back-
gammon and chess. And he'd listened to
music and read.

But Sam Tremaine hadn't ever tossed a
football.

Nor, of course, had Peter. The boy

who'd walked but never toddled hadn't played anything at all. But Peter was a natural athlete, and his life had taught him to walk through pain.

He ran through pain as he got older, an exertion that had nothing to do with play. Peter's restless limbs hungered for physical catharsis as his bright mind hungered to learn.

It was Sam, not Peter, who suggested they play catch with a football. A natural athlete, too, with restless growing limbs, Sam loved the newfound sport.

The Christmas Eve toss that could have killed Samuel Lancaster Tremaine was not a spiral pass misthrown by Peter. Sam twirled the football himself, a spin of pure exuberance that misfired.

When the ball flew behind him, Sam flew after it.

The car's driver, a neighborhood mom, was returning from last-minute grocery shopping before the holiday. She was a careful driver. She had children, too. She was mindful of balls that appeared from between parked cars and the young legs that might follow right behind. But she had no experience with balls that spiraled down from on high.

Unconscious and bleeding, Sam was

rushed to Massachusetts General Hospital. A cortege of cars followed the ambulance. Peter would've been left behind had he not flagged down a neighbor.

Peter stood apart from the circle of love that surrounded Sam's grandparents in the Emergency Ward waiting room, his gaze fixed on the double doors behind which the doctors were trying to save Sam's life.

Finally, two white-coated physicians appeared. As they approached the circle, Peter moved just close enough to hear.

Sam's head injury wasn't nearly as bad as it had appeared at the scene. Only a mild concussion. He was already awake and oriented. The cuts and scrapes no longer bled, and once properly set, his fractured arm would heal. The primary concern was a possible ruptured spleen. It would be better to look and see than wait and see — so, with his grandparents' permission, they'd like to do Sam's exploratory surgery soon.

With that, the doctors and the Tremaines moved toward the double doors. At the last moment, one of the doctors turned, scanned the waiting area and walked to Peter.

He knelt, introduced himself, then

asked, "Are you Peter?"

"Yes."

"Sam says to tell you he's okay."

"*Is* he okay?" Peter's question spoke volumes: nine years of mistrust.

"Yes, he is. Not perfect at the moment, but definitely okay. It'll take a while for him to get completely back to normal. But he will."

"Really?"

They were eye to eye, doctor and boy.

"Really, Peter. I promise."

Peter never saw him again. But the white-coated doctor hadn't lied. Sam's spleen hadn't ruptured, after all, and his broken arm would mend so flawlessly that neither his violin-playing nor his football-tossing days were in any peril.

As promised, Sam would recover completely. His convalescence would begin on an around-the-world cruise after which he and his grandparents would live in their Parisian home.

Unlike Peter's parents, the Tremaines didn't vanish in the night. Nor did they forget to say goodbye. Sam's grandparents even told Peter, as convincingly as they could, that Sam's accident hadn't been his fault. They knew who'd thrown the ball. They even confessed to Peter, as they'd been confessing to everyone in sight, that it was they who'd been derelict. They should have taught their grandson the dangers of footballs and cars.

Not that there'd been such danger in the gated enclaves where Sam had spent his first nine years. And, although what happened wasn't Peter's fault, the simple fact remained: if not for Sam's friendship with Peter, Sam would have been inside that Christmas Eve, playing his violin.

Peter harbored the same thoughts, and then some. He never answered the postcards Sam sent him at the orphanage, and eventually the one-way communication stopped.

Peter ran hard and fast during the restless hours away from school. Harder, faster, and ever closer to the hospital where a doctor had looked a nine-year-old in the eye and told him the truth.

One day, Peter went inside. The hospital became a sacred refuge for him, cathedral and home in one. He belonged in this place that was open around the clock, as if churning with the restlessness that sent him running at midnight. This place where injured children were saved.

The never-adopted boy graduated first in his class from Harvard Medical School, one of three graduating seniors whose last name was Hart. He was the only Hart in the pediatric surgery residency at Mass General — although there were several in other residencies — as there were in Dallas, where Peter did a two-year-fellowship in trauma, and Seattle, where he held a faculty position until he was recruited to become chief of pediatric surgery at SMC.

He'd be the only SMC pediatrician named Hart. But within six months of his arrival, the center's Drs. Hart would number four. The second, an internist-hematologist, was on staff already. The third and fourth, a husband and wife, would come onboard once their residencies in rehabilitation medicine were through.

Peter had been at SMC for three days when he responded to the stat page for Dr. Hart — no first name. It was ten at night. Peter wasn't on call, merely restless and roaming.

He knew he wasn't the Dr. Hart needed *stat* in room AT14-222. Asquith Tower was the medical wing. But his roaming had taken him nearby, to the Tower's eleventh floor.

The fourteenth floor oncology ward was

three easy flights away. Peter and the crash cart arrived simultaneously.

"What's the history?" Peter's voice was quiet, calm, as he assessed the patient in room 222. Very frail, she was gasping for breath — and getting none. Her trachea was shifted. Her lips were blue. Her eyes were frantic.

"Acute leukemia now, Hodgkin's years ago, a pleural mass that may be a chloroma."

"Was it biopsied?"

"This afternoon."

"Give me the largest bore needle on the cart." Peter smiled gently at the suffocating woman, looked straight into her bewildered eyes. "You're going to be okay. I promise."

He kept talking, kept reassuring, as the sixteen-gauge needle was placed in his outstretched hand and his practiced fingers palpated the necessary landmarks just below her clavicle. "You have a tension pneumothorax and in about two seconds —"

"Joanna."

Peter didn't turn to the voice behind him. But he saw the patient's reaction. Relief, despite her panic.

Peter would have bet she couldn't speak.

304

But she could. A whisper. Through a
faint blue smile.

"Robert."

30

Brooke had compartmentalized like the professional she was during the copy-making hours spent at Kinko's. Concentration had been imperative. The thousands of pages had to be fed into the copier one at a time and copies of the Post-its had been needed, as well.

The task had been tedious . . . and welcome.

She'd even managed to keep the compartments closed until after she'd seen Rafe.

The floodgates opened then, beginning with *I'm going to ask him to be the baby's father.*

Brooke hadn't seen it coming. Had, no doubt, clung to Lily's admission that she wasn't "involved." But that wasn't much of an excuse; Lily had been foreshadowing clearly enough. Brooke knew the real reason she hadn't seen it coming: because she'd chosen to not look.

So there it was.

And, once revealed, Lily had further

explained her decision.

"Rafe's so wonderful with children. You should see him with Faye's grandkids and with Lorraine's Sarah. He wants to be a father, I think, would *love* to be. If I could give him that happiness . . . I'd been thinking about it for a very long time, Brooke. But it wasn't until Curtis told me you wanted to return to the Farm that I actually made the appointment to see Dr. Davis. Your courage gave me courage. . . . Of course, I don't know if Rafe will say yes. But I think he will. Whatever his answer, I know it will be honest."

"He'll say yes," Brooke had heard herself whisper.

He'll say yes, he'll say yes, he'll say yes.

There'd been a compartment just for those three words. And when its door flew open, they swirled around the cottage, stealing heat, hoarding oxygen, and joining forces with more words that were true.

And he'll want her to marry him. And she'll say yes, yes.

Rafe and Lily were parents already, to their lilacs and their ponies; had been for years. And they'd made plans — and Rafe had made commitments to those plans — into the future.

"Emma" and "Charles" would be shared

with the world this fall. And there was a name to be chosen for the golden lilac. And there were more daughter lilacs, rows and rows of seedlings that had yet to bloom.

And the FoxHaven babies that Daphne and Shadow would have.

Rafe and Lily had twelve years of being together, *choosing* to be together, and making promises for years to come.

And Rafe and Brooke? Twelve days of talking, two nights of touching, and the promise of . . . More, Brooke had learned on this stormy night. Rafe wanted more days and nights with her.

How many more? Brooke didn't know. Would never know. She knew only that — before Lily's revelation — she would have said yes to anything Rafe proposed. The occasional rendezvous of passion, or sleep, or talk, or dreams? Yes. Or more time, much more, to see if — over time, over years — they might have what Rafe already had with Lily. Oh, yes.

But, Brooke knew, her yes would have been swiftly trumped by Rafe's yes to Lily. *My life is with Lily,* Rafe would have told her. *Lily is daring to make this long-term commitment and I'm going make it with her. I want to.*

Rafe wouldn't confess that he'd always been a little in love with Lily. But of course it was true. Nor would Rafe say, or even imply, that he and his bride would be married in every way. Love . . . and lust.

He would say though — and with such tenderness for Brooke — how grateful he was for her offer to carry Lily's baby. The ectopic risk didn't worry him, he'd admit. If the studies showed even the slightest Fallopian tube narrowing, he and Lily would simply choose the in vitro technique. And as for the immunologic risk for Lily, if there *was* any at all, he'd insist she let Brooke carry the baby for her.

Which Brooke couldn't. Not possibly. Not when Lily's baby was Rafe's.

Brooke began the short walk from the cottage to the mansion just before 9:00 a.m.

The sun was warm, the sky was blue. But Brooke might have been trudging through a winter's accumulation of never-melted snow. She looked down as her weighted limbs plodded, and hugged Lily's charts to her chest.

So much for being her brilliant mother's brilliant daughter. Much less a hieroglyphics wizard. The records were filled with unfamiliar medical abbreviations and acronyms. And Marla, having mastered that shorthand, had also created her own.

In time, and without distraction, Brooke probably could have deciphered both the scientific and maternal stenography.

But she'd only had eight hours. And her concentration had been slashed by a relentless onslaught of thoughts — her very own Wind of Knives.

Forsythe women always married for love.

Their husbands always cherished them.

Lily would be no exception.

And: Lily would want Brooke at her wedding to the man Brooke loved — just as Carolyn had wanted her best friend Marla to witness her marriage to John — whom Marla had loved even then?

Was that why Marla shot him? Because John had changed his mind about marrying her . . . because he still, always, loved Carolyn too much?

The knife-sharp thoughts sliced, and there were even thoughts about the thoughts. Was this how it felt to have DIC? To bleed from every pore? To exsanguinate from even the most glancing wound?

And then: How *pathetic* to compare anything she might be feeling to what Lily had experienced, especially when Lily had triumphed over the real thing.

The intrepid Forsythe daughter had refused to die. The era of Forsythe women would live on. And what a spectacular hybrid Lily's daughters would be, the marriage of sunshine and midnight, lady and Plumed Serpent, artist and conquistador.

Brooke hadn't found the diagnosis that would enable Lily to carry her own children. But Dr. Robert Hart would find it. Even Marla had known he would.

Brooke *had* managed to decipher the many-colored stars Marla had drawn around the doctor's name, exuberant galaxies that reappeared every time he did. If anyone could solve the mystery, it would be her Georgetown housemate.

"Let me carry those for you."

Rafe. Standing directly in her path. Despite the mental "To do" list her fatigued brain had crafted for the day. *Give Lily's records to Dr. Hart. Spend time with Lily. Avoid Rafe.*

"No, Rafe. Thank you. I've got them."

"Did you accomplish what you'd hoped?"

"Not really. My mother was onto something, though. I'm sure of it."

"But you couldn't tell what?"

"No. I'm hopeful that Dr. Hart will be

311

able to." Brooke looked from too-tender blue eyes toward the mansion. "Is that his car?"

"Yes. He just arrived. You didn't remove the Post-its from the files."

"No, and I didn't even — oh! Here's Lily."

And the nice hematologist whose name Marla had wreathed in stars.

"Brooke. You look so tired."

"I'm fine, Lily. Really." And better as she gazed at the man who'd been her mother's friend . . . and who, she'd kept telling herself — a hope throughout her hopeless night — would find a happy solution for them all. Now, in the sunshine, she knew he would. "I'm Brooke."

"Hello, Brooke. I'm Robert."

Brooke let him take from her the charts she'd declined to let Rafe carry. "The Post-its are my mother's. She cross-referenced Lily's symptoms, lab results and treatments from admission to admission. She also wrote on the pages themselves. I was planning to delete those comments, but as I was just explaining to Rafe, I think she may have been onto something so I left them as is. Unedited."

"And pithy and direct?"

"Well, she did write 'bogus' a few times.

More than a few. Among other things. And the occasional frowning face. You got stars, though. At least on the pages I managed to get through."

Robert smiled. "Stars or no stars, I'm delighted to have Marla's help. Not only was she extremely bright, she was also a very good sport. Living with five medical residents meant incessant shop talk, case after case, dilemma after dilemma. She never complained. In fact, it wasn't long before she was jumping right in. Any and all of Marla's insights, positive or negative, are more than welcome."

"Oh, good. I'm glad."

"And I'm very glad to meet you."

"This is interesting," Lily mused. "A taxicab heading right toward us."

Interesting, but not alarming. The cab was coming to a stop on the cobblestones, and its occupant was most welcome.

"Faye! What a *wonderful* surprise!"

Lily hugged Faye, who hugged her back, after which Faye touched Rafe on the arm, a pat that said hello and thank you for grabbing her suitcase.

Then she smiled at Brooke.

"Wow."

"Hi, Faye." Like Robert, Faye looked the way fifty-something could look these days.

Young. "Wow, too."

Lily waited for Faye and Brooke to hug. But they didn't, never had, a fact Lily recalled before the moment became uncomfortable. "And, Faye, this is Dr. Hart. Robert. He took care of me at SMC, and he and Marla knew each other from Georgetown."

"And," Robert added, "my wife and I were married here thirty years ago. We never met the talented artist who made our wedding cake. She was getting married herself and had some prenuptial event that day. But it seems to me her name was Faye."

"What a memory."

"It was a memorable cake." *And a memorable day.*

Robert's nostalgic thought, although unspoken, floated in the April air. The others sensed it . . . and honored it with a silence that might have become awkward had Lily not once again intervened. "Speaking of weddings, Faye, isn't this a busy cake-baking weekend for you?"

"Very busy. Springtime weddings galore. But Jen has everything under control. Besides, after Rafe's mysterious phone call, I *had* to come."

"Rafe's mysterious phone call?" Brooke asked.

The silence *was* awkward then. Just for the heartbeat or two during which Faye glanced at Rafe, frowned — and then smiled. " 'Beckoning' would be a better word. *Tantalizing.* Rafe let on that a party was happening and that I was invited. So here I am. Ready to party — and to cook. Yes, Lily. I *want* to."

There'd been extravagant house parties on the Farm once, the kind where guests enjoyed the grand estate however they pleased. They'd stroll in the gardens, or chat in the parlors, or ride the FoxHaven horses until it was time to reconvene for the next lavish meal — after which the strolling, chatting, riding would begin anew.

This house party's morning plans were discussed over a breakfast of chocolate croissants. Brooke and Lily would begin in Lily's studio, and maybe do a little more mansion wandering from there. Faye would "play" in the kitchen. Rafe would see to the horses.

Robert would review Lily's records. Like the houseguests of old, he could settle wherever he liked. John's study. The verandah. The guest suite that was his.

"Actually, if Faye doesn't mind, right

315

here in the kitchen would be great."

"I don't mind at all. I do tend to talk to myself as I putter, though."

"I have a feeling I do, too."

Lily's studio was a remodel of the existing sunroom. Natural light filtered in through glass walls and skylight, and floor-to-ceiling drawers had been built into the structural walls where glass alone wouldn't do.

In an ideal world, Lily explained, every tile not in active use would be stored in its designated drawer. And the basketful of photos of her various mosaics would be assembled into a portfolio. And she'd even find a filing system for future ideas — other than tossing them into a large ceramic bowl.

But the artist's world was a cluttered one, as Lily's half of the girls' playroom had always been. A Lily Forsythe Rutledge mosaic in itself.

The two most treasured playroom mementos had homes in Lily's studio. The rolltop desks stood side by side and open. A vase, filled with blossoms rescued early this morning after the storm, sat on Lily's desktop. And on Brooke's, the paint-by-number collaboration for Carolyn, forsaken since her death.

"I've rejuvenated the paints," Lily said. "A little paint thinner was all it took. You could do some painting while you're here, if you like, or take it with you . . . or not."

Brooke touched the brush, remembering how tightly she'd grasped it to be certain it wouldn't slip, and how intently she'd concentrated on every careful stroke.

The distractions had been fewer then. No slashing thoughts — and no view of the lilac garden where Charlotte and James had married, and Emma and Charles, and Carolyn and John, and Robert and Joanna . . . and where another wedding would soon take place.

"Have you spoken to Rafe about the baby?"

"No. I'd never planned to until after my follow-up visit with Dr. Davis."

"But if Robert finds something this weekend . . ."

"I'll bet he's as careful as you are. He'd want tests, don't you think, to confirm his diagnosis? And besides, Brooke, I'm not sure I'll ever make the baby proposal to Rafe."

"What? You were so sure last night."

"I know."

"And you said you'd been thinking about

it for a long time."

"True. But I've been thinking about you, too. And Rafe."

"Oh."

"So there *is* something."

"*Was,* Lily. You weren't the only seventeen-year-old to fall madly in love with him. I imagine *we're* not the only ones. But it was a nine-day infatuation twelve years ago."

"And now?"

"Now. You said it yourself. He's pretty terrific. And it's been very nice to see him again. But —" *he'll say yes, he'll say yes, he'll say yes* "— that's all. Ask him, Lily. He'll want to be your baby's father. He'll be thrilled."

"Was I talking to myself?" Robert asked when, looking up from the charts on the kitchen table, he found Faye looking straight at him.

"No." *Just worrying in silence.* "At least not out loud."

Robert smiled. "Did you know Marla well, Faye?"

"Not really. We met at John and Carolyn's wedding. I didn't see her again until she and Carolyn and I discussed the cake I'd make for yours. The next time was ten

318

years later, when my marriage fell apart. John and Carolyn invited me to live on the Farm. I'd been here five weeks when Carolyn died."

"And you stayed after her death."

"Yes. Marla and I lived under the same roof for seven years. But did I know her? Not really."

"What about Brooke's father?"

"I haven't the foggiest idea who he was. He was out of the picture, I gather, long before Brooke was born. From time to time, I thought I saw glimpses of various men I know from Forsythe in Brooke — including my ex-husband."

"Would that have been possible?"

"For my ex-husband to have had a fling with Marla? Why not? He had flings with virtually every other beautiful woman he ever met." Faye tilted her head. "There was a time when I didn't think that was so funny."

"There was a time when it probably wasn't."

"No. Not at all. Seeing Brooke today, I realize the only person she ever really looked like was Marla. The resemblance wasn't so striking when she was younger."

"I can't remember ever seeing Marla as haunted as Brooke seems today."

"Do you know what's haunting her, Robert?"

"I hope not."

"But it's haunting you. Might it help if I told you the questions Rafe asked me when he called last night?"

31

Faye's revelation of Rafe's questions helped Robert decide to do what he'd been thinking about doing for a while. Talk with Rafe.

Faye watched the conversation — in the paddock — from a kitchen window. Solemn at the outset, in moments both men appeared relaxed, as if the worry hadn't been so serious, after all, and had now been entirely resolved.

It was time, Faye decided, to find out just what that worry had been.

She'd almost reached the two men, who were walking to greet her, when she heard the hushed call from behind.

"Faye!"

"Lily! Why are we whispering?"

"Because Brooke's napping."

"In a cottage so far away she couldn't possibly hear us even if we were shouting?"

Lily nodded. "It's wishful whispering, Faye. I *want* Brooke to be sleeping."

"Brooke's sleeping?" Rafe asked as he and Robert joined them.

"I hope so," Lily replied.

"Is she all right?"

"She was very tired, she said. Exhausted. Halfway through the basket of photos, she decided to stop fighting it and go to sleep. Are you thinking, Rafe, that there might be something more than fatigue?"

"Did she say there was?"

"No. But I have to wonder. I feel as though there's something going on and I'm the only one who doesn't know what it is. I can't help worrying that it has to do with my diagnosis. I know that sounds paranoid, but we have the discovery of the records, the mysterious phone call to Faye, and even the way you're all looking at each other right now. It's bad, isn't it?"

"No, Lily," Robert said. "In fact, it's wonderful."

"Wonderful?"

"As wonderful as it gets."

"You mean . . . ?"

"I know what you had and it's gone."

Lily drew a breath and inhaled pure joy. "Thank you *so much*."

Oh, Lily, don't thank me. "I'd like to wait until all the labs are in and I've had a chance to talk with Rachel before going into the details with you."

"That's fine. The details don't matter.

I'd been hoping for this for so long, but I'd completely underestimated how . . . buoyant I would feel. How free. I'm sorry for my paranoia."

"It wasn't paranoia, Lily. You were right. Something *was* going on. We each had pieces of the puzzle. Rafe and I just now fit them together."

"So Brooke doesn't know?"

"No. Neither does Faye."

"Were Marla's notes helpful?"

"Extremely."

"Oh, good. Brooke will be so pleased. Won't she, Fleur?" With outstretched hands, Lily greeted the roan mare who'd ambled over to join the group. "We could take a walk while Brooke's sleeping. The ground might be a little soggy but —"

"Who cares?" Faye asked. "It's an absolutely glorious day."

"It certainly is." Lily gave the horse a farewell pat — Fleur was moving on to Robert — then looked at her dear friend, her best friend, who seemed so very far away. "We could swing by the greenhouse and you could show them the golden lilac. Have you told Brooke the name?"

"Not yet." *I'm waiting for her to tell me.*

"What's wrong, Rafe?"

"Nothing, Lily. Sure, we can go see the photos."

"It looks to me," Faye said as a sudden silence began to linger, "as if Fleur's found a friend."

Robert smiled. "I've found a friend."

Fleur nodded her happy nod as if she agreed.

Brooke watched from Marla's bedroom window as the others returned from their stroll.

It was time. She was ready.

She waited until the horses were corralled and the foursome had started their walk across cobblestones to the mansion.

They'd been heading to the kitchen, but veered when Brooke opened the front door.

She wore her dark-blue suit, with not a roan hair on it, and polished heels scrubbed free of dirt.

She wore makeup, too, the discreet adornment the experts prescribed. The darkest color on her translucent skin was nature's own, a deep purple beneath her eyes.

Brooke hadn't napped. Obviously. Lily's query — "Are you okay?" — was abandoned in favor of a more pertinent one.

"What's wrong?"

"Nothing, Lily. In fact, everything's terrific. It's *over.* You're cured."

"I know, Brooke. Robert told me. Your mother's notes were tremendously helpful."

"I'm sure they were." Brooke looked at the physician who'd bored holes in Lily's bones; he'd hated to, but had no alternative. "Did you tell Lily what she had?"

"No. I want to wait until next week when all the lab tests are back."

"But that's not necessary, is it?"

"I think it is."

"Well, since I won't be here next week, or even tomorrow —"

"What does that mean?"

The question, low and harsh, was Rafe's. Brooke replied without meeting his gaze. "It means I'm on this evening's seven-fifteen nonstop to Cairo."

"Would someone please tell me what's going on?"

"I will, Lily," Brooke said. "You deserve to know everything — now. Rafe could have told you yesterday, when *he* made the diagnosis, but it's clear he chose not to."

"I'm right here, Brooke. You can talk directly to me."

She did. "It was John's handwriting on

the memo pad, wasn't it? That's why the pen and pad were askew. Even in haste, my mother was compulsively neat. I hadn't done a tracing, but I'm guessing what John wrote was something like MJ 503? Or MSD 97?"

"Something like that."

"The note in John's study," Faye said. "No one could figure out what the letters and numbers meant, not us, not Curtis, not the police. The law firm's filing system was somewhat similar, but . . . It was decided that either they were reservation codes — hotel, plane, car — for an upcoming trip, or partial license plate numbers John had noted during the drive from Dulles that afternoon. No one believed they had anything to do with the deaths. But they did?"

"Yes. John figured it out that afternoon. He confronted my mother, not knowing she had a gun, and she killed him."

"Figured what out, Brooke? You're *scaring* me."

"Come upstairs, Lily, and I'll tell you. Show you. It's my right to. She was my mother, after all. My *monster.*"

The bookshelf in the sitting-room alcove of Marla's suite still contained the texts

Marla had carefully bookmarked for John, Brooke, Faye. The *PDR* especially had been instrumental in the archeologist's excavation of the truth.

Dr. Brooke Blair was highly regarded as a public speaker. And in private she'd always been a wonderful storyteller.

The story she told today was excruciatingly private, but there was science, as well.

Brooke began with a confession that was both personal and professional.

"I violated a cardinal principle of archeology. Of science in general. I approached Lily's medical records, particularly the notes my mother had written, with a preconceived and rose-colored vision of what I believed I would find: that Marla's analysis would point the way to a diagnosis. Which, arguably, it did. But because of my emotional bias, I couldn't see it."

"You're her daughter, Brooke." Robert's reminder was very gentle.

So was Faye's. "And bright as you are and as much as you've studied the medical texts, you're not a physician."

"But *any* objective reviewer, lay or otherwise, would have seen what I didn't. It was simply a matter of paying attention to what she'd written and being open to what it

meant. Her notes were crucial, I think."
Brooke looked at Robert. "Would you
have made the diagnosis without them?"

"No. I wouldn't have. And didn't. I
missed the diagnosis for seven years,
Brooke. Didn't even consider it — even
though it was in plain view."

"Hiding in plain view was one of her
specialities. Like always leaving her key
ring on the bureau in the foyer. All her
keys were on that ring. Her car key. Her
office key. Her cottage key. Her desk key.
For anyone to see — to take, as John did
that afternoon."

Brooke reached for the photograph she'd
placed facedown atop Marla's jewelry box.
The image, a tableau of ribbons and bows,
was familiar to Faye, Rafe and Lily, so
Brooke explained its significance to
Robert.

"This was the first mosaic Lily made
after the deaths. As you can see, she used
mosaicking tiles and something else —
pills. At least one of every pill that had
been prescribed during the seven years she
was so ill. Faye had kept all the extra pills
until three years into Lily's renewed good
health, when she decided it was time to
throw them out. Lily, being Lily, rescued
them, and made this beautiful celebration

of weddings — and of Faye, whose shakes enabled Lily to take her life-saving pills, no matter how sick she felt. The mosaic's in Faye's home in Chicago. But the photograph was in a basket in Lily's studio . . . something I think Rafe didn't know."

Brooke had asked her audience to sit. Rafe refused. He leaned against a nearby wall, watching her, worrying about her, furious with himself for failing to protect her.

She was talking about him. Rafe waited until she met his gaze. "No," he said. "I didn't know."

"Lorraine took the picture," Lily explained — without understanding yet the significance of what she was explaining. "Years ago. She found it recently and gave it to me." She looked at Brooke. "It was after seeing the photograph this morning, and asking me about it, that you left so abruptly. Why, Brooke? What is it?"

"I'm getting there, Lily, and I'm sorry if it feels like I'm playing games. I guess after having been so shamefully unscientific last night, I'm being overly methodical today. This mosaic is the reason Rafe called Faye, to confirm, I assume, that it was what he'd always believed it to be — a visual record of every drug your doctors prescribed. It's also the reason my own blinders came off. But you're right. How any of us got to the diagnosis isn't really relevant."

Brooke set the photograph aside and touched the jewelry box. "This, however, is. It was in the cottage, locked in her desk." Brooke lifted the lid and removed a white pill with blue speckles. "This is MJ 503. You can see the letters and numbers engraved on the pill. 'MJ' indicates the name of the pharmaceutical company and '503' identifies the specific drug. Using the *PDR*, it's very easy to find everything you'd want to know about MJ 503, from what it looks like to what it does. Its scientific name is cyclophosamide, and it's a wonder drug in the treatment of certain cancers — so much so, I imagine, that its side effects are tolerable . . . and can, in the instance of nausea and vomiting, be treated by giving other drugs at the same time. Cyclophosamide causes hair loss, usually temporary, and because it works by attacking rapidly growing cancer cells, it causes collateral damage to rapidly growing normal cells — most significantly, red blood cells, white blood cells and platelets."

Brooke returned the blue-speckled pill to its velvet compartment and removed a lilac one from an adjacent compartment.

"This is warfarin. In addition to its medical uses, it's the active ingredient in rat poison. Warfarin is marketed in a rainbow of colors, each of which contains a different amount of the drug. Lilac is 2 milligrams. Pharmacologically, warfarin is an anticoagulant. It's given to patients with prosthetic heart valves, so that tiny blood clots — which could become cerebral emboli — don't form on the valve, and it's also given to patients with deep venous thrombosis. Again, the purpose is to prevent clotting and emboli, in this case to the lungs. I gather from the *PDR* that dosing is a delicate balance. You have to get just the right amount of anticoagulation, enough to prevent the unwanted clotting but not so much that you bleed."

The Ph.D. storyteller's next visual aid was oval-shaped and white. "This is procainamide. It's used for treating cardiac arrhythmias, specifically life-threatening ventricular ones, and often when the patient is in the throes of an acute myocardial infarction. But procainamide can also *cause* abnormal rhythms, including asystole — no heartbeat at all — and like cyclophosamide, it can lower blood counts. One of its more interesting tendencies is to

331

cause a false positive ANA, the antinuclear antibody that's an indicator of autoimmune illnesses such as lupus."

The last of the pills Brooke had had time to identify and review was a pentagonal tablet the mauve of Marla's bedroom. "This is dexamethasone, an extremely potent corticosteroid. It's indicated for use in a variety of illnesses, from autoimmune disorders to ulcerative colitis to serum sickness, cerebral edema and TB. Its toxicities are varied, too, but include disturbances in electrolytes, muscle weakness, vertigo and, in high doses, confusion and disorientation."

Brooke replaced the dexamethasone, closed the lid, and opened the first of the three jewelry-box drawers. "As you can see, there are other pills to look up. Some of them must be diuretics, and who knows what else? But the ones I've described give you the general idea. These are powerful drugs with major side effects. All except this." Brooke displayed the over-the-counter eyedrops. "The label says the active ingredient is tetrahydrozoline. I didn't have a chance to find out what happens if you swallow it."

"Immediate gastrointestinal distress," Robert said.

"Fulminant and explosive diarrhea?"

"Yes."

"Did my mother know?"

"She's the one who told us — her housemates — about the pharmacology of just a few drops. It was a tried-and-true cocktail-waitress trick she'd heard about in college, a way to get rid of a rowdy customer in a hurry. It also worked well, she said, with undesirable dates. Marla told us about tetrahydrozoline. Much of the rest, I'm afraid, we probably taught her — if not specifically, at least as a roadmap to finding whatever information she wanted."

"But how did she get the pills?"

"Easily. I remember how amazed she was to learn that prescriptions were — are — often called in to pharmacies not by the doctor, but by someone in the office. The doctor's name is given, of course, and if it's a narcotic, the DEA number. But most prescriptions aren't for narcotics, have no abuse potential . . . in the traditional sense. The drugs she used fit into that category. Not drugs you'd choose to take unless you had to."

"Or had no choice. She didn't learn about the syndrome itself when she lived in the house in Georgetown . . . did she? Had it even been described thirty years ago?"

"No. I'm quite sure it hadn't."

"Or nineteen years ago? There's no mention of it in any of the textbooks here."

"My guess would be that case reports had begun appearing in the pediatric literature by then. It takes a while for a newly described syndrome to make it into the standard texts."

"So she came up with it all on her own."

"Came up with what, Brooke?"

"*It*, Lily. Your . . . diagnosis. What you had. *It* was never really yours, of course, except for the ruptured appendix and the septic shock. The shock and its consequences became her blueprint. She highlighted the symptoms you had during that first admission, so when variations of those symptoms recurred it would logically seem they'd been triggered by the original illness. If it hadn't been for the ruptured appendix, she might never have discovered how much *fun* it was when you were deathly ill, and how wonderful it was to be perceived as the *perfect* mother — as perfect as Carolyn — as well as a dazzling entrepreneur. And she might never have discovered how much she loved being needed by John —"

"*Brooke*. Please. What are you saying?"

"Don't you know, Lily? Haven't you guessed?"

"I don't *want* to guess."

"You don't want to know, you mean. But," Brooke said softly, "it's true. After surviving the septic shock, you should have been as healthy as you've been since my mother's death. She made you sick, Lily. She *poisoned* you with wonder drugs. *These,* none of which can be found in the mosaic you made for Faye. There's absolutely no doubt. She made you sick in ways she chose and when she chose. Time for a bone marrow biopsy? Better sprinkle a little cyclophosamide in Lily's shakes so her blood counts will plummet. Or for a change of pace, how about a spinal tap? A handful of dexamethasone should do the trick. And when Lily wants — so much — to go to her first dance, is *determined* to go against my mother's wishes and despite the dizziness from all the other drugs? A few drops of tetrahydrozoline should induce the desired mortification. Have Rafe tell you about Tlaloc sometime, Lily, the Aztec Rain God who demanded the tears of children. I think you'll agree my mother puts him to shame."

"She would never —"

"Yes, she *would.* And did. But only when

it was convenient for her. You were ill at her pleasure. Do you remember her ever having to cancel something she wanted to do because you were sick? I don't. But when she was in the mood for attention from John, or admiration for the supposed sacrifices she made for the sick little girl who wasn't even hers — or when she just felt like matching wits with the doctors — your illness came in very handy. And, of course, there was the Geneva trip. It had been decided in the fall that the next time your electrolytes were seriously out of whack, they'd send you to the clinic. My mother chose spring. The perfect time for romance. The edelweiss would be in bloom, after all, and —"

"Stop it, Brooke! Stop sounding so —"

"So crazy, Lily?"

"*Yes.*"

"So like my mother?"

"No!"

"It's called Munchausen Syndrome by Proxy. You've heard of it, haven't you? In the newspapers, in *People*, on TV?"

"Yes. But . . . Yes. I have."

"I saw John in his study that afternoon. He'd probably just come from the cottage. We'll never know why he went there, what made him know to search or if he had any idea what he'd find. He was standing very still when I saw him, absorbing what he'd just discovered, I think, and deciding what to do. We know he tried to reach Curtis, for his input probably. Maybe to discuss when he should involve the police. In the end, John decided to confront her himself. And why not? He had no idea she had a gun. And, of course, even *she'd* forgotten it . . . until I reminded her."

"She would have remembered the gun, Brooke." Rafe's voice was quiet. Fierce. "You know she would have. Confronted with John's accusations, she would have remembered it right away."

"Despite the giddiness she was feeling from jet-lag? And even if she and I *hadn't* been reminiscing about rape? I don't know. We'll never know. What we do know is that in John's final heartbeats of life, his thoughts and his love were with Lily."

Brooke looked at Lily, so beloved and so betrayed. "He killed her to protect you, Lily, to save you. I'm *so sorry* for who she was and what she did."

Lily couldn't speak. Nor could she stop trembling. But she managed a faint nod, a delicate *I know.*

"I'll leave the jewelry box here." Brooke touched the treasure trove of such evil and spoke to Robert and Faye. "Please throw it away when everything's learned that needs to be learned. And the pills, too." *Do not let the gracious rescuer attempt to make something beautiful out of this.* "Well. I guess that's it. Time for me to go."

32

Brooke's heart stumbled as it had four days ago. Just four days. She'd been hopelessly stalled then, needing to face the past in order to go on.

The past had been faced. And the woman who walked down the mansion steps into April sunlight?

She was stalled. Still. And hopeless. More.

Too bad.

"Aren't you going to say goodbye to Fleur?"

She hadn't heard his footsteps behind her. They'd been silent above the chaotic pounding of her heart.

She didn't look at him, couldn't, but glanced toward the paddock and Fleur. She was whinnying, wanting more hugs, daring Brooke to once again cover her tidy blue suit with wisps of roan.

It had taken a while to pluck off each and every hair, and — the truly pathetic part — Brooke had put them in an envelope . . . as someone who was hopelessly stalled might provide safe haven for a wish.

"Fleur was never mine." *Nothing here was ever mine.* "And given her attention span, she'll quickly forget I was ever here."

Fleur wasn't forgetting yet. And her attention span seemed infinite.

Brooke turned away, resumed her faltering journey to the cottage.

The sure-footed warrior walked beside her.

"So you're just running away?"

"I have a plane to catch."

"A few hours from now."

"Wouldn't it be nice if my mother's impulse had been to leave, not to murder? The beauty of leaving is that you don't kill anyone in the process."

"Don't you, Brooke?"

She had no reply, nor did she speak again until they reached her car. She'd left it the way she needed it to be, luggage loaded, keys in the ignition, ready to go.

Rafe's hand got to the door handle before hers did. His fingers rested there, a deceptively casual gesture, given what it was — an absolute blockade of her escape.

"What do you want, Rafe?"

"Answers."

"What happened to *truth?*"

"I was hoping for truthful answers."

"I can't believe this. You knew what she'd done, knew the truth, and concealed it from me. When did you figure it out? Before or after I was telling you how proud I was of her?"

"After."

"At which point you decided to destroy the memo-pad evidence —"

"That's right."

"And if you'd known about the photo of Faye's mosaic, you would have destroyed it, too?"

"Hidden it, anyway."

Brooke looked at the fingers that held her captive without touching. Her thoughts might have drifted to remembrance of his touch, but she forced them to different memories — of her mother . . . and Lily's.

Both mothers had kept journals. Carolyn's was a hopeful record of the daughter lilacs she might one day breed. And Marla's? Her diary — the notes she wrote in medical charts — chronicled the torture of a daughter and the poison-by-number recipes for the same: what pills created the desired effects and in what doses they needed to be given and for how long.

"I would've realized — eventually — what her notes truly meant."

"Maybe," the voice behind her conceded. "Or maybe not."

"You asked Robert to keep the diagnosis secret until after I was gone."

"It didn't take any persuading."

"Was Lily ever going to know the truth?"

"Yes."

"And when *I* happened to ask Lily what Robert had found?"

"He was planning to talk to a pediatric immunologist and come up with some rare but real childhood illness that doesn't follow the patient into adulthood. There's actually a pediatric variant of lupus he thought would do."

"So you convince Lily to lie and everyone's destined to know the truth but me. What gives you the right to make that kind of decision about my life?"

"What gives me the right, Brooke, is that I love you."

"*No.* You can't. It's too late."

"I think it's about time. And I can, Brooke. I do. Is it really so bad?"

No. Just wondrous. Merely impossible.
"Yes."

"Why? And don't tell me because of your mother. We're way past believing our ancestral sins have anything to do with us. Or that we're responsible for them."

But we're not way past what you'll say to

Lily. We won't get past that once you know. She wants to have your baby. "Ancestral sins, yes," she affirmed. "But there's no ancient history here. Let's say you were in the parent-selecting phase of creating a daughter lilac. I seriously doubt you'd decide to cross Murderess with Rapist."

"I would if I knew I'd get you."

Brooke looked from car door to window — and saw love. Wondrous.

Impossible.

"Star Light," she murmured. "That's what you should name your golden lilac."

"That sounds good for the springtime blossoms. But it forgets the autumnal blooms, doesn't it?"

"They should be forgotten." *Star Bright should be forgotten.*

"I'd have to fill out the Lilac Society paperwork all over again."

"I thought Lily was still working on the name."

"She was, but the paperwork's been filled out for a while. Lily came up with the name, realized what it should be, Thursday night."

"I think she'll change her mind when she tumbles to the fact that my mother very likely murdered both her parents."

"Carolyn died of a ruptured ectopic."

"So my psychopath mother said."

"The doctors said it, too, Brooke. Faye was there. She heard the postmortem diagnosis at the same time John and Marla did."

"You asked her about it last night, didn't you? You wondered if my mother had murdered Carolyn, too. You knew she was capable of it, might even have done it . . ." *If an innocent little life hadn't stalled partway down a Fallopian tube.*

"What I wonder, Brooke, is if what happened is a result of the rape. The way your mother dealt with it — or didn't."

"The rape was irrelevant. She'd have happily murdered her high-school boyfriend just for breaking up with her. She didn't do well with rejection. Ever. She must have hated John for not loving her, and hated Carolyn for being loved instead, and hated Lily for being their child. My grandmother has a similar, although not so overtly lethal, streak."

"Which explains why John wrote your name and Curtis's that afternoon — on the same sheet of paper as the codes for the drugs. But only the codes were on the sheets I removed from your mother's desk. John wrote your name *after* returning to the study and already knowing what your

344

mother had done. He wanted to become your legal guardian, I imagine, so that with your mother behind bars you wouldn't be sent to live with Elise."

"Something else we'll never know." But Brooke did know. Her heart did. John would have protected her, too. "I do know that the Blair women should never have children, not Elise, not Marla, not Brooke."

"That's nonsense."

Would you trust me with your babies, Rafe? Brooke couldn't ask. At this moment, before Rafe discovered it was a question Lily, too, would ask, Brooke believed his answer — to her — would have been yes. Yes . . . and then no.

"I have to go."

"One of those archeological emergencies?"

Oh, yes. The kind where it's necessary to spend the rest of your life in a tomb.

"What happened to leaving Monday morning?"

"I didn't know how long it would take me to go through my mother's things. Monday morning was the longest-case scenario, and one which would've made me late in joining the dig. It's best to be there at the outset, when we discuss our approach to the site. If I leave tonight I'll be in time for those discussions and I won't have to impose on anyone to fill me in."

"Fair enough. Why don't I come with you?"

"Lily needs you."

"Did you hear the part where I told you I love you?"

"I can't hear that part, Rafe. Don't you see?"

"No. Make me see."

"We barely know each other."

"That's not true. And what we don't know, we'll discover. It'll be one long, interesting dig. Look at me, Brooke, and tell me you don't love me."

She obeyed what she could. Looked at him. "Lily loves you, Rafe."

"And I love Lily. Just as you love Lily. This isn't about her, Brooke. It's about us. You and me."

"And Lily. She saw an obstetrician on Thursday. It was something she'd been thinking about for a very long time. She wants to have a baby, Rafe. Lots of babies, I imagine, now that she can. Her babies . . . and yours. She wasn't going to ask you until she saw the doctor again next week, but now there's no reason to wait."

346

Brooke watched his reaction, and realized that he was right. They knew each other more than barely.

And that she was right. He would say yes to Lily.

But it would be more difficult for Rafe than she'd imagined. She saw the longing for what might have been. The sadness for what would never be.

It was always difficult to say goodbye.

"I'd better go," she said. *I have to.*

His hand had relinquished its casual imprisonment of her car. It had drifted to his side, clenched there. Her car was free. She was free.

He was letting her go.

"I'll drive you."

"No. Thank you."

"You're exhausted."

"I'm fine. It's broad daylight, no traffic." Brooke curled her fingers around the door handle. His hand didn't join hers, didn't stop her, but its heat lingered on the chrome. "I need to drive myself."

"Okay. But I need to know where you're staying in Cairo." He smiled faintly. "Don't tell me some remote encampment. I know the Giza Plateau is about three minutes from the Cairo Hilton."

"The Nile Hilton. But . . ."

"Don't just show up? I won't. I promise. As long as you make me a promise in return."

"What promise, Rafe?"

"That we see each other a week from Monday. I'll come to Cairo or — have you ever been to the Wind Chimes Hotel in London?"

"No."

"Neither have I. Meet me there, Brooke. A week from Monday at four."

Twelve years ago, twelve Aprils ago, Brooke had failed to keep their Monday teatime rendezvous. She'd detoured to a conversation about guns and rape.

"Why?"

"Because I love you. And I haven't yet heard you say that you don't love me."

"You need to talk to Lily."

"I will."

"If you're not there, Rafe, I'll understand."

"And if you're not there, Brooke, I won't."

33

Lily insisted she was fine. *Really.* Her assertion went unchallenged by what remained of the FoxHaven house party. Rafe, Robert and Faye merely closed ranks around her, permitting her to guide the conversation wherever she chose.

Their hostess chattered about lilacs, horses, Faye's grandchildren and wedding cakes. But she'd stop midsentence, suddenly remembering what they'd learned about Marla. Seconds would pass. Minutes. Finally, unable to talk about it yet, she'd shrug and return to other topics.

Faye and Robert left together on Sunday afternoon. Both offered to stay longer. As long as Lily liked. But it was obvious that Lily needed time with Rafe, just the two of them, the familiar companionship of the past twelve years.

Faye and Robert didn't have a dozen years' companionship. But both looked forward to their drive to the airport.

"Talk about being an enabler," Faye began. "I made the shakes first thing each morning, so they'd be chilled when Lily came downstairs . . . and ready, in the meantime, for Marla to sprinkle in her poison. I was *in* the kitchen when she did it. I must have been. But was I paying much attention when she went to the refrigerator to get milk for her tea? No, never. I suppose she enjoyed the risk. Thrilled at it."

"I'm sure she did."

"I made the shakes every day, even when Lily was doing well. They'd become a habit for her, for *both* of us, reliably soothing to her queasy stomach . . . and a way in which I could help. Some help."

"Shakes or no shakes, Marla would have given Lily the pills. She could've simply handed them to her, said the doctors had called and wanted her to take them. At least you were on to her, Faye. You shared the same house for seven years without ever becoming close. I, on the other hand, spent two years under the same roof with Marla and never thought she was anything but terrific."

"I wasn't on to her, Robert. Everyone thought she was terrific. Including me. And there's no doubt her Lilac Cottage was a remarkable success. Which makes what she did all the more incomprehensible." Faye paused. "She did it well though, didn't she? Brilliantly?"

"I'm afraid so. From what I know of the syndrome, she avoided all the usual mistakes."

"Such as?"

"Most MSP perpetrators do everything possible to keep the child in the hospital. It's where they, the perpetrators, *want* to be. As a result, the child often suffers setbacks during hospitalization, particularly when discharge is at hand. But Marla always seemed eager to get Lily home. Appropriately eager. Appropriate," Robert mused. "That's what syndrome perpetrators typically *aren't*. They're inappropriately calm about the child's illness, untroubled by the severity of the symptoms and even vaguely satisfied when painful procedures are required."

"Wasn't Marla calm?"

"Yes. She was. But no different than I'd always known her to be — or, for that matter, than John was most of the time. And, like John, Marla was concerned about the procedures. She knew of Lily's fear and wanted to be certain every test was necessary. It was ultimately John's decision, of course, not Marla's."

"John did what was best for Lily."

"Always."

"And thanks to Marla, what was best — necessary — for Lily hurt her and was a torment to John. And," Faye added quietly, "to you."

"I believed Marla and I were friends. Good ones. I suppose I was blinded to the truth because I owed her so much."

"You owed Marla?"

"She's the reason Joanna came back into my life. Joanna and I had known each other in high school, but we'd never dated. There was a connection, though. We went our separate ways — med school, law school, D.C., Denver — until, one New Year's Eve, Joanna called the house in Georgetown. I was at the hospital, and would be for the next thirty-six hours, but she and Marla talked. And talked. Joanna had just been diagnosed with Hodgkins. Stage 4B. Her prognosis was grim. She didn't want to die without saying some things to me. Marla convinced her to say them in person. Five months later, Joanna and I were married."

"And, Robert?"

"We had twenty-nine years."

"Marla's not responsible for that," Faye said. "You're the one who saved Joanna's life."

352

Robert smiled briefly, then frowned. "A month before her death, Joanna had a pleural biopsy that was complicated a few hours later by shortness of breath. I was paged *stat* and arrived just moments after another Dr. Hart, a pediatric surgeon named Peter, had made the diagnosis — tension pneumothorax — and was taking the steps necessary to save her. He did save her. Without the slightest hesitation, he put a large bore needle into her chest. That's what you're supposed to do. Even an internist knows it. But when I saw her . . . all I could think was *someone help her — please.*"

"You were a husband at that point, not a doctor."

"But what I don't know, what I'll never know, is what would've happened if Peter hadn't been there. Would I have been able to do what he did? He saved her life at the exact moment, the only moment, it could be saved. If she'd arrested . . . Peter gave us the chance to say our final goodbyes, and Joanna the chance to do a little match-making of sorts."

"Matchmaking?" Faye asked.

"Between Peter and me. When he came to see her the following morning, Joanna — being Joanna — was far more interested in learning about this other Hart from Boston than in her own declining health. Peter had been abandoned at age four. So he needed a family, Joanna decided. A father. And I needed a son. Joanna's treatment for Hodgkins made it impossible for us to have children. She worried a lot about how lonely I'd be after she died. It took her about two seconds to conclude that Peter was lonely, too, and that he and I were very much alike."

"Are you?"

"Like Peter? Not in any way that's obvious to anyone but Joanna."

"Are you his father? Could you be?"

"No to both. He's thirty-six, so I would've been nineteen. I was on a work-study scholarship to college and not involved with anyone. Not even once. And Peter's equally certain that the father who abandoned him wasn't me. Biology was never really the issue. Peter had no father. I had no son. We were, Joanna believed, meant to be close. She orchestrated as much as she could. Including," he said in a soft voice, "when she died."

Faye's voice, too, was soft. "Peter was with her then? With you?"

"He was in the other room, as Joanna had asked him to be. She died in our home, in our bed. I knew in advance the calls I'd need to make — coroner, funeral home . . ."

"Peter helped you."

"Yes, Faye. He did. Again."

"He sounds like a fine man."

"A very fine man."

So you are alike. "And your surrogate son?"

"No. We've become less close, not close at all, since Joanna died. He's very private. And he feels an awkwardness with me . . . toward me. I'm sure Joanna noticed it. She didn't want to explore it, though. She didn't want to make things even more awkward, since she was convinced there could be — *should* be — a genuine bond between us."

"Have *you* explored it?"

"The awkwardness? With Peter? No."

"Men," Faye murmured.

"Men?"

"Yes, Robert, *men.*"

Six hours after Faye's flight departed from Dulles, Rafe greeted Lily in her brightly lighted studio with, "You couldn't sleep."

"I tried."

"So now you're doing what?"

355

"A little spring-cleaning."

Rafe surveyed the immaculate studio. The clutter was gone. Tiles, grout, glue, plaster had been consigned to their designated drawers and works-in-progress had been stowed on shelves beneath the tables. The baskets of ideas and photographs had been moved to a distant corner and the rolltop desks were closed.

"More than a little."

"The place needed it, and I needed to do it. Rafe?"

"Lily."

"I'm worried about Brooke. Do you know where she's staying?"

"The Nile Hilton. I also know she arrived safely."

"You've talked to her?"

"No. Just to the front desk." Rafe paused for a beat. "I will be talking to her, Lily." Two beats. "We're meeting in London a week from tomorrow."

"Good."

"I'm sure Faye would be happy to stay here while I'm away."

"I think I'd rather be by myself. I'd like to be. At the very least, it would be an adventure in spring-cleaning."

"I thought I'd ask Sarah to look after the horses. School will be on spring break, so she'll have the time. I know you could do it, but . . ."

"It's a vote of confidence for Sarah, who still feels responsible — although she shouldn't — for Daphne's accident."

"Yes."

"You're going to be such a wonderful father." Lily smiled at the suddenly worried blue eyes. "Brooke told you, didn't she? About the baby?"

"Yes. She did. Lily . . ."

"Don't say a thing."

"There's a lot to say."

"But it's all unnecessary. I know how you feel about me, Rafe, and you know how I feel about you."

"I'm not sure you know, Lily, what it meant to me that you would ask."

"You would've said yes, wouldn't you, once upon a time?"

"Yes. I would have."

"Well, that's good . . . because, once upon a time, I would've needed you to. At the moment, however, what I really need is a little help rearranging these work tables. I'm thinking I'd like to try them at the perimeter of the room. . . ."

357

34

Emergency Room

Swedish Medical Center

Tuesday, April 17

Twelve-Fifteen a.m.

"Oh! Dr. Hart, I didn't realize you were still here." The surprised voice belonged to the admissions clerk.

"Was someone trying to reach me?" Peter asked.

"No. It's just that these medical records arrived for you, and I thought I'd let you know. In case you'd been waiting for them."

Peter hadn't been waiting for medical records.

But he had most definitely been waiting to hear from the sender. Lily Rutledge. FoxHaven Farm. 12222 Canterfield Road. Forsythe, Virginia. 20118.

"How did these arrive?"

"By cab."

"When?"

"About eleven. I'm sorry I didn't page you right away. The main point, I thought, was for them to be available when your office opened in the morning."

"You did everything right. Thank you."

Ten minutes later, in his condominium in the Wind Chimes Towers, Peter read the cover sheet that accompanied the hospital charts.

Lily's charts.

The neatly typed information was more playbill than letter. The setting was Swedish Medical Center. The time span was the seven years of Lily's girlhood from ages eight to fifteen.

Just one character was identified in the drama. Marla Blair. Her role was mother-surrogate to Lily, and it was her color-coded handwriting — like an omniscient narrator — that appeared throughout.

An envelope containing an assortment of pills and labeled "Found in Marla's desk" was stapled to the cover sheet. There was a newspaper clipping, too, a succinct yet devastating description of the deaths on FoxHaven Farm.

That was it. The stage was set.

And as for the title of the four-volume play?

None was provided. But titles came to Peter as he read.

Miracle. It was the appropriate title for Lily's hospitalization for the ruptured appendix. But a subtitle was called for: *The Courage of a Little Girl.*

The titles changed as he read.

Mother. Evil. Fury. Horror.

Peter waited until 5:00 a.m. to call her. It was early, but if he waited much longer it would be too late. He had surgery beginning at six and for most of the day.

He expected a soft and dreamy voice to answer. Something twisted deep within when he imagined the voice might whisper *Rafe.*

The voice he heard was soft . . . and awake.

"Hello?"

"It's Peter."

"Hi."

"You're not asleep."

"No. Online, in fact, doing a Google search for Munchausen Syndrome by Proxy. Now that I have a diagnosis, I thought I'd better do a little reading about it."

"You've just learned the diagnosis?"

"On Saturday. The records had been locked in Marla's desk. Once they were discovered, Robert took a look and . . . you're probably wondering why I sent them to you."

"Wondering but not objecting."

"Thank you. My plan had been to call Edith in the morning, explain much more than was included in the package, and ask her to ask you about reviewing them — if you wanted to and if you had the time."

"I have the time. I want to. I already have."

"Thank —"

"You're welcome, Lily. So?"

"So? Oh, why did I send them to you? I . . . don't know. I have some thoughts, however, the most logical being that I should've gotten back to you first thing yesterday morning about the 7-North mosaics and this was a way of letting you know why I hadn't."

"Don't worry about the mosaics."

"I'm not. Very much. Although even before the Munchausen by Proxy revelation, I'd done some rethinking and decided that it might be better — best — to have the children make the mosaics themselves. It's something children of all ages really

361

can do. Each child could come up with his or her design with as much or as little help as needed. There's still a crafts program for pediatric inpatients, isn't there?"

"Yes. There still is." A vastly improved program over what had been in place during Lily's inpatient days. And her idea of letting the children create the mosaics was a terrific one — a project the very enthusiastic MaryAnn, the crafts-program director, would love to oversee. But . . . "There's no rush for you to make a decision, Lily."

"I will be making it, though. This weekend. Saturday. That's when I'm planning a repeat of my sentimental journey to the Pediatrics Pavilion, especially 7-North, to find out whether the friendly ghosts of last Thursday have subsequently become ghouls. Between now and then, in addition to giving myself a crash course on MSP, I'll be spending time with the ghosts — well, the one ghoul — on the Farm. I have to make peace with her here, in my home. Whatever's awaiting me at SMC is a little more expendable."

"You're only giving yourself a week to deal with this?"

"That's how much time Rafe is giving Marla's daughter, Brooke — and, let's face it, the issues she's dealing with are far more difficult than mine. Besides, I've already spent years worrying about what I had and fearing it would come back. I have the answer now and basically it's a relief."

"But not an unqualified one."

"No."

"That's hardly surprising."

"I know. But I'm determined to come to grips with it and get over it. This week. I know what Marla did had everything to do with her and very little to do with me. I *know* it. But, at the moment, it's feeling quite personal. Learning about the syndrome will, I hope, enable me to be more objective. Maybe understanding why the Marlas of the world do what they do will give me the distance I need."

"I think it will, Lily. Because you're right. It wasn't personal. Was learning about the syndrome one of your reasons for sending your records to me? Did you think I might have some special expertise?"

"No. It really wasn't one of the reasons. How illogical is that? But . . . *do* you have special expertise?"

"No. Although I have seen a number of cases. Pediatric surgery, especially trauma surgery, involves me with a spectrum of child abuse."

"You choose to be involved," Lily said. "Made the choice to be. I wonder if I knew that? It definitely ties into another of my thoughts about sending you the records."

"Oh?"

"The way you looked in Rachel's office that first day — what I *believed* I saw — reminded me of my father's expression on the afternoon of the killings. Now I know that when I saw that expression, he'd just found out what Marla had been doing to me."

"In Rachel's office," Peter said softly, "when you correctly diagnosed my anger, I'd just come from admitting a battered child to intensive care. He was a baby Rachel had delivered ten months before. I wanted to be sure she'd be available to testify in the court proceedings against his parents. You were right about my potential for violence, too. At that moment I was imagining the irrevocable things I'd willingly have done to his abusers."

"Imagining. But you wouldn't have acted upon them. As much as you wanted to protect an innocent child."

"Your father did act that afternoon. He gave his life to protect you. Do you think what he did was wrong?"

"*No.* But I wish, always will, that he'd

been able to protect me in the way he'd planned. Legally, not . . . lethally. He didn't know she had the gun. And when he realized, too late, that she did, he shot her. As he was dying. When I think of what he did, what he gave, the notion of allowing myself even a week to deal with Marla's pathology seems incredibly self-indulgent."

"It's not, Lily. Don't you think your father would agree?"

"Oh, yes. I do. He would."

"He was a wonderful man."

"Yes. He was."

In Forsythe, outside her studio window, birds were just beginning to greet the dawn. Lily heard them in the silence.

In D.C., floors below Peter's condominium, a siren screamed.

"Do I otherwise remind you of him?"

"What? Oh. My father? *No.* I mean, not to say that *you* aren't wonderful, but . . . I wonder how one answers a question like that?"

"Truthfully. As you did. It wasn't a bad answer, Lily."

"Well . . . there is a Dr. Hart who reminds me of my father."

"Robert."

"Yes. A lot, and in so many ways.

Including his protectiveness of me — and the guilt he feels, as I'm sure my father did, about missing the diagnosis all those years."

"It couldn't have been made, Lily, not by either of them, without Marla's notes and her hidden cache of pills. From a clinician's standpoint, Robert's standpoint, the most important tip-off to the syndrome is that the child's illness makes no medical sense. Yes, what you had didn't have a name. But it fit very nicely into a spectrum of autoimmune illnesses that was expanding then and continues to expand. Robert shouldn't feel the slightest guilt."

"Would you mind telling him that?" Lily waited for a reply that didn't come. And waited a few heartbeats more. "You would mind. Why?"

"There's no better physician anywhere than Robert Hart."

"So it would feel awkward for you to tell him? Presumptuous?"

"Yes. Both."

"Oh."

Silence fell again. Awkwardly. But there was something presumptuous Peter needed to do — and soon, before he had to leave for the OR and Lily began learning all she could about MSP.

She'd be able to learn a great deal, he knew, without leaving her computer. It was simply a matter of visiting the official MSP web site, *www.AsherMeadow.com.*

The clock was ticking away not only the time Peter had left to talk with her this morning, but also the time she'd allotted her ghosts — and what she believed was the only ghoul.

Lily didn't know, but Peter did, that there were other haunting discoveries she would make.

"How did you feel during those seven years?"

"Feel, Peter? Helpless. Betrayed by my body."

"Did you like the attention?"

"No."

"Or the sympathy?"

"Not at *all.* And I hated causing such worry for my father. And Brooke. And Faye."

"And Marla?"

"Yes, of course. But I spent far more time worrying about the others . . . and thinking about my mother, how worried she would've been."

"Many MSP victims, especially older ones, begin to sense that how much they're loved depends on their disease. The sicker they are, the more love is lavished on them. A co-dependency can develop, in which the children actually make themselves sick."

"I wonder if I did that. Unwittingly, and for an entirely different reason. I wanted so much to be well that I started hiding my symptoms."

"Such as during the weeks before the dance? Given your electrolytes when you were brought into Emergency, you must've been having symptoms for a while."

"Yes. I had been. Having them and hiding them."

"To which Marla responded by increasing the doses of the medications she was giving you. You could easily have died that evening."

"Marla wasn't trying to kill me."

"No. Although the abuse typically increases over time. It becomes an addiction for the perpetrator. And, as with an addiction, the cravings escalate. More and more of what hooked the addict in the first place is required to get the fix. For the MSP perpetrator, the sicker the child, the higher the high. To achieve those highs, more risks are taken — which, for the child, leads to even greater harm."

"With my inadvertent help, Marla

almost caused the greatest harm of all.' "

" 'Inadvertent' being the word to remember. Have you been ill much during the past twelve years?"

"Only once. A cold. Rafe had it, too, and was far sicker than I."

"So you don't miss being ill?"

"*No.* Why are you asking me these questions?"

"Because you're going to discover two potentially worrisome bits of data about MSP victims. The questions, and more specifically your answers, seemed a good way of reminding you in advance that neither worry applies to you."

"You knew my answers before you asked?"

"I was pretty sure I did. I doubt you even think of yourself as a victim of child abuse."

"No. I really don't. Nothing ever felt like abuse to me. I was so loved by my parents. And Brooke. And 'victim' is wrong, too, for me. I didn't feel victimized as a child, and don't — won't — today. I think 'pawn' is a better word for me — a pawn in whatever game Marla was playing."

"What would you estimate your chance of becoming a Munchausen patient to be?"

"A Munchausen patient? Meaning

someone who creates illnesses in myself? Zero."

"So would I. But some MSP victims — which you've just pointed out you're not — spend their adulthood creating factitious illness in themselves. The theory is that they miss the attention they had when they were ill as children."

"That's not me. What I missed was the health I'd enjoyed until I was eight. What's the second worrisome bit of data?"

"A small minority of MSP victims become MSP perpetrators."

"They hurt their *own* children? I can't imagine ever hurting a child!"

"I never thought you could."

"Thank you. And for the questions, too. I might have dwelled on those bits of data for a very long time had I come upon them cold."

"The reading's going to be difficult enough for you. Disturbing."

"Because there *are* victims and it *is* child abuse."

"That's right."

"I need to do the reading, though."

"And talk with me later?"

"Yes. Please. If you have the time."

"I do, and I don't. Beginning in about three minutes, I'm surrendering all control to the whimsies of patient care. It may be tonight before I can call you again. Maybe late tonight."

"Any time is fine. I've surrendered all control of sleep to the whimsies of ghosts and ghouls. I've been staying up late, and napping at noon, and surfing the Net at dawn. Please call me, Peter. Whenever. If you like."

"I do. I will. I have one more question. Who's Rafe?"

"Oh." *My knight in shining armor. The man who would have been my baby's father.* The familiar descriptions swirled in her mind. They belonged to the past now, lovely not anguished. And the description of Rafe that would replace them? Lily hadn't realized she'd even formulated one. But it came without thought, and with a smile. "He's my wonderful friend who's in love with Brooke."

They talked at all hours during the days and nights that followed — *for* hours, sometimes, and sometimes just long enough to say hello before Peter was paged away.

They discussed, with quiet sadness for the victims not so lucky as she, what Lily had learned: that the mortality rate was between ten and thirty percent; that MSP perpetrators could not be rehabilitated; that the abuse stopped only when the victim died or the perpetrator was caught or the perpetrator found a younger child to abuse.

Perpetrators were often well-educated, upper class, and they were overwhelmingly women. Most were the victim's biological mother. Eighty percent had some exposure to the medical — hospital — environment, as workers, as patients, as both. Eighty percent also had a history of Munchausen's Syndrome. They'd induced fake illnesses in themselves before beginning their reign of terror in others. A history of psychiatric therapy was frequent, as was attempted suicide — either in the past or when it was discovered what they'd done.

The youngest reported victim was in its mother's womb. The perpetrator had learned how to cause fetal distress — fetal hypoxia — by changing positions, allowing the weight of her pregnant abdomen to impede blood flow through the umbilical cord. The oldest reported victim was in a nursing home. The syndrome was also seen in veterinary medicine.

Smothering was a typical means of inflicting harm, factitious SIDS a common presentation. When drugs or poisons were given, they were usually readily available ones: over-the-counter laxatives and emetics, caffeine, nail polish, acid. When the offender had access to needles, the injected substance was similarly opportunistic — dirt, air, acid, bodily fluids. Insulin-induced hypoglycemic coma had occurred, and a widely publicized case had been reported in which the father was alleged to have injected HIV.

There was no doubt about what Marla Blair had done. But *how* she'd done it had never been described.

"It *should* be described, though, shouldn't it?" Lily asked at ten-forty-five Thursday night. "In the interest of letting other physicians know?"

Peter's reply was preempted by a page, followed by a distracted goodbye. Four hours later, however, when the sleepy voice answered, he said very softly, "Yes."

"Yes," Lily echoed. Smiled. Woke up just enough. "Oh. The case report."

"Would you like me to call back another time?"

"Yes. Please. Another time *after* this time. Would you do the report?"

"I'd be glad to do it, but I'd need to talk to the doctors who cared for you first."

"I'm their case, not yours?"

"That's the protocol."

"I was seen by a lot of doctors."

"I know. There are only a couple I'd need to speak with, the ones involved with your primary care."

"The consultants don't have to be consulted?"

"Not unless the eventual diagnosis falls into their particular specialty."

"I've been worrying about my diagnosis becoming known in Forsythe. I'd rather no one knew."

"Still not interested in attention?"

"Still not. And I especially don't want negative attention for Brooke. From the case reports I've read, I realize patients are never identified by name. But even initials might be problematic."

"Whether I write it up or someone else does, I'll make sure the initials aren't even close. You can choose them if you like."

"I trust you to choose."

"I'll run them by you anyway."

Lily frowned at the sudden flatness in his voice, as if he didn't want her trust. Or was tired, she told herself. Or thinking about a patient.

Still, something made her bring up a

subject she hadn't been sure she would.

Or should.

Or wanted to.

"Rachel called today. I'd cancelled my follow-up visit earlier this week, since it was pretty clear the results of the pending studies would be normal, but this was the first time I'd spoken directly to her."

"Did you tell her you'd given me the records?"

"Yes." That was when *her* voice, Rachel's, became a little flat. "She said she suspected you knew as much or more about MSP as anyone at SMC."

"Did she suggest you also talk with someone else?"

"It wasn't really a suggestion. She just wondered if I was planning to."

"Because she believes you should. She knows I let people down."

"You do?"

"I do."

"Not your patients."

"No. Just everyone else."

"Everyone else probably expects too much."

"No, they don't. Their expectations are reasonable, Lily. They just don't realize how little they should expect of me, how little I'm able — or willing — to give."

35

Saturday, April 21

FoxHaven Farm

"Lily." Rafe's voice was fond but firm. "Go."

"It seems silly for me not to drop you off at the airport on my way into town."

"Only if my flight was leaving in the near future, which it's not."

"I know. But I could easily call Peter back and tell him I'll be there this evening as originally planned."

"You could. But he might not be as available to roam the Pediatrics Pavilion this evening as he is now. The surgical service is quiet at the moment, and he's on third call to the Emergency Room. Didn't you just tell me that's what he said?"

"Pretty much verbatim."

"So, go. I like having my car at the airport anyway."

"Ha! Okay. I'll go. You're going to bring

her home, aren't you?"

"I'm sure as hell going to try."

"You will. I have no doubt."

"Drive carefully, Lil."

"You, too."

Rafe's United Airlines flight to London was still hours away from its scheduled 6:28 p.m. departure when Rafe gave in to restlessness and began the short, safe, easy drive to Dulles.

The April afternoon was flawless. Warm and sunny, clear and blue. It was rather a good day, weather-wise, for a young mother's station wagon to have a flat.

And rather a good place, safety-wise, a wide-shouldered stretch of road.

And it was an ideal time. Rafe was a quarter of a mile behind her.

She gratefully accepted his offer of help.

Rafe paid attention to the task at hand. He positioned the jack beneath the chassis so that its footing was secure. And he was mindful of the *whoosh* of cars passing by.

But there was room for other thoughts. One thought. The only one. Brooke.

Life with Brooke. Babies with Brooke.

Love with Brooke.

Rafe didn't worry that a passing car would swerve into him, or that despite his care the station wagon would fall.

And nothing screamed. Why would it?

He was almost home.

Lily hadn't needed to make peace again with the FoxHaven ghosts. They were the spirits of her loved ones, after all. The spirits themselves seemed more peaceful, though, as if comforted that the truth had been revealed.

And the one FoxHaven ghoul?

It was remarkable, Lily told Peter late one night, what had happened to Marla. She had, quite simply, vanished. Each childhood moment had become a photograph from which every image of Marla had been excised. It hadn't required tedious mental editing on Lily's part. The images had disappeared as if some computer wizard had given a single Search, Find, Delete command.

There weren't empty spaces where Marla had been, either. The photographs had been seamlessly spliced. Only the true loved ones, the truly loving ones, remained.

It wasn't a matter of selective memory. The memories *were* there. She merely selected which parts of the memories she wanted to keep.

Choice, not denial, Lily decided, and Peter agreed.

And as for the ghosts — and the single ghoul — at SMC . . .

"How are you doing?" Peter asked as he and Lily wandered the Pediatrics Pavilion on that Saturday afternoon.

"Good. Great. Marla's not here, either, and the other ghosts are as friendly as before."

But there was this new presence, this gray-eyed one. He'd been only a voice for the past few days, like a cave into which she'd ventured without fear . . . and been rewarded for her boldness with sanctuary.

Now the sanctuary was walking beside her. But the physical reality was so much more than the voice into which she had curled, often as she lay curled in her bed; it was more than her memory — busy with deleting Marla — had chosen to recall.

Denial. Pure and not so simple. It was quite difficult to talk to him when he looked at her. Smiled at her.

And when he wondered, with his searching gaze, where her flow of words had gone, why she didn't chatter as coherently, and expansively, as she did from her cloistered home.

Peter had told her — no, it was a

warning — that it was a mistake to expect much from him. *Anything* from him. Well, Lily had a little something to tell him about expectations. *You're expecting too much of me, Peter. Believing this is something I can do.*

Maybe she'd tell him, the next time he called her.

If there was a next time.

She'd already told him she wasn't going to make the candy mosaics for 7-North. No matter how friendly the SMC phantoms might be. The children — his patients — needed to make their own mosaics. The more she'd thought about it, the more strongly she'd felt.

The voice on the phone had accepted her decision. He'd even spoken with the crafts director, MaryAnn.

After today, Lily would have no reason to return to SMC. Nor would Peter have a reason to call her at all hours, any hours — to call her at all. He knew the timeline she'd given herself for dealing with MSP and getting over it. And he knew how determined she was to adhere to it.

Lily had adhered to the timeline. This was it. The week ended today. Soon. They were nearing 7-North, the last stop on their tour of the no-longer haunted halls.

They hadn't discussed what they might do afterward. But Lily had made a reservation at the Wind Chimes, in case Peter suggested they go to dinner. In case? No. That was what she'd expected him to do.

It wasn't a grand expectation. In fact a reasonable one. She'd even imagined — from the safety of her cloister — that she might make the suggestion herself.

Their expectations are reasonable, Lily. They just don't realize how little to expect of me, how little I'm able — or willing — to give.

"No more paintings." The observation was hers, succinct and obvious. They'd reached 7-North.

"I had them taken down the day you came to my office. About an hour after you left."

"Because you were so sure I'd be doing the mosaics?"

"No. Because of what you said to Edith — that you thought they were wrong for the children."

"She said you thought that, too."

"I did, and I'd even convinced the center's administrators that we needed new art. But they agreed only because I insisted. They thought the paintings were fine. Everyone did, Lily, but you."

"And you. Your patients liked them?"

"I don't think so, although I never asked. It didn't seem fair to burden them with trying to figure out the answer I wanted to hear."

"Which is what they would have done. Even children who might've been quite decisive in another setting."

"They're helpless when they're here."

Yes, they are.

"I did watch their reactions to the paintings," he went on. "Those who'd never seen them glanced only briefly, and those who'd seen them once never looked again. Can you tell me why the paintings were wrong, Lily?"

Peter was looking at her. And it seemed that he needed something from her . . . which she alone could provide.

"There wasn't any hope in them," she began. "No promise that every dream is possible and all wishes can come true. To take hope, that *wonder,* away from sick and frightened children — was that what seemed wrong about the paintings to you? Or was there something else that — oh." Lily fell silent as his pager sounded and spoke only after he'd glanced at its lighted display. "Do you need to go?"

"I'm not sure. The number's to the adult

trauma center, not the pediatric one. I may find that my pager was dialed by mistake. . . ."

There had been no mistake. Thirty minutes later, from Peter's office, Lily was making a transatlantic call.

Peter had offered to make the call for her. But Lily had believed she'd be able to, *should* be able to.

But couldn't.

"Brooke, it's . . ."

"*Lily?* What is it? What's happened?"

"This is Peter Hart, Brooke. Rafe's been in an accident." Peter didn't pause. Suspense was cruel. He also always gave the good news first — assuming there was any. Tonight there was. "He's alive, conscious, without head injury or paralysis. Are you with me?"

"Yes."

"Good. His primary injuries are broken bones in his legs and pelvis. He'll be going to the operating room soon. The orthopedic surgeons have to stabilize the fractures."

"I need to . . ." *touch him, love him.*

"It's all arranged, Brooke. Your flight leaves Cairo in two-and-a-half hours. I know you could get to the airport before

383

then, in minutes, but it's the flight that will get you to Dulles the soonest — sooner, even, than if we chartered a private jet."

Peter provided Brooke with the flight information, then gave the receiver to the hands that wanted it again.

"It's me, Brooke. I'm better now. I don't know why I was so emotional. Rafe's *going* to be okay. Yes, the injuries are serious and it'll take him a while to heal, but . . . it could've been so much worse."

"Have you seen him, Lily?"

"No. The top priority was to get in touch with you. Robert's seen him, though, talked to him. He's still with him or he'd have been here, in Peter's office, speaking with you, too."

"Robert's seen him? That must mean . . . Rafe's bleeding, isn't he? *He has DIC.*"

"No, Brooke. Rafe is *not* bleeding. Rafe asked that Robert be called. To find me." No further explanation was necessary. But Lily had purpose now: to keep Brooke on the line, and as worry-free as possible, during at least some of what would feel to Brooke like the interminable wait until she could even begin the long flight home. So Lily said more. "Rafe knew I was with Peter, but since Rafe doesn't know Peter — and does know Robert — I'm sure it felt more comfortable to him to ask Robert to find us. And it's worked out well. Rafe wants to know that we've reached you and that you're on your way. That's why Robert's still with him, to let him know. Peter's calling right now, so Rafe can know before he goes to the operating room."

Lily also told Brooke what she knew of the accident.

Lily didn't know, and there was no reason she would, about the young mother Rafe had helped en route to the airport. That act of kindness had gone without incident. The jack hadn't collapsed, nor had a passing car swerved into him. There'd been a consequence to the kindness, however: timing. The minutes, the *seconds*, spent at the roadside conspired to place Rafe precisely where he was at the moment the mishap occured.

He'd almost reached the airport, Lily knew. He hadn't been rushing; he'd had plenty of time. And he'd been following what should have been a safe distance behind the flatbed truck with its cargo of stone pillars.

The pillars were secured with a crisscross of heavy cables, one of which snapped, freeing a single pillar.

The heavy stone cartwheeled, witnesses

said, end over end and straight toward Rafe. It happened very quickly. Still, some witnesses thought, Rafe could have swerved.

Had he done so, however, his pickup would have struck a much smaller car. Its passengers, a family of five, would not have survived.

Someone would meet Brooke's plane at Dulles. Lily had repeated the assurance several times. Brooke needn't worry about that. Or anything.

Rafe would be *fine*.

The someone was Robert.

Like Peter, he knew to share good news right away.

"He's out of surgery, Brooke."

"And doing well?"

Robert's answering smile — very gentle, a little wry — was surprisingly familiar to Brooke. Achingly. It was very like the smile of the man who'd been willing to adopt her, even after learning what her mother had done to Lily.

"He's doing very well medically, and as well as can be expected given his pain."

"Couldn't they be treating that?"

"Could and would if he'd let them. He will, he says, once he's spoken to you.

Until then, he's getting the minimum doses the orthopedists will allow. He wouldn't even be getting those if the decision was in his control. But it's not. The infusion of narcotic — he's on a morphine drip — is determined by his blood pressure. When it reaches a certain upper-limit threshold, a dose is automatically infused."

"Is his blood pressure dangerously high?"

"No. Not at all. But it's a good barometer of the pain in his legs and pelvis — as the pain increases, his pressure rises. And also, in response to the pain, his muscles contract. The orthopedists have the fractures stabilized just the way they want them. Too much contraction of his muscles, which are apparently very powerful, jeopardizes the alignments they've achieved. The problem, from Rafe's standpoint, is that even the minimum dose of morphine alters his mental status. He doesn't want any confusion when he talks to you."

"But . . ."

"I know. You don't want him to be in pain. Of course you don't. You can make that clear to him very soon."

Very soon. Very soon.

It felt, why did it feel, not soon enough?

Why couldn't she hear the reassurances and believe they were true?

Maybe if she heard them one more time, and directly, from this man who reminded her of John.

"He's going to be fine, isn't he?"

"Yes, Brooke, he is. Just fine. I promise."

36

He was so pale, her warrior, ashen from his ferocious battle with pain.

But he smiled when he saw her.

"Brooke."

"Hi. How are you?"

"Better now."

"In pain."

"I'm okay. I always knew he'd reappear."

Robert had told her about the morphine-induced confusion. So had Lily, during their brief hug and hello before Lily insisted that Brooke get to the place she wanted to be. Here. *He becomes confused,* Lily had said. *And it bothers him when he realizes it. So when he says something that doesn't make sense, just play along.*

"Who would reappear, Rafe?"

"Tlaloc."

Brooke smiled. He wasn't confused at all.

"He didn't crush me on the mountain, so he tried again."

"And failed again. According to witnesses, Robert said, the pillar shattered on impact."

"You talked to Robert?"

"He met me at the airport."

Rafe looked at her for a long moment. "You need to talk to him more, Brooke."

"Okay. I will. As soon as I tell you what I need to tell you, and as soon as you agree to more meds for your pain."

"What do you need to tell me?"

"That I love you, Rafe. I've always loved you. I should've told you before I left, but I thought that when you talked to Lily and remembered how much the two of you have shared and how important you are to each other —" *Rafe, what's wrong?*

Brooke didn't ask the worried question; she realized in time it was a new bolus of morphine that had clouded his gaze and had his hands fumbling with his hospital gown . . . as if searching for something.

There was nothing to find in the sheer

fabric. No pockets.

Only blood.

"*Rafe.*" She couldn't block this. "You're bleeding."

Her worry focused him. "Seeping a little, Brooke, not bleeding. Something pierced my abdominal wall. A piece of metal, maybe. Or —" he smiled "— a slice of obsidian. The doctors were concerned it might've gone deeper, into the abdomen itself, so they did a mini-exploration by opening the wound a little more. It's okay, Brooke. It's not a penetrating injury. They left the wound open, though — to prevent infection — and covered it with gauze."

Rafe's explanation was clear. He was clear. Again. Until . . .

"*I need Lily.*"

"Rafe?"

"Get Lily for me."

It was simply a matter of beckoning. Lily stood with Robert on the other side of a glass wall.

She came right away.

"He needs you."

"He's confused." Lily mouthed the words to Brooke. Then, "What is it, Rafe?"

"I can't find it. Where did you put it?"

Lily retrieved something small nestled just above his left shoulder.

"Right here, Rafe." She put it in his hand, smiled, and said, "I'm leaving."

Rafe stared at the small and sparkling object — a diamond ring — and frowned. Brooke could see him struggling to will away the narcotic fog. Heard the struggle in his voice.

"This made sense when I bought it for you. I'm trying to remember the reason. I hadn't forgotten your aversion to all gems except celestial ones, but somehow convinced myself this would be okay. The question is why."

"It doesn't matter, Rafe. It's so beautiful."

"Beautiful. Like you. I'm remembering now. I thought, maybe, you could pretend the diamond was a chip of star . . . ? I have my own star, you see, my own Star Bright. But what do you have?"

"The man I love. And this beautiful ring. I love it, Rafe. I love *you*."

"Will you marry me, Brooke?"

"Oh, yes."

She saw his happiness. His eyes had never been more blue.

Then suddenly gray.

"Would you have married me, Brooke?"

He was using the subjunctive tense in this language, his third, he'd learned so well. He was asking her what would have been, what could have been, if only . . .

His eyes were clouds. His skin was snow.

But he did not seem confused.

"I *am* marrying you, Rafe. Right now. It's just a matter of tying my blouse to your —" *blood-soaked gown.*

The small circle of seeped blood had become a pulsing pond. And even as Brooke called for help, the blood pressure monitor was shrieking that a different threshold, dangerously low, had been detected.

The unknown shard had pierced deep, after all — a stab wound to his aorta.

Rafe's pressure would only get lower, lethally so, until the severed vessel was clamped above the bleeding site.

The exsanguination site.

It wouldn't take long for Rafe's powerful and dying heart to pump its final crimson tears. The death would happen here. Soon.

There wasn't a question of making it to the operating room. There simply wasn't time. Nor — yet — on this Sunday afternoon were there surgeons.

The Code Blue had been called, was still being called, and if only it had been a Monday at teatime . . .

But there was an internist in the ICU. A husband who hadn't known, would never know, what would've happened to his Joanna if a surgeon named Hart hadn't arrived.

He'd been a husband then, not a doctor.

Robert was a doctor . . . and more . . . now.

He didn't hesitate. He plunged his hand into the churning pond of blood, then deeper, through the wound in the abdominal wall. Then deeper, feeling the pulsing current, moving against it, finding its source. Then deeper, and with pressure now, he pinned the ruptured vessel against Rafe's vertebral column and *made* the bleeding stop.

It was a temporary fix. But it was enough. The first two surgeons who reached Rafe's bedside placed a surgical clamp where Robert's fingers had been — and already the vascular surgeons were arranging to transport him to the operating room for the definitive repair.

Everyone who'd rushed to the ICU cubicle assumed that Rafe was unconscious, and had been the entire time. Feeling nothing, surely, and unseeing through his open but motionless gray eyes, and not even hearing the whispered words of love from the woman who clutched in her hand the gift he had given her, the shining splinter of a star.

The assumption was so certain that there were those who would maintain the rasping whisper could not have come from him.

But it did.

And it sounded like a command.

"Tell her, Robert. *Tell her.*"

Robert didn't tell Brooke then, not when he was drenched in Rafe's blood and Brooke already had what she needed most — Lily, holding her, comforting her, making reassuring promises like the one Robert himself had made.

Dr. Robert Hart was also needed in the operating room. Rafe hadn't presented with DIC, despite the crush injuries he'd sustained, but his clotting parameters — thrombin time, prothrombin time — had been prolonged.

The protracted bleeding times hadn't been clinically significant before. Rafe hadn't bled excessively from his shattered bones.

But now his injury was a tattered aorta.

Robert waited outside Operating Suite 8 while the vascular surgeons stitched and sewed.

After about thirty minutes, he wasn't alone.

"I heard what you did," Peter said.

"I hope it was enough." Robert drew a heavy breath. "I promised Brooke that Rafe would be fine."

"Then he will be."

"I wish I had your confidence."

Peter saw the wish, and the worry, and didn't hesitate. "It's not confidence, Robert. It's experience. When you make a promise, you keep it. That's something I've known for twenty-five years. You made a promise, once, to a nine-year-old boy. He was a mistrusting kid. An angry kid. It was Christmas Eve. The boy and his friend had been playing football. The friend had been hit by a car. The boy thought you were a pediatric surgeon. But he's come to realize you must've been doing research on trauma-associated DIC. I'm not sure he became a pediatric surgeon because of you. I think that was what he was destined to be. But he became a doctor because of you. I think it's safe to say you saved his life."

"And he saved mine, Peter. By saving Joanna. I remember you. I do. You looked me straight in the eye and prepared to deal with whatever I was about to tell you. Did Joanna know about that Christmas Eve?"

"No. I thought about telling her. But it

would have meant telling her everything." Which would have been awkward, he believed. And presumptuous. But now, as he saw Robert's hope, it felt as if he was being saved — as if they were saving each other — again.

"Everything, Peter? Are you my son? Somehow?"

"No, Robert. I'm not. But until I met you my last name wasn't Hart."

37

Robert gave Brooke and Lily the news that Rafe was in the recovery room, would be there awhile, but that it all looked very good.

Brooke thanked him. They both did.

Then, and fearfully, Brooke asked, "Is there something else? Another problem?"

"With Rafe? No, Brooke. There's not."

"But there's something he wanted you to tell me."

"Yes."

"Maybe I should leave?" Lily asked.

"No."

Robert and Brooke spoke at once. And smiled.

Their reasons were different, but both wanted Lily to stay.

"Rafe told me about the rape," Robert began. "I asked him to. You'd mentioned it was something you and your mother had talked about the day she died."

"Yes."

"It wasn't rape, Brooke, and you were conceived on Christmas Eve, not New Year's Eve. Marla was alone that New

Year's Eve, talking to Joanna, convincing her it wasn't too late for the two of us, Joanna and me. I'm not sure why Marla decided to reunite us, whether it was a test or a game. Nor do I know," he said to Lily, "whether it was John she was punishing by making you so ill — or me. Both of us, I suppose."

"Punishing?"

"For not being in love with her, even though — and I imagine this was true for both of us — she always made it clear that she wasn't interested in more than a casual fling. Maybe she wasn't, with either of us, until we found someone else. I think the reason Marla said she was raped on New Year's Eve is because that night set in motion my falling in love with Joanna. I was in the hospital on New Year's Eve — I didn't even see Marla. Your mother and I hadn't been together since Christmas Eve. I had no idea she was pregnant, Brooke. Even at my wedding to Joanna, when Marla would've been five months along, I couldn't tell. The possibility didn't occur to me. And when Lily told me about you, I just assumed you'd been conceived after Marla moved to Forsythe. I would never have abandoned you had I known."

"Are you saying . . ."

"That I'm your father? Yes," Robert said softly. "At least that's what I'm trying to say. We could do blood tests to confirm it, but I'm very sure we'd discover what Fleur already knows. Besides," he confessed, "I *want* it to be true."

And she didn't, he thought as his confession — his wish — was greeted with silence.

"I'm sorry, Brooke. Terribly sorry that I didn't know." *And that it's too late.* "I would've protected you, loved you. I would have."

"I *had* a father who loved me. Protected me. Lily and I both did."

"I know and I'm glad. John was a wonderful man."

"Yes, he was. And . . ."

Robert steeled himself, but asked gently, "And Brooke?"

"And Lily was always so willing to share her father with me. I wonder . . . would it be all right if I shared you with her?"

Emotion flooded his eyes, then hers. And after a moment, but at the same moment, they smiled remarkably similar smiles. Her frowning silence had been caution, a carefulness like his.

It was the first — albeit blurry — glimpse of what would become for Robert

and Brooke a joyous refrain. Like father
. . . like daughter.

Lily didn't imagine, when she answered
the phone at 10:00 a.m., that it would be
the call she'd been hoping for, lying awake
for, night after night.
"Hello, Lily."
"Peter."
"How are you?"
"Good. Fine."
"And Brooke and Rafe?"
"Happy." *So very happy.* "Rafe's started
doing a little weight-bearing."
"After only three weeks?"
"Yes." Only three weeks since Rafe's discharge, when she'd seen Peter last.
Lily had reminded herself, just moments
before the page about Rafe's accident, that
her week with Peter was coming to an end.
But there'd been a grace period. Ten additional days. When she'd been in the hospital because of Rafe, and Peter had
dropped by, often, and they'd talked. She'd
gotten a little better at talking when he was
looking at her and there were so many
things they could find to talk about *other*
than MSP. Or so it seemed.
Lily had begun expecting things from
Peter again.

Expecting, at least, that it wouldn't all end just because it was time for Rafe to leave the hospital.

But it had.

"Is this a convenient time to talk?"

"Sure."

"I wanted to answer the question you asked me that day on the ward," he said.

"About why you thought the paintings were wrong."

"Yes. It wasn't because I could see what was missing in them. I couldn't. But what I could see reminded me of my own childhood. It was a place without the wonder you described. Or the hope."

"I'm sorry."

"Don't be. *Yet.* There just may be a happy ending. See what you think. I glimpsed the hope once, as a child. It belonged to a friend, not to me. But it's occurred to me that if I can steal a name — and find a father — I can steal a memory, too, and make it my own."

"And delete the other memories while you're at it?" *The ghoulish ones?*

"I'm told such things can be done."

"Yes, they can. You'll have your happy ending, Peter." *You deserve to have it.*

"Lily?"

"Yes?"

402

"I was hoping — that word again — you'd be interested in being part of the new memories I'm planning to make."

"I'm in the mood for a walk."
"In the middle of the night with a man who can't walk?"
"No," Brooke admitted. "I'm pretty happy right where we are. For now."
"But?"
"But maybe sometime we could climb a mountain."
"Brooke."
"Not if you don't want to, Rafe. If it feels too difficult — emotionally — for you to do so. But it's so beautiful on your mountain, and I even thought we could do some planting."
"Planting?"
"Yes," she said softly to the flower magician she loved. "Planting."
So they would go to the place where a father's maize had kept his family fed . . . and a father's love had nourished a young boy's soul. And there would be more magic on the hillside. Twice a year, in autumn and in spring, the entire mountain would glow gold, and the fragrance of lilacs would drift like puffs of smoke from the snowy mountain, and everyone would

believe, as the lovely storyteller wanted them to believe, that the flowers had been a gift from Quetzalcoatl to the precious sisters who'd been lost in the mud but who'd ascended to the heavens.

It was a modern Nahuatl legend. And there was more, if you believed. The sisters floated above the mountain. You could see them even during the day. Just there. In that shimmer of rainbows.

And the names of those sisters who sparkled in the azure sky were the names of the other sisters rescued by the blue-eyed man.

The same names, perhaps, of sisters everywhere who'd been healed by love.

Star Light and . . . Star Bright.